THE

Angel

AND THE

Raven

FARRELL MASON

Live in Hope
Farrell

for DAVID — my *Protector*

for LOVEY — my *Guardian*

and for CHARLIE, BELLE, ELISE, ROSE, AND PERCY
— my *Winged Ones*

Table of Contents

The Prologue

We are all on a pilgrimage towards something. Some of us are looking for home, or some semblance of home. Others are journeying away from a place of hurt or betrayal. And then there are the daring who embark on the sacred path of the unknown. A path paved with stones of wonder, mystery and sacrifice, all carefully seamed together with Love. But heed the pilgrim's warning: Where there is Light, there is Darkness. Where there is Darkness, there will always be glimmers of Light.

Some say the purpose of the pilgrim's journey is to find one's Truth, the first step through the Holy Door. But I know that is only part of the story. With a mysterious wind swirling in anticipation outside, I allow my mind to walk those same dusty footpaths that have led me to this hour. There is indeed a story etched here. A story of much love and intrigue, loss and regret, but always the sacred.

There is much to my story that appears the wiliest mischief of a child's imagination, but one day I hope you will have the courage to look back over your own story and see the demons, the saints and the angels who have intersected your own path. And then you too will begin to believe in the beautiful Truth. It will break open the world for you. It did mine. Although frightening, you will understand that your life was architected by and designed for Love from the start. I will travel the path again, hoping that I will have the words to make you believe. Believe in visions, wings of redemption and a magical place of Light that exists just beyond the dreaming. Most importantly, believe in Love.

a Percolating Miracle

A world without angels is a world without wonder. A theology without angels
is a theology without mystery. And if our theology cannot accommodate the
mystery of creation, in the end it will fail to accommodate God.

— KARL BARTH —

CHAPTER 1

They tell me I was set apart for a special purpose long before the fibers of my lungs contracted and stretched enough to push forth the first inkling of my humanity. I have always been different. I knew that from the beginning. First it was the dreams. These haunting visions that came with a fury each time I looked into the eyes of the innocent. Through each iris looking glass, I was invited into their raw, secret truths. The fears, the mistakes, the regrets, the hopes—each carefully tucked behind the quivering of eyelashes.

These visions have the power to unsteady the footing. And yet they have proven faithful companions, my teachers on the pilgrim's road. I ran from or tried to ignore them for years without much success. It was not until I met others like myself that my secret was set free. Mine is considered a gift—to see beyond the eyes to the real story beneath the surface, constricting and expanding with all the pains and joys of mortal existence. I shall speak more of these gifts later.

But first, all stories worth telling must begin with the words, *In the beginning.* What mother, architect or Creator does not instinctively curl up the edges of his or her mouth in a grin, remembering the beginning of a creation, a percolating miracle?

I have come to trust in the creative Spirit who has proven time and time again the power to weave its jaunty threads into a masterpiece of divine proportions. This mysterious force tilts the universe ever so slightly here and there, encouraging creation forward on its destined path. There is divine applause when the story unfolds with grace. Think of it as the most elegant mathematical equation skipping across the line of time in perfect pirouettes. Of course, one cannot ignore those nettlesome, ever-changing variables that ensure each equation tells an interesting, sometimes tragic, but always sacred tale. Rest assured, the value—or, shall I venture, the sanctity—of each story is admired equally. There is a calling for each one of us, angel and mortal alike, once released into the world from the Creator's hand. It is an honor to take one's place in the sequence of creation. For me, it was the path of the winged—an angel sent to Earth.

My name is Gabrielle. The sisters at Sacred Heart priory believed themselves quite clever as they took the cerulean blue thread, wet it through with their prayerful lips and then carefully sewed my prophetic name into the muslin baptismal gown on the evening of my arrival. Sister Anne winked and said the cumulus clouds filed out in vertical attention, like puffed-up royal sentries to herald my arrival. If only the sisters had known the whole truth, that an angel of the line of Gabriel, no less, had shared the sweet air of their abbey for a time. That is, until the Spirit deemed I was ready to join the others like myself and fulfill my destiny on earth.

I was born on the pilgrimage road of Santiago de Compostela on the propitious evening of the Feast of the Assumption. My papa was a Roman Catholic priest, and my mother, Valentina, was his secret love, but I would not glean my true origins until much later. In the indigo-inked pages of my father's private letters, I would learn that my mother passed through the Door shortly after I took my first breath, but not before she looked into my eyes and whispered my name for the first time in this world. Valentina knew she had fulfilled her destiny. The eyes tell all. And mine held the Light.

My arrival had come much earlier than expected. My mother was concerned that I was twisted in her womb and for weeks had caressed her belly with rose oil, coaxing me to turn. Stoic, and under a blanket of prayers and clenched fists, she quietly submitted to her fate and stepped into the shadows so that I could live in the Light. Papa believed it especially providential that I was born on the celebration day of our immaculate Holy Mother Mary's ascension into the clouds, for she was one of the best of our kind, the Angel Queen. Papa never doubted that my life was created for holy things. All his tender instructions for me were written in the language of angels and awaited my maturity to be discovered in the *Angel Holy Book*.

I was brought into the world under the twinkling lights of the Milky Way amidst cheers from a parade of adoring villagers as they processed through the village behind the painted statue of Our Lady, and tenderly anointed by the quiet tears of my mother. Papa said Valentina was taken on the wings of a chariot of angels that very night. I never knew my mother, but I often clutched her precious rosary for a whisper that she was with me. Much later, in Paris, I found the scarlet glass prayer beads and a curl of her hair, identical to my own, fastened in a blue silk purse and tucked safely in the crease of chapter seven of the *Angel Holy Book*, the chapter that unraveled the tale of my genesis.

My father had seen me in a dream before I was born, wrapped in a white linen scallop-edged cloth, being blessed with holy water spilling from a giant shell, the sacred symbol for the Way of St. James. He set out that very next morning with my exceedingly pregnant mother on a journey to the Cathedral of Santiago, where I would be anointed by the Light. But I was born too soon, in a little hamlet called Auvergne, famously known for its hospitality to traveling pilgrims. Papa claimed the entire village had helped carry my mother on a pallet in a solemn procession the remaining kilometers to the Cathedral. Somehow he convinced a group of French and Spanish strangers to help our family. I imagine it was his priestly collar that encouraged them to make the journey with the hopes of a plenary indulgence or at least a wink from Above.

Upon birth, I was consecrated to the Holy One in the presence of the whole celestial court. Laughing cherubim accompanied by the singing seraphs hovered with the grand archangels. They came to ordain my mission, my mortal journey on earth. Papa raised me up high, and humans and angels alike joined in communion to celebrate my arrival, for my incarnation meant another piece of the Light was released into the world. Sadly, perched on a dusty beam that secured one of the Cathedral's magnificent groin vaults, the Dark Deep's minion, a black Raven, loomed. The presence of Darkness is never far from the Light. It's just that way here on earth.

How much of this story is believable to mortal eyes is hard to say, for most live contently in blindness. But inside the gilt-edged *Angel Holy Book*, its pages worn and splattered with candle wax, I would learn that I was destined to be one of the Chosen from the very beginning. This, despite the fact that for my entire childhood, I was led to believe I was a gift from the Virgin Mary to the sisters of the Sacred Heart order. I was to be a nun like them. The convent was the only home I had ever known. It had been chosen as a safe refuge until I was strong enough to look the Raven in the eye and challenge the Darkness of this imperfect world with my Light.

CHAPTER 2

My papa was a priest who took his mortal profession of the cloth very seriously. He accomplished his purpose, happily genuflecting under the vaulted ceilings, anointing with blessed oil by flickering candlelight and intoning the ancient liturgies of the Holy Church to his parishioners. However, his ecclesial oath held no weight when it came to his angelic destiny. Falling in love with my mother was always part of the divinely-appointed plan. He discovered Valentina, a gypsy beauty, in the town of Chiclayo in Peru. Papa claimed he never felt guilty about their forbidden relationship or secret betrothal. He trusted in the Almighty plan.

Papa saw meaning in dreams just as Saint Joseph had. In a dream the night before he met my mother, he saw a beautiful, otherworldly creature drawing water from a well. As he drew closer to her, they melded into one. Any ordinary priest would have awakened in terror, fearful the devil was working in the dark, but Papa steadfastly believed the Divine to be in charge, beautifully aligning the stars. And his life was proof of that.

The son of a famous Austrian composer living in Paris, Papa never knew his mother, not even her name. He imagined she was a famous dancer or a player on the stage. But underneath he intuited that she had more in common with the nightingales of the street, a sad angel who had fallen prey to the Darkness. His father drank heavily, testified by his bulbous nose and depressive nature. He slept his days away in a dark cave on the third floor and could be heard roaming the house at all hours of the night, pounding away on his piano, occasionally scribbling mad compositions across the cracked plaster walls. As a child, Papa imagined invisible armies of musical notes battling it out for his father's soul. But later he would come to understand that it was the Dark Deep that had taken hold of the flesh of both of his parents long before he had the powers to save them. The Dark comes looking for any and all, and thus my papa warned me that I must remain in the Light at all costs. He knew the danger of despair too well.

When Papa turned fifteen, he found his father swinging grotesquely from the rafter above the piano. It did not come as a surprise, since for months he had been wrestling with that awful vision. The alcohol and dark chaos waging war for his father's soul had finally won. That night, Papa saw the Raven for the first time perched on the windowsill next to his father's grand piano. You see, the presence of the Raven signals the Darkness is near, vying for souls.

There was no inheritance. All of those precious golden ducats had gone to the greedy coffers of establishments that oozed of sweet perfume and drowning whiskey. His virtuoso parent, wounded by life, was no match for the cunning of the Deep. And my papa was left an orphan.

Papa next became a ward of the Monastery of St. John. They took him in as charity but quickly realized the child had unique powers. The gift of his prescient dreams and supernatural visions marked him as special. The monks renamed him Brother Josef for his uncanny ability to interpret dreams. One night, kneeling on the stone floors of his cold cell, a true miracle happened. Papa was invited into the mysteries of the angels who battled the Darkness just beyond the veil of this material world. He could now see things most could not even conjure in their human imagination. Papa was invited into the world just beyond the dreaming.

In those early years, cloistered in the quiet safety of the monastery, Papa secretly spoke in tongues, the enchanting language of the celestial world. First it sounded like nothing more than a delicate melody. Kneeling beside the brothers in meditation, Papa slowly learned to open his mortal hinges so that the door to his very soul could open. Human words proved now only mere symbols for the full thoughts and ecstatic emotions spoken by the spirit within. This was the beginning of Papa's secret postulancy as the next in the line of Gabriel.

In two years' time, prostrate before the abbot and encircled by his brother monks, Papa took his final monastic vows. He would become one of God's most loyal earthly vassals while secretly training to become the brightest light in the celestial court on earth. Papa relished the life of solitude within the ivy-covered walls of the monastery. He carefully concealed his other gifts, waiting for Divine direction. But the ecclesial establishment had other plans in store for their gifted monk. Tonsured, and clad in his black-hooded frock with a simple wooden cross about his neck, he was called to Rome. For centuries, the monastery had proven a fruitful feeding ground for recruiting the Pope's most obedient acolytes. Papa had been handpicked for his visionary gifts, as the abbott had betrayed my father's secret talent for the Pope's favor. Papa's mind was a divining rod; he could see coming events in visions and dreams, an enviable asset to the throne of St. Peter.

Brother Josef became an influential and trusted member of the pontiff's inner circle. Some said Papa was so close to the Pope that he knew the very rhythms of his sleeping breaths. In the Vatican Library, there is correspondence between the Pope and my father from his travels. A modern rendition of *The Last Supper* in the bishop's refectory portrays a beloved disciple who bears an uncanny resemblance to my father. On the Pope's deathbed, as Papa performed the Extreme Unction, he gifted my father with a holy seat in Paris. And so Papa found himself uprooted again, yet assigned a jewel of a church on the Île Saint-Louis. There he blurred the lines of the visible and the invisible, life and death, mortal and angel, earth and heaven.

I must admit that the love story of my mother and father, recorded for my eyes later in the *Angel Holy Book,* caused my cheeks to blush with color. The vision of my mother behind a lace veil took Papa down the forbidden path for a priest. He did not need to unroll ancient scrolls or read papal decrees to be reminded of the church's position on celibacy. With the snap of a finger, a priest was defrocked and any offspring relegated to shameful bastardom. But Papa's pilgrimage toward his own truth included a love that could only be found in the feminine body and lighted soul of another with wings like his own. And that is how my magical story began. Papa was a priest, a husband, a father and an archangel, all under the pontiff's pointed nose.

My mother was a precious surprise from Above. The sensual love she shared with my father was a holy gift. At the baptistery inside the Cathedral of Santa Maria, Papa felt the light leave his fingertips as he made the sign of the cross on Valentina's forehead. My mother fell backward in a swoon. When she awoke in Papa's arms, they both knew they were destined. The Holy Spirit had spoken, and Papa surrendered yet again to a new variable in the equation.

It was like Jacob wrestling the Divine for a blessing to win Valentina's hand. It took all his powers, both angelic and human, to convince her guardians to release their brazen gypsy to a scandalous suitor, a wayward priest. The Valencia patriarch had ambitious betrothal plans for his exotic beauty of a daughter. Garcia Valencia intended to marry Valentina into the Marquez family for its prestige and many acres of fruit trees. But ambition for his family would be no match for celestial intervention. Sparks flew in the chapel. Consummation was inevitable. Next Papa delivered a glorious, near supernatural homily that had Valentina and the shocked Valencia clan baptizing the stone floor with tears. Before Papa could change from his priestly vestments, the dowry trunk was packed, and Valentina was waiting on the boat with her hat, monogrammed handkerchief and mischievous smile. She had always known her life and her future offspring were meant for higher things. Valentina would become one of the most unique of our kind.

My father ordained their union in the lower cargo pit of the ship among the chickens, coal and gifts for the Holy See. Papa bowed to the angels and saints levitating above their union as witnesses. On that fateful first night, my father took a beautiful rosary of rose gold, scarlet glass beads and an emerald-encrusted cross from the cache for the Pope. It would be the secret symbol of their marital union. My mother could not wear a ring as Papa would have been condemned. I have that rosary now wrapped in her monogrammed linen handkerchief. Much later, I would often wear it under my flour-dusted pastry jacket. Sometimes I would lift it to my nose, sure that I could smell her scent of gardenias. Papa recorded that they were her favorite flower, and that they could often be found pinned in her hair or in a silver bud vase next to their marital bed.

My mother cut her long curls before the boat reached the port at Venice, and traded in her silk organza dresses and mother of pearl earrings for the humble garb of an apprentice. This would be their alias to mortal eyes. Valentina never questioned the legitimacy of their relationship because she knew a love, an intimacy, that transcended her earthly existence. Papa awakened her young body and honored her soul with his love. Heaven was on their side, he said.

Valentina, however, was destined for her own pilgrimage and angelic mission ordained from Above. She became well known for her arts of healing. On all of their travels, she was never without her carpet valise of precious flowering herbs and medicinal plants. Many sought her out, eager to touch even the hem of her flowing skirts. Included in my father's stories in the ancient *Angel Holy Book* was a picture of my mother tenderly bathing a sick child in a grotto known for its miracles of healing. Valentina would stir the waters in hopes of releasing their powers, enabling the ill to travel inward to the quiet place of the soul, where she knew all real healing took place.

My mother's early passage through the Door touched every wing and was responsible for many a salted tear. Papa laid her mortal form to rest next to a camellia bush with a view of the sea. A stonemason took pity for his tears and carved Valentina a beautiful tombstone—an angel, of course, with wings extended, curving in protection over her grave.

It simply read, "Mother to an angel."

Years later, when I made my own pilgrimage to Santiago, I found her tombstone, its hovering angel statue with one wing missing, but my fate engraved for eternity. It took a long time to believe I was the legendary Valentina's daughter, an angel no less.

Papa was a blind man stumbling down the pilgrim's road away from my mother. Even our kind cannot avoid the plight of humanity when on earth. Loss spares not one of creation. It must have been a sight to see a weeping priest, drunk with grief, bearing a child swaddled in a tablecloth. The Spirit took mercy, and her name was Sister Karis. She approached Papa at the border between France and Spain, having walked for three days along the pilgrim's road from her home at the Convent of the Sacred Heart. She too had had a vision, an annunciation, in which an angel clothed in light had revealed her important task. A special child awaited her on the pilgrim's road. This would be her angelic test, her special destiny.

When Papa discovered Sister Karis kneeling at one of the altars to the Virgin Mary on the road's edge, he knew our paths must diverge if I were to be protected. For several nights his dreams had shown a forked river; on one side a winged figure protecting an orb of light in her arms; on the other side, a Raven, black as night, wings contorted, ready to swoop down on its prey. Always good and evil. And the cruel truth: the Dark Deep will go to extraordinary lengths to destroy the Light.

CHAPTER 3

Looking back I am surprised I did not question my origins. The only family I knew were the sisters of the Sacred Heart convent. Never did I ask, and Sister Karis never divulged, the secret of my true parentage. I grew up believing I was a gift from the Virgin Mary to the sisters at the convent. Every year, to commemorate my birth, the sisters would parade me into the chapel and hang a wreath of camellias around the chiseled stone neck of our Mother Mary statue in thanksgiving for my life. Later I would discover my father had passed through the Holy Door soon after my birth, sacrificing his own mortal life for the life of another. My father refused to lose a single soul to the dark side on his watch. A day would come when I would witness in the flesh the price he paid, for I would do the same for another's salvation.

Although the sisters never lost their tenacity in prayers for my salvation, it became clear early on that I was not cut from their same cloth. A life cocooned within the strict simplicity of prayer, service and celibacy was a challenge from the beginning. To the chagrin of the sisters, I had no aspirations of ever donning the habit of Christus's bride. Instead I was the plucky child who floated through the herb garden in homespun paper wings, satin ribbons tied about my waist and twisted through my hair. I would conjure up words to a language I was sure was angelical. I tried to convince the sisters that the white-speckled donkey in the paddock was my winged Pegasus. I even hung sheets from the top of my bed to create a secret chamber, painting the fabric in the watery blue colors of a starry night sky. Winged creatures were always part of my imaginary world. I see now that my imagination even then had a hint of the secret world that I was destined to be a part of. It was only a matter of time before my spirit would stretch and breach the abbey's disciplined cloister for the freedom of the world outside.

It would take many years before I could appreciate the gifts found in those whispered prayers, incense and the lighting of candles offered within the sisters' chapel. Although disdainfully dismissed in my childhood, they would one day provide the door that would open my life to the sacred and allow me to hear my native language, the language of my true country.

Sister Karis was ordained as my Protectress. She raised me in a flour-dusted blanket of love, prayers and buttery croissants. She understood her responsibility in caring for me as her holy calling. And she would prove to be a master at keeping my secrets. When I turned eight, I had my first dream, too insignificant to classify as supernatural. Until the propitious evening Sister Karis found me tangled in the sheets, bathed in sweat, screaming from a painfully sinister vision. I saw a hooded man entering our dormitory in the middle of the night, carrying a coiled rope in his large, dirty mitt of a fist. On that very night, Sister Karis would run barefoot down the dormitory hall and save young Sister Isabelle's life from the clutches of her crazed, jilted lover. Sister Karis never divulged to the others that my dream had saved Isabelle's life.

The dreams presented a problem when they began to haunt me in the light of day. Soon they no longer remained tucked neatly in the closet of my nighttime slumber. I was given a front seat to the inner musings of the nuns, some quite unholy by the way. Just by looking into their eyes! I trained myself to blink away the visions, unless of course they would serve in my getting my way or staying out of trouble with the nuns. But then there was the vision that would haunt me for years, until it finally manifested in the devastating passing of my beloved Sister Karis. She was in a dark room, as I had dreamed many times, pale, leached of her happy, rosy color. Death, I fought it. It still came. Beloved Sister Karis departed this world.

Without her I was utterly alone. I became frightened of my powers, or lack of powers. For I could not stop the relentless decline of the woman I loved so dearly. The suffering of Sister Karis twisted something inside of me. Without her, I was not connected to anyone or anything at the abbey. Although I had spent my entire life at the convent, Sister Karis was my true home, my touchstone.

A Percolating Miracle

As Father John performed the last rites on my faithful guardian, Sister Karis reached for my hand and whispered her final mysterious words to me: "Trust your visions. They will help you discover your wings." As I was moving to leave her side, frightened by her delirious state, she suddenly reached again for my hand and said, "Love is the Message, Gabrielle."

CHAPTER 4

I was twenty-three when Sister Karis passed to the other side. I tended my grief by furiously planting a garden by her grave, determined to create a beautiful view for her eternal rest. I planted lavender so that its fragrance would tickle her freckled nose and ease her worries about me. I designed a pattern of roses and lilacs that I knew would inspire a smile. I had no concept then of sacred time, other planes of existence or the invisible war between the evil Dark and heaven's Light. Nor that I would one day see her again.

I stayed at the convent through the summer to tie up loose ends and to train Sister Pauline to take the reins at the Sacred Heart bakery. It had been Sister Karis's holy chapel. "Feed the soul through the stomach, little one," she said. Under her flour-encrusted apron, I learned to knead a perfect round of dough by the age of five. Between the smoke-stained stone walls and cracked tiled floor of the bakery, Sister Karis imparted her love and the magic of baking.

The love affair began on my sixth birthday. I will never forget Sister Karis excitedly waking me before Lauds, dragging me down to the wood and marble kitchen table to unveil my spectacular birthday gift. It was a cake. But no ordinary cake. Sister Karis had copied one of my childish watercolors of the garden and replicated it to perfection in sugared pastry dough and cream. It was the most beautiful piece of art my young eyes had ever seen. At first I didn't want her to cut into the design, but she giggled and with abandon swiped her finger across the crimson-frosted peonies. Thrusting her frosting-covered fingers into her mouth, she was transported to another plane, exclaiming, "Ooh la la!" It was the most sensual act I had ever witnessed. If Mother Superior had observed our sybaritic behavior, we surely would have found ourselves with bruised knees from scrubbing the chapel floor in penance. From that day forward, I became Sister Karis's devoted apprentice in the bakery.

We were a team, Sister Karis and I, in that humble alcove of a kitchen just below the chapel. She expanded my world from the strict black and white of the wimple and habit to a rich palette of delicious color. My life before had been meticulously carved into eight sacred wedges of prayer. We were alerted to the time of the day when robust Sister Sarah would lumber up the medieval iron spiral staircase of the bell tower and tug the rope to call us to our knees. Time was measured by the bells for the nuns, but the ovens and the calculated rising of dough would become my most favored timepiece.

The bakery under Sister Karis became quite well known in the town for its airy sourdough baguettes and almond brioche. But it was her creations for the holiday of *Pâques* that earned the smiles of children and adults alike on Easter morning. Each year we created hundreds of *cloches volants,* or flying bells. They were made from sweet pastry dough and chocolate, honoring the tradition that all the church bells in France fly away in mourning to the Vatican on Good Friday. But on Easter morning, the bells return, ringing for the resurrection of life, laden full with gifts of chocolate bells and decorative eggs for the children. The mingling of the joyous sounds reverberating from the bell tower with the arousing experience of biting into one of Sister Karis's succulent crème-filled or dark-chocolate bells was as close as some would come to an ecstatic religious experience.

The kitchen was an intimate space, holier to me in some ways than the abbey's solemn chapel with its famed stained glass. Sister Karis had an enormous, worn brown leather bible of recipes passed down from generations of bakers on her mother's side. This collection of handwritten scratches, measurements and temperatures became my sacred text. In the afternoons, I would take my sketchbook into the garden and, in watercolors, bring to life bejeweled cakes with shimmering ribbons of spun sugar, marzipan and swirls of crème. I dreamed of the day I would create sublime and even seductive creations in my own bakery. Milles-feuilles with pistachio layers, éclairs with caramel-walnut crème, cakes covered in a tapestry of pastel macaroons and chocolate fountains spilling over choux pastry sculptures had me up late into the night, sketching under candlelight, each a secret and tantalizing delight. Mother Superior once found my sketchbook and happily assigned me washing duty of all the stained-glass windows in the chapel, plus an endless number of Hail Marys as penance before I could rejoin Sister Karis in the kitchen. It did not matter. I was where I belonged.

Everything changed the day I scattered three handfuls of dirt on a wooden coffin and returned to an empty kitchen. I sat at the oak farm table after Lauds with our same matching rosebud teacups and saucers, sipping our favorite vervain. All I wanted to hear was, "Gaby, take a peek at the rounds of dough in the oven. I think the tops are browning too fast." But the room was still. Sister Karis's voice was buried beneath the dirt. I knew I had to leave.

Sister Karis had wrapped her bible of recipes in her old patched flowery apron and left it for me to find in the drawer where we kept all of our beaten-tin measuring cups. Tucked inside an envelope between the recipe for a tarte au citron and her favorite lemon-scented cake with raspberry ganache were her final words to me.

Gabrielle,
Take my recipes and go to Paris. On the Île Saint-Louis, you will find a bakery on the corner of rue de Bourbon called the Levain Bakery. It is run by a dear friend, Lille. She knows you are coming. Send my love to Pierre and Sophie. Make friends with Baabar. Take your sketchbook. Lille will cheer your designs. I love and believe in you, my little angel, with all my heart. The journey has just begun for us.
Until we see each other again,
Karis

— PART TWO —

Baker's Heaven

For now we see in a mirror dimly. Then we shall see face to face. Now I know in part, then I shall know fully, just as I am fully known.

— 1 CORINTHIANS 13:12 —

CHAPTER 5

The future proves a dusty footpath, unknown to the wayfarer, and that in itself creates a knot in the throat and rough stones for the feet. But all must press forward into the night, trusting in the Light to guide the way. If not, one will miss the blessings that await.

Weeks went by with my bag neatly packed, but I could not leave the protection of Sacred Heart. Ironically, it would be my nemesis, Mother Superior, with a bevy of the sisters in tow, who would formally lead me in a taut procession to the train station. The sisters had kindly packed a leather satchel with my sketchbook and paints, a picture of Sister Karis in the garden, a knapsack of brioche rolls carefully wrapped in a linen napkin, and a slim leather clutch tied with a blue ribbon, containing the bulk of the offering plate collected over the last month.

The sisters followed closely the Rule of Saint Benedict. All possessions were considered communal property. My only frocks were two simple white linen habits with my name embroidered in pale blue on the back. Most of the sisters who had taken their final vows and were officially betrothed to Christ were distinguished by the black scapular, veil and cowl. In preparation for my journey, kind Sister Mary had quietly hand-stitched two simple jupes and matching linen shirts from a pattern purchased in the village. Everyone knew it was time. I was not one for grand displays of emotion; nonetheless, the tears spilled from my eyes as the train pulled away from the station. The choir of nuns, who waved furiously at me down the platform, had been my blessed family.

Thankfully, I shared my car on the train with the elegantly coiffed, most proper Madame LaTouche, who took pity on me. She was returning to the city after a weekend visiting her ailing mother and shared her thermos of milky tea, a pear and some generous conversation. She was only a middling couturier in Paris; nevertheless, her bejeweled *chaussures* were from a fairy tale to me. They were frivolous, but they distracted my fear and filled several pages in my sketchbook on the train passage into Paris. I imagined her shoes reincarnated in a rich vanilla cake and wrapped in a rose cream with elaborate ribbons spun from lavender marzipan.

As the train pulled into the Gare Saint-Lazare station, I carefully tucked away my sketchbook and pencils, and I could feel the condensation bubbling up from my palms. Madame LaTouche recognized my fright and offered to see me safely to the taxi line.

The moment I walked out of the station into the bright light of the sun, I was hypnotized by everything, even the difference in the air. It was as if the oxygen filling my lungs was lighter, waking my spirit from a long slumber. Then I noticed the gathering of black ravens perched on the tarred gate, all at perfect attention, beady eyes glaring at me. As I crossed through the metal opening, they began a shrill of caws, threatening to alert the entire city to my arrival. A weird chill fluttered down my spine. And yet I was drawn to them.

Just as I saw my reflection in the shiny black buttons of their eyes, my traveling companion bustled me into a cab, handing me her calling card. I tore one of my sketches of her shoes from my book and passed it to her, signed with a swirly *G*. I looked over my shoulder as the cab pulled away, thankfully the ominous ravens were gone.

My cab driver was named Pip, a jolly old gentleman with a bald head, a skinny silver curled mustache and a crooked smile decorated with an ebony carved pipe dangling to his wrinkled chin. He said his parents could never agree on his name.

"My mother preferred Pierre," he said, "and yet there was a long line of Phillipes on my father's side. In order to prevent another revolution *à la française*, they settled on Pip."

Pip's companion rode up front, a chocolate poodle named Mignon with a red handkerchief tied fashionably about his neck. Pip's taxi was anything but conventional. It was a moving chapel: Prayer cards with pictures of all the saints had been haphazardly pasted along the sides and ceiling. I recognized one as Saint Thérèse of Lisieux with a bouquet of flowers in her hand. I remembered she was the "Little Flower of Jesus." We had her statue in the abbey's rose garden, her arms outstretched around a stone birdbath. The sisters would leave crumbs at her feet for the birds, encouraging them to sing during morning chores.

Pip peered at me through his rearview mirror and insisted I take one of the prayer cards for protection as a newcomer to the city. He excitedly described the City of Light as if the French Revolution had never occurred and a regal queen still sat on the throne. He could hardly contain his zeal, so happy to present his city in all her majesty to my virginal eyes. Pip's Paris was bejeweled and swathed in the richest robes of history.

As we made our way along the Right Bank, cutting across the Place de la Concorde that divided the Tuileries gardens from the Champs-Élysées, he reminisced about walking hand in hand down the grand boulevard beneath the clipped horse chestnut trees and kissing his wife Clara under the Arc de Triomphe. He pointed to the Eiffel Tower, nodding with pride, and made the sign of the cross as we passed by Notre Dame.

Pip parked on the Île de la Cité and jumped from the driver's seat with Mignon following close behind. It was break time, and he invited me to join him. We walked along the left side of Notre Dame to the Pont Marie bridge, then crossed over onto the Île Saint-Louis. A bustling café with bright green-striped awnings, the name barely legible in a cursive scroll of gold across the top, came into view. The waiter, introduced to me as Jean-Paul and dressed in the most elegant evening suit, motioned Pip to his usual table facing the afternoon sun. There was a bowl already filled with water for Mignon. Jean-Paul, with a pretentious flourish, dropped the daily paper in Pip's lap and then presented to us the first of many espressos. I wondered how I had gotten here.

Next Pip pointed up to the row of gargoyles that lined the heights of Notre Dame.

"Those monsters protect our Grand Lady from the Evil One. The ravens never cease pecking away at her stone armor, intent on pillaging the treasure within. It's the same with the soul. The Darkness is determined to extinguish what remains of the Light. May we all be blessed with the protective eye of the gargoyle, Mademoiselle Gabrielle."

I nervously giggled at his warning. He wagged his head from side to side in true Gallic manner and told me to make peace with the frightening stone creatures. At the time, I had no idea the gargoyle would play a part in my own story. Pip would be profoundly right. When faced with the evil of this world, we must fight to protect the beauty that rests deep inside. A lesson hard learned for most. The irony is that it is often our ugly and imperfect humanity that guards the soul, the inner place of our divinity.

I waved *à bientôt* as the waiter placed a buttery tarte tatin with a perfect caramelized top before Pip. A flush of excitement rose in his cheeks as he anticipated that first bite. I applauded and envied the baker, who had gifted such joy to another. Sister Karis would have loved it. I thumbed the prayer card curled in my left pocket and then edged forward, one hesitant foot in front of the other, beneath the shadow of the gargoyles, the final steps to my new life.

CHAPTER 6

The Île Saint-Louis is a jewel tucked seductively in the décolletage of Madame Paris. Crossing one of its five bridges is like stepping back in time. The tree-lined quays provide an enchanting backdrop for young lovers giggling cheek to cheek on French vert iron benches. The Pont Marie bridge is a theatrical stage for a street musician named Bernard with his beat-up violin, its case an alms plate, to kick up in a jig around the ancient street lamps. At the river's edge, the neighborhood children happily entice the ducks with sweet brioche and release their toy boats to the bewitching flow of the Seine. The handful of streets on the Île Saint-Louis are anchored by elegant mansions that recall the time of horse-drawn carriages, gaslights and stolen kisses. These architectural grand dames still watch like proud parents over the bustle of cafés, crêperies, chocolate and bonbon shops, bookstores, art galleries, cheese and flower shops and, of course, the legendary Levain Bakery.

From the Pont Marie, I turned left and located my new home at 11, rue de Bourbon. At that moment, I knew my true life would now begin, forever transformed by this mysterious and magical place.

The Levain Bakery has an illustrious pedigree. The oldest bakery on the island, it still bakes in the original seventeenth-century wood-burning oven cut into the stone wall, but its greatest claim is its founder, the legendary royal baker Monsieur LeNotre. Visit the Musée des Art Décoratifs on the famed rue de Rivoli to find mention of Monsieur LeNotre in the private diary of the famed and often controversial queen, Marie Antoinette.

On the seventeenth of Janvier, 1792, the queen wrote, "LeNotre was my magician today. He waved his wand and I was back at Hofburg Palace in Austria, perfectly recreated in pastry dough and crème. I could almost hear my brother playing the violin and see myself kneeling at the foot of my mother in utter contentment."

Monsieur LeNotre was ingenious when it came to self-preservation. The moment he caught a whiff of the smoke from the bomb fires that peppered the city and witnessed his first guillotine spectacle, the baker extraordinaire abandoned his garish court clothes emblazoned with the fleur-de-lis for the humble garb of peasant woolen breaches and cap. With true French flair, LeNotre escaped the angry mobs of the revolution by hiding in a wooden cart bearing the royal garbage.

He sought refuge for his wife and two children on the Île Saint-Louis with a distant uncle and quickly took on the new surname Levain. It was a clever but sober reminder that fermented sourdough kneaded by hand would allow his family to rise above the horrors of the French Revolution. Although the bakery was small, it became very popular for its humble sourdough baguettes. Several generations later, with the guillotine a distant memory, the Levain Bakery resurrected the Versailles recipes, and a new breath of creativity infused the spirit of the ancient bakery.

Today the bakery is celebrated for its innovative creations with choux pasty and crème. The Levain especially commands an audience for the unveiling of its store windows for *la fête de Noël*. The bakery not only creates lifelike renditions of Mary, Joseph and the babe Jesus in pastry dough, but every year it adds to the community of French men and women who follow the star to the stable. Next to the traditional ensemble of shepherds, wise men perched on camels bearing elaborate gifts, and honored members of the animal kingdom, there are shoemakers, fishmongers and professors with books in hand. There are seamstresses with needle and thread, frocked priests and *garçons* on bicycles tossing *le journal*. Parisian women of the highest couture file in beside street performers and *les intellectuels au berets*, all to take a peek inside the crèche. There are even tributes to the artists of the neighborhood such as Chagall and Picasso. But it is the legendary Levain family of mice, creatively hidden within the holy scene, that garners the biggest grins. One must blink twice to be reminded that these edible *santons* are not flesh, fur and bone but rather pieces of art brought to life in pastry and crème.

On Christmas morning, the line twists around the block, all hoping to take home a treasure from the mystical scene to be the centerpiece for their own Christmas tables. The bakery clerks wrap each figure in gold tissue, with Levain's signature rose ribbon tied in a flourish. As tradition goes, the family with the newest born in the neighborhood takes home the baby Jesus as a special blessing from the Levain Bakery.

Something mystical was baking at the Levain Bakery alongside its delicious breads. Carefully hidden behind the perfect golden croissants and baguettes standing tall as soldiers in their bins, breathed a secret society with gifts of supernatural proportion. In time, I would become one of its most loyal disciples, invited into the sacred mysteries of the winged. But first, I must become the newest darling of pastry dough and cream.

CHAPTER 7

On that fateful first day of June, I approached my new home with a gut seized by fluttering wings, a salty dew spilling with a fury from my palms. Was anyone at the Levain Bakery expecting my arrival? Sister Karis had simply written down the address, 11, rue de Bourbon, and the proprietor's name, Lille. For two hours, I sat across the street on a green iron bench with its gold pedestal feet and watched the line of people wrap around the corner, all eager for their morning brioche and café au lait. Old matriarchs slowly pushing their rickety wooden grocery carts, elegant madames with their leather bags and perfectly coiffed dogs, businessmen in bold patterned silk ties, chattering students weighed down with books and bearded artists with paint-stained hands, all waiting for their daily baker's blessing. At half past two, a beautiful blonde woman in red, impossibly high heels flipped the sign on the door, announcing the *pâtisserie* and *thé du jour*. Now the afternoon line commenced for teatime in the salon.

The Levain Bakery, with its bright-vermillion painted exterior, smiled at me that first day as I timidly stood, satchel in hand. The words *Levain Boulangerie et Pâtisserie* were calligraphed in rose and swirled across the elegant striped aqua awning of the building. For many, including the words "*boulangerie*" and "*pâtisserie*" in the same sentence would be sacrilege, much like marrying a beast to a princess. The making of bread required brawn, sweat upon the brow and the flames of heat from the dark pit of an oven, whereas pastry making was considered an angel's art. Inside the storage room of the bakery, hanging above the bags of flour and sugar, was a tattered charcoal cartoon. With humor, it mocked the union of *boulangerie* and *pâtisserie*. There was a lug bourgeois *boulanger* kneading dough with his feet. Sitting pleasantly next to him was an angel painting an elaborate design on a choux pastry with the tip of a feather.

Sister Karis always said, "Kneading dough keeps your feet on the ground, whereas the art of the *pâtisserie* allows your spirit a little adventure."

I was enchanted. The Levain Bakery was the antithesis of the humble bakery back at the convent. I imagined the storefront selling wares of lace and satin instead of creations from wheat, butter and sugar. I blushed at the thought of Sister Mary, in all of her primness, barring my entrance as if this place were more brothel than bakery. On either side of the ornate curlicue iron doors, there were painted wood panels of life-size, Rubenesque nymphs wearing seductive smiles and tourmaline eyes that urged you forward. Someone surely had a sense of humor here.

Through the frosted glass, I could see the same blonde woman in heels flipping through the day's receipts while nibbling on a very decadent, chocolate-dipped madeleine. I rapped on the door ever so slightly, and my knock drew her astonishing eyes like two pointed arrows to mine. I should have known at that very instant that Lille was a different being. Her blue eyes bore through me until they reached deep, too deep. I was left standing naked before her. The fragility of my emotions were exposed with the simple batting of her gold-flecked eyelashes, and I didn't like it.

I pulled the iron ring of the door, and the ethereal notes of a piano immediately lifted me off the ground. The familiar perfume of butter, sugar and cacao beans took me by the hand and drew me farther into this haven of sweetness. Above was a celestial trompe l'oeil fresco with plump angels, wreaths of wheat upon their heads, holding hands and dancing in a circle. High up in the corner, a young cherub was peeking over the gilt molding, his dimpled hands holding a golden box wrapped in the bakery's signature rose ribbon. My eyes moved to bluebirds with cherry-red breasts, peacocks with elaborate turquoise fans, golden butterflies and even a grand owl in a violet sky. The floor seemed to vibrate beneath my feet, a dancing mosaic of colored tiles. The beauty of this otherworldly space overwhelmed me. A baker's heaven. My heart skipped into a gallop. Something was happening here. Something was happening to me.

Lille interrupted my trance, real or not, with her dulcimer voice and the whisper of her soft lips against my cheeks, lightly imprinting me in a warm greeting. I found her voice to be the most beautiful I had ever heard. The delight in her intonation was reminiscent of Sister Karis's lullabies coaxing me to sleep. Even Lille's homespun perfume of camellias with hints of verbena reminded me of Sister Karis, as if they were carved from the same rich block. Lille was much shorter than me, and her pixie hair was the color of new wheat. Sea-blue eyes and a peppering of freckles that danced in a constellation upon her flushed cheeks announced her benevolence. It was as if Lille had just been told something wonderful and her joy spilled out into the air, an offering to whoever crossed her path. I imagined many a Parisian lady would have emptied their silk purses for the secret of Lille's vibrant skin and sheer magnetism.

"You must be Gabrielle," she said. "You have the Gabriel marking. It is unmistakable in your eyes. It has been such a long time, my dear. We have been waiting patiently for your arrival, fearing you would choose the safety of the familiar wimple and habit. I have already sung your praises in the neighborhood for those exquisite chocolate Easter bells. You must do them for the bakery this year."

I stood dumbstruck. How did she know about my Easter bells. And my eyes? The Gabriel marking? This was too fast, too much.

"*Mon petit,* I suppose Sister Karis kept us her little secret. And for good reason. Many have awaited the time of your coming out. And sadly, not all wish you well."

Lille offered me a seat on the banquette under the arched window. She was lightness next to me, like a luminous wind percolating with emotion. She called to the back for a cup of tea, and a tall, robust and frighteningly dark creature named Baabar emerged majestically from behind the painted curtain. He brought a silver-filigreed tray bearing two perfect blue porcelain cups of mint tea and a saucer of warm *punitions*. I was a child again in Sister Karis's kitchen. French children happily take their first steps in the world for the reward of a buttery *punition* cookie. They were called *punitions* because it was truly a grave punishment to wait at the oven's edge for the cookies to cool.

Lille grinned. "I make a batch of *punitions* every Friday for *les enfants* in the neighborhood on their way home from *l'école.* They especially love when I add chips off the block of dark chocolate. Have one."

I now recognize the irony in Lille offering me a *punition* that first day at 11, rue de Bourbon. She was tempting me to take my first steps into her world. A world of mystery, invisible boundaries and wings of light.

I was unfamiliar with the term "Protector" that first day in the bakery. He was introduced simply as Baabar. And like Sister Karis, he had been tapped from the beginning to be a Protector. But no ordinary Protector. He had been created as one of the Protectors of the Order of Gabriel. His earthly task was to ensure that I was shielded from the Dark Deep long enough for me to discover my destiny here on earth. And then it would be up to me whether I would have the strength and courage to deliver the Message of Gabriel.

Baabar was mysterious, even frightening at first glance. He was exotic and strange, a mystical creature like I had never seen. A gentle giant, he was much too grand for the small space of the bakery. Baabar could have stepped from any one of Sister Karis's fairy tales, spun so brilliantly for me as a child, even down to the perfectly cut emeralds for his eyes. His skin was the color of a roasted cacao bean, a rich burnt brown. He smelled of mint and honey, and his bald head gleamed in the sunlight. There was a boxer's strength in the way he turned, beat and flipped the dough in his huge hands. But I would never meet a more tender spirit. It would be Baabar who would teach me the greatest lesson—the lesson of sacrificial love.

CHAPTER 8

The Levain Bakery was much more than a fabulous pastry shop. A secret world was living and operating deep inside this mysterious corner building on the Île Saint-Louis. Here was an earthly home for angels. Behind the tall, carved olive wood doors with gilt wings etched in their top panels was an invisible boundary to a celestial oasis. Maybe it was the warm glow of candlelight flickering from the ancient Venetian glass globe in the entry, or the lemony perfume of verbena that edged the cobbled courtyard; regardless, my spirit knew I had stumbled upon a mythical place. Only this wasn't a myth.

The baroque mansion was designed around an interior courtyard, neatly hidden from the street. A clever footpath of ancient horseshoes led to a secret garden. It was amassed in cherry blossoms, lavender and rosemary. Coral roses attended a gurgling marble fountain wreathed by a necklace of violet water lilies. Generations prior, it had been the humble watering trough for *les chevaux*.

Stepping inside, the Rococo-inspired entry was anchored by a grand central marble staircase that curved seductively up into the girth of the ancient building. A true work of art. My eyes were immediately drawn upward to the art deco stained-glass skylight high above in the grand hall. Thousands of slivers of mirror and gold glass beads winking in the sun hung from nowhere it seemed. The first time, I shook my head in disbelief, adrenaline pumping. Adding to the otherworldliness were hundreds of twinkling lights that danced on golden cords hanging in the darkness, just barely kissing the white and black parquet floors below. When the windows near the eaves were open, the lights swayed like a company of fireflies spinning and swirling.

Eleven, rue de Bourbon was ever grander upon inspection, boasting several royal apartments, each occupying an entire floor. The space also included an elegantly appointed salon on the first floor, shared by all the residents, as well as the bakery on the street, the ballroom on the second floor and a string of lilliputian rooms on the top floor for guests like myself.

The Sun King would surely have approved of the grand salon for one of his royal ballets. It did not take much imagination to hear the harpsichord and be drawn back in time to silk bouffant gowns swishing across the parquet floors. I could close my eyes and see a parade of ladies with their mounds of powdered hair, rouged cheeks and ostrich plumes, exchanging coquettish smirks and coy curtsies with a line of noble gentlemen clad in velvet coats with gold fleur-de-lis buttons. There was a magic to the room, and not only because of the thousands of twinkling crystals that danced above in the massive chandelier. The room was just alive, glowing with an otherworldly light. I didn't know it then, but in the salon, postulants like me had received celestial instruction for generations.

The mansion was enchanting but that did not rival the mystical creatures or their fantastical stories carefully protected within its elegant frame. A fruitwood *secretaire* in the salon held a series of large leather-bound tomes organized by angelic name that carefully recorded our kind's earthly history. These books remain important, because they document every winged spirit sent to earth. I would soon learn that there were many like myself, created as morning stars and charged with the task of bringing illumination to this world. Not all fulfill their missions. For whatever reason, some never accept their supernatural gifts. They become mere shadows of what they were created to be. Others succumb to the material world, living lives on the surface, never willing to look inside to the spirit and claim their true powers. And then there are those, such as the line of the archangel Lucifer, who relinquish their holy Light to the Dark Deep. This is why 11, rue de Bourbon is so important to the story. For centuries, there have been sacred enclaves, such as this one, where Guardians have been entrusted with the task of protecting the winged spirits on earth, helping them realize their lighted destinies. Ultimately, it all comes down to the Light winning out against the Darkness.

As you will come to see, my experience at 11, rue de Bourbon likened more to a magician's cap that never ceased to shock and amaze. These little surprises, well hidden in the silken lining, challenged what was real and true on this plane. If the building could only tell its own story, it would say with a certainty that angels indeed live among us here on earth.

On my first day, Lille shared the story of one particular angel Guardian, a gentleman by the name of Louis Latour, who had at one time lived in Apartment 3. In his earthly life, he had been a world-renowned ornithologist, a bit eccentric, who frequently traveled the world, always returning with yet another addition to his collection of exotic birds. Professor Latour was often found politely asking his birds to instruct fledgling angels on the gift of flying. At first I was sure Lille was jesting to put me at ease.

On a tour of the apartment, Lille pointed to a row of crooked hooks lining the wall. Long ago, they had held bamboo cages for Monsieur Latour's avian family. Lille recalled his rainbow lory, *petite* Chou. Chou-Chou would fly out of Monsieur Latour's window and land on Lille's shoulder in the garden, patiently awaiting a brioche treat. It was Monsieur Latour with his dear Chou who encouraged Lille's own spirit to soar on behalf of humanity.

I often found myself conversing with the stone walls of the ancient building, peppering them with questions, hoping to coax a word about those who had come before me, especially my papa and Valentina. But like its residents, the building proved a master at keeping secrets. And so I had to wait patiently for Lille or some of the others to offer little morsels of the secret story that lived and breathed within the mortar and stone of 11, rue de Bourbon.

I'll never forget Lille giggling, "Gabrielle, are you familiar with the painter Paul Cézanne?" I almost choked. I remembered my twelfth birthday, when Sister Karis gifted me a book of the artist's paintings. Karis claimed it was a surprise find in a *bouquiniste* stall, bought on one of her mysterious trips to Paris. It became one of my favorite treasures. When Sister June ripped from the book what she considered a scandalous nude sketch of a courtesan, I wept for days.

Lille said, "Well, Cézanne's mistress, Hortense, sought refuge here to give birth to their son, Paul. Karis performed the midwifery duties. It was she who refused Cézanne entrance during the birth, so he sat here on the bottom stone step with a bottle of absinthe, pencil in quivering hand, and sketched this *Madonna and Child*. It remains one of his only religious pieces."

I could not believe I was looking at an original Cézanne.

Lille pointed to a place just above the thick trim molding. "If you look closely here, you can just make out his autograph."

But the greatest surprise came when Lille ushered me down the spiral staircase to the corner apartment on the second floor. Opening the door she said, "This was Sister Karis's room before she was directed to the Sacred Heart convent."

My mouth dropped open. The mysterious tapestry of my life continued to unravel. There, on the Louis XVI desk, was a framed picture of me in pigtails, sitting on Sister Karis's lap in the garden at Sacred Heart, our smiles glowing out of the frame. There was so much I did not know about Sister Karis. Next, Lille unfastened the brass latch on the tall French windows and called a bonjour to the familiar street performer on the Pont Marie bridge.

Turning her jubilant gaze back in my direction, she said,

"That is Bernard—such a sweet man. He and Karis were a pair of lovebirds, you know. It was before she was called to you. He used to set up below her window by that rose bush and tease her from her dreams with his magic violin. While you were growing up, Sister Karis came back once a year for a visit. It was a treat for us all, especially our romantic Bernard. Those visits were how we know so much about you. You were her life, you know. But one day she and Bernard will pick up where they left off. He is still called to be on this side for now."

My mouth was gaping open. Who were these people? I remembered Sister Karis's annual trips away. They were the first two weeks of every August, and she would pack her old, battered bible of recipes, two fresh loaves of bread and a journal and gleefully set off. Very few details were offered about her journey upon returning except for a new recipe or two, a sack generously filled to the brim with cherries for the sisters and a funny story or two for all. Sister Karis would also return with a special gift for me. Away from the nosy eyes of the sisters, she would place a beautiful gold paper box tied with a rose ribbon into my hands. Inside I would find two macaroons, one for each of us. Those delicious macaroons foreshadowed the life she knew was ahead for me at the Levain Bakery.

CHAPTER 9

Getting acclimated to my new life at 11, rue de Bourbon was easier than I imagined. My days were surprisingly disciplined, ordered much like St. Benedict's rules at Sacred Heart. Instead of the psalms, I meditated on measurements, litanies of ingredients, and took solemn posture before the ovens. Stumbling into the bakery each morning at half past three, I worked straight through the day until I heard Lille flip the sign on the front door to *A Demain.* My evening ritual consisted of the partaking of a demi-baguette and a slice of Emmentaler cheese, sometimes *jambon,* in my room for dinner. Most nights after climbing the ninety-nine steps to my elfin room on the roof, I would fall directly into my dreams. The cheese and bread remnants I left became a welcomed feast for the family of mice living behind the gable. I never realized the peace I shared with them. Or that a wise owl and his enemy, the vexing pugilist Raven, took their positions of duel on the stone sill, each determined to win me to his side.

My introductions to the other residents were slow in coming. But nothing could have prepared me for the Guardians. These were the most sage of our kind, charged with introducing postulants like myself into the angel mysteries and channeling our unique gifts for good. From the window by the oven, I would sneak curious peeks at Pierre, who often read in the garden. Here he was the head Guardian, but he was also an esteemed eye doctor by earthly trade. The residents of 11, rue de Bourbon honored him as one of the best of our celestial kind, using his superior gift of visions to further the divine plan. I was lucky to have him as my teacher. Pierre had a gentle face, punctuated by owlish eyes, behind large tortoiseshell glasses.

A glass beaded chain hung just below his heart and secured his ancient gold pocket watch. He often rubbed it with his thumb and forefinger during our lessons. It kept a different kind of time. Lille and he were a happy pair and lived together in Apartment 4.

There was Baabar, my Protector and unlikely partner in the bakery. I was awakened each morning by the beautiful, deep hum of his morning prayers in some mysterious language. In the kitchen, his large hands moved with a quiet discipline over the dough as he chanted melodically the salat. There was a peace and surety about Baabar that grounded me. And I loved his crooked, shy smile and the way his eyebrows lifted in humor to reveal the two flashing emerald lights usually hidden behind his lacquered lashes.

There was also an intriguing resident in apartment 3 who appeared at teatime in the bakery every day. I could not engage her, but I knew she was special too. I came to learn she was a painter. When I asked Lille about her, she just chuckled, "Oh, yes, a painter. But so much more, dear."

Pierre responded, "You mean our resident firecracker, Sophie? Trust, she did not get her name for her *cheveux rouge*. You will meet Sophie on her timing; she is superstitious like that."

There was also petite Jobe, the "keeper of the keys." One could not miss this lilliputian character, who jangled a brass ring fastened at his belt, weighted down with a collection of keys. Everyone came to attention when he entered a room, all eyes on the glittering assortment of unusual keys. I called out to him one day in the garden, and he appeared not to have heard or seen me. Later I asked Baabar about him.

"Oh, Jobe has only the sixth sense. He has proven our savior more times than I can count. Only his soul speaks for him. He was tapped to encourage angels-in-training to use their inner compass instead of relying so on their fragile flesh and bone. Sometimes on the pilgrimage of life, even angels must be reminded of the intuitive powers of the soul. We call him the gatekeeper because he holds the keys to our true home, the place of continuous Light."

I had no idea then what Baabar meant, nor the depth of Jobe's faith. But he would prove to be my redeemer, opening and closing doors when I needed direction or help seeing with my spiritual eyes.

On the third day of my seventh week at the Levain Bakery, Lille surprised me at the oven with a formal invitation to join Pierre and her for tea in their apartment.

"Gabrielle, knock on the door to Apartment 4 when you have finished the last pralines for Madame Coutier's party on Saturday. I will have Baabar turn off the ovens and close up the shop for you."

The door to apartment Apartment 4 opened, and I was ushered in by the tinkling music of the piano playing inside. Its ethereal notes set the mood. They had the power to awaken the sleepy soul. The hubbub of the bakery was long gone. I was on another plane.

Lille smiled. "This is Pierre's welcome song, written just for you. We have all been anticipating the day you would come to us. Since the hour your father sent word of your birth on the pilgrims' road, we have waited."

The trembling started. She knew my father? I carelessly dropped the gift bag of pistachio macaroons on the lacquered red side table. Lille clapped her hands.

"Oh, Gabrielle, your macaroons are Pierre's favorite. Thank you, *ma chérie.*" She ushered me through the entry vestibule.

Pierre and Lille's apartment was like a fantastical museum to rival any keen imagination. There were handsomely carved mahogany bookcases lining three walls, full of wondrous curiosities and eclectic mementos. I ran my finger across the spine of an old book with the title *Saints and Demons* etched in gold and black. There was a massive rose glass jar of miscellaneous coins that surely included the world's currency for the last three millennia. Hanging on the open wall was an onyx African peace mask, a pair of exotic butterflies preserved in a lighted glass teardrop, an albino peacock feather with a gold tip and a linen necklace strung with a collection of rare Tahitian black pearls. All glowed with a strange light; their source, I could not see.

Numerous framed photographs of random people from different time periods were scattered atop ornate tables. In one Lille and Pierre were dressed in Victorian attire but looked just as they did now, clearly escaping the cruel dance with time. There were sepia pictures of Lille and Pierre walking on a black-pebbled beach, another of the two sitting beneath a baobab tree, even one with Lille holding a baby. Most unusual were their eyes. Even in the faded tint, you could see this mysterious light emanating from them. But it was the next picture that clutched my heart. It was of a young woman sitting on a bench in a garden. I looked at Pierre. What? How? It was a picture of me, it seemed.

Lille came up behind me and reached for the picture in my hands.

"Gabrielle, your mother was quite astonishing. Most of us still cannot get over your likeness to her. You too have that gypsy, dark, wavy hair, olive skin and hazel feline eyes. You even share her voice. But it is your eyes, always the eyes, that proclaim the line of Gabriel is in you."

I did not know what to say. How does one react to hearing others speak with such familiarity about you? But Lille and Pierre did not see it as unusual. I would only later understand the imperative for protection of the line of Gabriel. No chances could be taken with the sacred birth of the Light on earth. Only later would I learn too of eternal time. Even those marked by the Light come to earth for a set small quantum of time.

Lille called me over to the large round table, gold-trimmed and mounted on curved legs, in the center of the room. There was a luscious pomegranate split and tempting on a green oval majolica plate. Lille motioned for me to partake. "Welcome to our home, Gabrielle. Let me offer you this sacred fruit."

The seeds exploded with promise in my mouth as if I had never tasted a pomegranate before. Somehow all was different to my senses. I stepped deeper into the salon and leaned gratefully on the shiny black piano for support. The tall windows on either side were framed by soft velvet drapes in a rich ecclesial purple. On a lush charcoal-tufted Napoleon III divan next to the window, a pair of silver Weimaraners sat regally, watching me. Lille broke the now uncomfortable silence.

"Gabrielle, breathe. You have nothing to fear. We are here for you."

Pierre invited me to the bamboo chair with its heart-shaped, painted footstool, and then joined Lille on the sofa across from me. For what was either a minute or an hour, they just stared at me, or was it *through* me? Suddenly, a shimmery glow encircled the room, and I looked around for the light source. There was none. Returning my view to my hosts, I became aware of a golden aura arcing above their heads like those medieval frescos of angels with gilt halos. Spreading her arms Lille then introduced Pierre with a grand formality.

"Gabrielle, Pierre is your Guardian. You were always meant to join us here at 11, rue de Bourbon. Now the time has come for you to understand who you really are and to begin your training."

"What? But I am a just a humble baker." A nervous giggle escaped my lips. Was this a joke? I looked around to see if anyone else was laughing at Lille's theatrics. Maybe this was how these strange but kind people entertained themselves. There was no question they were different. A troupe of gypsies, right? Now I was beginning to question why Sister Karis had sent me here. I looked around the now claustrophobic room for the quickest exit. I'd go back to the abbey and happily wear the habit and scapular.

My squirming in the maharani seat did not discourage Lille in the least. She continued.

"Pierre is what mortals would call a clairvoyant. When he looks into a person's eyes, he is invited into their story—past, present and future. He sees the emotions, the invisible wounds, the joys, the fears and hopelessness. More importantly, though, he sees what the Holy One aspires for that human vessel. Many come to Pierre complaining of their dimming vision when often it is life that is blocking their view. Pierre helps them to see again, but not like they suppose. He guides them back to the Truth, placing the compass of hope in their right hand. He helps them pursue their destiny. Gabrielle, does this sound at all familiar to you? Most of us morning stars envy *your* gift."

I must have shot Lille a look of fright, because she quickly switched the subject back to Pierre. How did she know about my visions? They were my carefully concealed secret. Over the years, I had become quite good at scattering them before they had a chance to take hold of my mind's third eye. The visions frightened me. Seeing into the intimate stories and sometimes futures of strangers, and especially people I cared about, was not a gift but a fearful burden. Especially when you couldn't stop something from happening or couldn't rewrite their stories for them. I had no way to end the pain, to fight their demons, to wipe their slates clean. My visions were my curse, I thought.

Pierre took my hand. "You will give this world, one person at a time, a reason to hope. The eyes are the windows into the soul. And you are blessed to see more than most. As your Guardian, I will help you to use your gifts for good. If you study creation at any length, you will see that each created being is wired with a unique sacred threading of light. It is the Divine One's signature. Each minuscule fiber is imprinted with Love. We—and that includes you, Gabrielle—can *see* through to their souls. With our gift, we have the ability to stimulate, or jump-start, if you will, those electric fibers. The human creature then remembers his or her divine value and purpose. You have the extraordinary power to change people's lives for good. Within, you carry Gabriel's message of Hope. With a simple nudge at the spirit, you can proclaim the sacred message that Love will always triumph. A lost human can then move away from the Darkness and into the Light again. Because of you."

Weren't those Sister Karis's last words to me?

Lille patted Pierre and me on our knees. She was beaming.

"You both have the gift of helping mortals and even angels see themselves again as the Holy One sees them," she said. "You remind them of their inner divine spark, long forgotten, so they have the courage to recover, heal, renew and believe again."

It was the way Lille said "believe again" that unsettled me. There was an angst in her voice; it felt out of place. I would understand why soon enough.

With a tender voice, Pierre said, "Gabrielle, this is a lot to take in. You are truly one of the exceptional of our kind. I do not believe I have seen a light-bearer so bright with potential during my time here. It will be an honor to be your Guardian."

Pierre turned to an unsettled Lille. "Dear, you are forgetting that time has no power over us. He will return to us. The Holy One always works for good. You must trust, my love. Where is your faith?"

The tears pooled in Lille's eyes. "But Pierre, what if we are too late? He is still our son."

They both seemed to forget my presence.

Pierre tenderly embraced Lille. "He is the son of the Holy One first. How about you check on the tea in the kitchen? Don't forget to include Jobe's healing rosemary honey."

Lille retreated to the kitchen. But her secret still floated in the air between us. A son? Where was he? Who was he?

Pierre elbowed the dogs off the sofa and invited me to come and sit next to him.

"Gabrielle, my dear, the Holy One has brought us together. Nothing here on earth or in heaven is by chance. It is my charge to invite you into the angelic Mysteries."

I sat stunned. Speechless.

"Imagine the divine plan as much like that spiderweb there in the corner of the windowpane. The intricate pattern of the web is exceptionally beautiful. At first glance, the fine silk thread appears impossibly delicate, unpredictable, so fragile. Much like the human story. But I assure you, the silk spun from the mind of the Master Architect endures for eternity. You must trust in the sacred design.

"And that leads us to your gifts. I was tapped as your Guardian because you are from the Order of Gabriel. The Order of Gabriel was created from the beginning to be the Holy One's trusted and sacred messengers. The archangel Gabriel was the first warrior to brave the Dark Deep with his Light and divine proclamations of mercy and hope. He is your heritage."

In my head I was reeling. Was there a place called the Dark Deep? Pierre knew my thoughts before they even raised the red flag of panic.

"Gabrielle, the Dark Deep is invisible and yet all around us. It can take the form of evil or despair. It feeds on violence, pride, greed and hurt. You've seen it in the eyes—the anger, the defeat, the hopelessness. It leaves humanity with a pervading sense of emptiness and despair. The Dark Deep has someone in its ugly mouth when he or she begins to question the sacredness of life itself. We lose some to the bottomless black hole of the Deep. All of creation suffers and struggles against this Darkness every day here on earth. Even with your gifts, you will struggle against the dark forces too. It takes much faith to deflect the power of the Dark, hungry for the soul. The Raven, disguised in the sinister cloak of night, is a messenger of the Darkness. Be on your guard when the Raven crosses your path. Protect your light."

He frightened but intrigued me with his confident talk of destined plans, light-bearers fighting the Dark Deep, Guardians, Protectors and the Order of Gabriel. I was the child who would scurry away and hide in the broom closet or under my bed when the sisters gathered in the chapel under candlelight, chanting for hours to an invisible Presence. I, on the other hand, was always more comfortable organizing my life in measurements, like the 50 grams of sugar necessary for spun caramel. And yet I could not deny the mysterious whisperings of something more deep within me.

I worried Pierre could hear my internal dialogue. He reached for my hand, and the same warmth I had experienced from Lille on my first day in the bakery enveloped me. I could feel something inside me loosening from its protective corset. Pierre next said something that would forever imprint me.

"Gabrielle, we become the creatures the Holy One created us to be only when we choose faith over reason, what we intuitively know over what we see. It does not mean we will not face obstacles along the way, but we have a choice. We can offer Light or hang our heads in defeat and allow the Dark Deep to win. You were created as a spirit of Light—never forget that. I can help prepare you for the journey, but you, my dear one, must choose to become the Master's winged messenger of Hope."

My mind swirled like a tempest, desperate to find a grounding in a stormy sea. In the past, whenever my mind was twisted in a corkscrew, I carefully put things back into proper order by reciting recipes in my head. It gave me such calm clarity. Just as I was going through the ingredient list for a baba au rhum—one tablespoon good dark rum, half a cup milk, two tablespoons sugar—I looked up and blinked not once, or twice, but three times. Were those angel's wings tattooed on the backs of Pierre's hands I saw as his fingers glided across the black and white keys of the piano? Lille returned with an elaborate tray of teacups and saucers, and an elegant sandwich tree. She saw my disbelief and smiled.

"Oh, you will be seeing a lot of those markings around here. They are the golden wings. Sophie, in Apartment 3, is our resident artist. Her sacred markings etched in light are exceptional. She inked Pierre on his pointer fingers so that when he composes music, they become an angel in flight. Mine are here, hidden beneath my ring. Our golden tattoos remind us of who we are and why we are here on earth. One day, you too will be marked with the wings."

Pierre stopped playing and said, "We pray you will choose to join us, honoring the great destiny that was bestowed upon you. But first you must achieve mastery over your gifts."

And then he did a strange thing. In parting, instead of a cheek-to-cheek à bientôt, he touched his heart with his hand, and then he brought his hand to me and touched my furiously beating heart.

"Gabrielle, I offer you my spirit. It is all I have of any true value. You will know when you meet others like yourself, because they too will touch their hearts and offer the best of themselves to you. It is our secret sign, honoring the presence of Love in this world. You will find there are many of us out there. Join us. Accept your destiny. You are an angel from the line of Gabriel."

CHAPTER 10

For the next several days I muddled about, inebriated by a nettling uncertainty that spilled over the edges of my reality. I even feared for my sanity. The boundaries of my existence, which I had always assumed to be neat and fixed, had mysteriously shifted. Like in a dream, the words had casually floated off Pierre's lips, *"You are one of us."* And I was now supposed to hang my apron on this bizarre revelation? As a child, I reveled in the possibilities of magical worlds, of fairies in the forest and shining castles in the clouds. But as the years had tumbled forward, my imagination was sobered by ugly reality. How could I make sense of what Pierre and Lille had suggested—this amazing new way of life for me? They had an expanded vision of creation, and it included, of all things, mystical eyes and lighted wings. Was I to believe there really was an invisible curtain that separated the world I could see from another world, a spiritual one? A world of angels? And I was one of them?

In my distracted haze, I forgot to put the eggs in the dough for the croissants, and after my fifth attempt at the perfect double-chocolate amaretto soufflé for Madame Tulipe's *anniversaire,* Baabar took the reins and gently set me down, like a confused child, on a stool in the corner of the kitchen. I watched as he kneaded little rounds of dough and wrapped them around chunks of dark chocolate. I stared at him from across the wooden table and imagined a mighty gladiator from a time long ago. A brave warrior who stirred a mixture of fear and admiration. Baabar placed the tray of prepared dough into the oven and came to quietly kneel before me.

"Gabrielle, do not be frightened. You were always meant to come here, just as I was. There is much for you to learn, but be patient. You will see in time, all will be revealed to you."

His deep, melodic voice was reassuring and calmed me. I wanted to believe him. And yet my rational, cynical brain was having a difficult time surrendering to my intuitive heart.

"I remember the first time I met Lille. She was browsing through the *Marché Dejean*, the African market in the eighteenth arrondissement. She came with her large woven basket and clearly knew her way around the African bazaar, purchasing melegueta peppers, dried mangoes and brightly colored African linens. In a sea of my dark brothers, Lille was out-of-place, an alabaster *Sacre Coeur*. I had just arrived from Morocco and couldn't find a job. Lille walked with purpose right up to me and said, 'Baabar, you have finally arrived. I was sad to hear the news of your father's passing. I know you miss him. He was a great man and will continue to serve from the other side.' Kissing my cheek and touching my heart, she proclaimed, 'I will expect you in a white, *très* starched apron at the Levain Bakery on Monday.' Before I could so much as utter a *bon mot*, she was gone. It took a while but I began to understand my destiny, here at 11, rue de Bourbon. So many spend a lifetime and never discover their purpose here on earth. Gabrielle, it is not my job to invite you into the secrets of our kind. I only serve as your Protector against the Darkness that always goes greedily after the Light, especially one as brilliant as yours. I will be here for you now and always." He stood and, with a formal bow, turned back to the wall of ovens.

From that day, we began a friendship where I gained much more than I was able to give. He taught me much about faith. He was never without his father's gold-filigreed, leather-bound Koran. As I pinched the dough around the tartes, he would read from his holy book. I learned of Allah, the all-knowing, all-powerful One who created the earth and the heavens. Baabar did not believe Allah created hell. He said we did that ourselves. He never doubted that the Creator continued to transcend time and space to engage with creation. I was still too afraid to believe in anything beyond what I could see with my own eyes. I was much more comfortable seeing life as an artist's still life, where the boundaries were predictable and fixed.

I tried to forget my visions entirely. But Baabar was persistent. He spoke of the stories of Joseph and his clairvoyant dreams, the visitations by angels, the birth of prophets and saviors and the ongoing redeeming of humankind. He never doubted that there was more to the unfolding love story of creation.

As a child in Morocco, he believed in the Chosen—Muhammad, Abraham, Moses, Christus, John, Mary, the Buddha—each with inspired knowledge and grand missions on behalf of the Creator. Unlike mine, Baabar's postulancy at 11, rue de Bourbon was not focused on convincing him there was an invisible world but rather that he was worthy to be a part of it. Baabar's humility was his greatest gift.

That first autumn, I learned much from Baabar under the canopy of flour and the incense of chocolate in the blessed Levain Bakery. He believed the longer the spirit was held within the boundaries of humanity, the more difficult it was to remember life before with the Holy One.

Baabar said, "It's the reason Christus instructed his disciples to become again like children to enter paradise."

Baabar was often on his knees. He would roll out his mat beside the oven and his spirit would depart the space of the busy kitchen on a woven carpet of prayers. I was too cynical then to even consider a conversation with the Divine. It was not until later, in absolute desperation, that I too would knock at the Holy Door, head tilted in submission, knees bent in humility, prayers my life preserver to endure the pendulum swing from joy to sorrow and back again. To live in hope was never promised to be easy.

CHAPTER 11

Lille and Pierre were well prepared for the skepticism of their new postulant. They had been training angels for a long time and knew when to send in holy reinforcements. And thus, the hand-painted invitation mysteriously arrived one morning. It was a watercolor of the Sacred Heart convent with no date, time or signature. It simply read, "Come for tea at Apartment 3 when the Spirit moves you."

I had decided to avoid anymore 11, rue de Bourbon invitations to tea. I even took to buttoning up my baker's coat to my chin. It's called hiding. Pierre and Lille had tried to rattle me, but I was determined to remain a simple, happy baker. I was always at my best in the kitchen, doing what was my passion. Peace was in the bread.

However, the celestial powers were determined. Just as I was counting stair number seventy-seven on my ascent to the top floor, exhausted from a long day postured at the ovens, the door to Apartment 3 popped open to reveal the fiery red curls of Sophie d'Or.

"Surely you are a wee bit curious about the gypsy in Apartment 3?" Sophie giggled.

And thus commenced my second tea with angels. My introduction to Sophie was like seeing the world in color for the first time. She made life, even breathing, extravagant, magical, like sequins shimmering on a beautiful swath of blue-green silk. When I stepped through her door, the teakettle heralded my arrival with a happy whistle. For a little while, I would be a star invited to orbit her wild sun.

"Come in, Gabrielle. I have a rose mélange tea steeping just for you. You still go by Gabrielle, right? What delightful irony that those dowdy, devout sisters at Sacred Heart had no idea their little pixie was a secret angel, one of the Order of Gabriel, no less. Not since your mother and father have we been blessed with this kind of hope on earth. But don't let it go to your head. And don't think I will ever become one of your handmaidens!"

I still had not spoken a word. Never had I seen anyone more exotically beautiful. But in a peculiar way, she looked strangely like Sister Karis. I couldn't quite put my finger on it, because her hair was wild, a mass of red ringlets the color of cinnamon, with streaks of gold framing a heart-shaped face. Her pouty lips were ruby red and her gray eyes clear as the water from the spring back at Sacred Heart. I suddenly felt the tears welling up. Sophie spoke and I was sure I was hearing Sister Karis's voice again.

"Gabrielle, my sister loved you dearly. I remember when she had the vision of you wrapped in that lace tablecloth on the road from Santiago. She said you were her destiny. She would be your Protector, take on Mary's veil, sacrifice her life here with us to take care of you. You had to live on the sacred ground of the convent for protection. We all feared for your safety and hers. The Dark One is vicious and so cunning. When the Holy One sends a Light-bearer of your magnitude down to earth, the serpent usually strikes. Karis became a nun so that you, the chosen herald, could survive. If only you had known her before! I'm sure sweet Bernard will sing you a love song about her moonlit eyes. Karis was the one who encouraged Pierre and Lille to move to Paris and take the helm of the Levain Bakery as cover. Surely you sensed her spirit in that baker's chapel?"

Sophie was Sister Karis's sister? I watched as she poured tea from the kettle into a chipped rose pottery mug. I recognized the identical mannerisms of Sister Karis. The tears were coming fast now, uncontrollable. Sister Karis had been my only experience of love. Sophie put her hand gently on my shoulder. I wept like a newborn.

"Gabrielle, you gave her earthly life a mother's purpose. She lives brighter now because of her sacrifice for you. Her love for you earned her the highest celestial brand. She was sad to say goodbye, but her work was done. Karis's mission was to imprint you with love so that you would be strong when the time came to…well, you'll see soon enough."

Sophie swirled into the kitchen for the *miel des fleurs,* then leaned her head back out the door. "Oh, and my sister really appreciated the garden you planted around her mortal burial. She brought me a bouquet. Look here, I dried some of the posies in the pages of my diary."

My mouth opened. No words came out. I was stunned. Sister Karis came here, to the bakery, after I dropped the three handfuls of dirt on her grave? I walked to the bookcase leaning against the shelf to regain my composure. The white, crackling plaster was wallpapered in an elaborate and haphazard collage of photos, paintings, embroidered pieces and charcoal sketches. A wall to inspire. In the room's center stood a whimsical sculpture of a spreading plane tree with branches that seemed to stretch across the room. Golden leaves shimmered all over, each bearing a name, but no ordinary name, one that was strange and unpronounceable.

Sophie pointed to a leaf and said, "Ilayael is Lille's angelic name. And there, that one, Xiron—that is Pierre's. Mine is on this branch, Oe. Maybe one day I will be honored to imprint you with the golden wings, and your beautiful angelic name will find its way here upon the Tree of Ascension."

I stepped away from the art wall and explored the rest of Sophie's studio, a kaleidoscope of images and changing colors. I felt like I had stepped into a living, breathing piece of art. The patterned tin ceiling soared fifteen feet, and its magnificent chandelier boasted hundreds of white squares of linen paper floating in the air, like fluttering butterflies suspended from invisible strings. Some of the sheets had words in black calligraphy, others just thick coats of shimmering paint or watery washes of rainbow colors, little secret messages floating above me.

Watching me, Sophie whispered, "I created this mobile long ago to tell the story of Love. Each swath of linen is a tale of its own. Love comes in many forms. If you look right there, the one with the two women flying above the silver steeple—that is Karis and you, *mon amie.*"

I pointed to a larger square in the center, with a cluster of white wings edged in gold that formed a circle around a golden orb of light.

"That one tells the story of the Light. We, angels, project and protect it here on earth."

Against the far wall were seven floor-to-ceiling canvases, each framed in uniquely carved wood. On closer inspection, I realized the paintings depicted enchanting doors. Sophie had painted the doors to appear slightly ajar, just enough to suggest the magical places behind them. She joined me before one of the surreal paintings. Behind the first door was a glorious weeping willow whimsically dipping its green fingers in a cool spring. For a second, I actually thought I felt the wind blowing through its graceful branches. I suddenly felt a shift in the equilibrium of my spirit. An inner vertigo threatened to topple me. I was spinning, no longer sure what was real.

"Forgive the mess, Gaby, but I'm working at a worker-bee's pace to finish this series for my upcoming art show."

I escaped to the nearby open French doors for a breath of fresh air, the curtains billowing around my feet, and wrapped my fingers tightly around the iron railing to steady myself. Punched in the gut, I could not catch my breath. How could Sister Karis have been here after I saw her buried in the garden? Was resurrection a reality? I collapsed to my knees. Looking through the filigreed iron gate, I saw Jobe clipping roses in the garden. Suddenly, he looked right at me. I felt a chill run down my spine. I was sure Baabar had said he was blind. And yet his lips were moving as if he were speaking to me. Sophie kneeled at my side.

"The gatekeeper knows what you are thinking right now. He is whispering words of comfort to your confused spirit. It is time you started believing in what you cannot see. Look at my doors in these paintings. Open one with your angel eyes and accept your holy sight. You will be able to join your mother, your father, Karis, Pierre, Baabar, me and so many others. You belong with us; You are an angel too."

I launched into a recitation of ingredients for a Mille-Feuille— mascarpone cheese, a teaspoon of balsamic, mission figs, crushed pistachios—but it was not working. My mind was reeling. What to do? What to believe? I got up in a panic and stumbled out the door, tripping as I went, then rushing pell-mell down the stairs past the back entrance to the bakery. Baabar caught my fall, but I wrestled free, tears now flowing. I did not stop until I was across the Pont Marie bridge and through the ornate heavy wooden doors of Notre Dame.

It was my first visit inside this holy chapel. The air was laced with incense as the young priest swung his brass thurible up and down the central aisle. I heard the familiar words of a mass taking place at the high altar. An elderly priest was reading from the Book of Genesis.

"In the beginning, God created the heavens and the earth. The earth was without form and void, and the Darkness was upon the face of the Deep; and the spirit of God was moving over the face of the waters. Then God said, 'Let there be Light,' and there was Light."

The words were a soothing balm to my soul. They transported me back to Sacred Heart, where I had been safe. I found refuge in an empty pew in the corner of a dark cordoned-off private alcove. An aged monk in a brown cassock and leather sandals shuffled across the stone floor after emptying coins from the woven baskets at the altar. Wrinkled, bent over but beatific, he approached me, touched his heart just as Pierre had done, and lightly brushed his hand over my heart. Warmth suddenly spread from my chest to my toes. He then offered me a single golden coin and whispered, "I see you are in need. Take this and light one of those candles. Open your eyes, Gabrielle. You have been traveling too long in the shadows."

I took the coin, bowed my head in confused gratitude and dutifully proceeded to the velvet-trimmed altar. I knelt down on the embroidered prayer bench. I remembered now Sister Karis's words: *"Courage is fear that has said its prayers."*

I could still see the kindly monk's shadow on the stone relief wall beside me. He was whispering a litany, surely praying for my salvation; clearly I was a lost soul. I lit the candle and stood mute before the universe that seemed ready to topple me. And then I heard a beautiful chorus of whispering voices behind me. Chanting, angelic, otherworldly.

"We are here for you. You bear the ancient marking of the Divine. Sent to light the way for many out of the Darkness. Fear not, for we will be with you for the entire journey."

I quickly turned around, but no one was there.

I made my way back across the bridge toward 11, rue de Bourbon. With my head bowed low, I nearly tripped over a group of rosy-cheeked children sitting in rapt attention at the feet of a street performer. It was Bernard. He was blowing and twisting balloons in the shapes of swords, crowns, flowers and even a boat ready to set sail down the Seine. He looked up, and there was a familiar kindness in his eyes. He understood what I was going through.

"Mademoiselle, you appear lost. May I help you find your way?"

He was right. I had never felt so lost in my life. I yearned to hear Sister Karis's voice calling me to check the ovens. I even missed the confounded ringing of the chapel bells. They had always grounded time and space for me. Where were they now?

I responded, "Thank you, but I am headed to the Levain Bakery."

With a mischievous grin, he said, "You will not be lost for long, mademoiselle. All find themselves lost on the pilgrim's road at one time or another. But you should know…that's when the angels gather."

PART THREE

Constellation of Hope

Now faith is the substance of things hoped for, the evidence of things not seen.

~ HEBREWS 11:1 ~

CHAPTER 12

Baabar called my experience a wink of grace, a little nudge to say that there is more to the story than meets the eye. My curiosity was moving at a canter, and I had no choice but to hang on. Careful not to frighten me, Pierre determined the bakery would become my first classroom and Lille my first teacher. Within a week, I had been introduced to the entire neighborhood, her family, as she liked to call them. It was French tradition to stop by the local *boulangerie* for each day's bread, and Lille never missed an opportunity to illuminate each customer. Even the most curmudgeonly on the island could not resist her baguette handoff and radiant smile. Lille encouraged them to include her in the most intimate details of their lives. She knew when one of the Laurier children was sick, when the train arrived bearing home a wounded young Philippe on leave from Afghanistan, when Monsieur Le Tour was unfaithful to his wife, and when Papa Lebrun was forced to sell the family car to pay off his card losses. Lille may not have been gifted with my visions, but she had her own gift of clairvoyance, somehow knowing that the tumor was growing in Madame Coucher's left breast before she did, and that the baby inside Evangeline's belly had taken its last breath.

One day I gasped and flushed bright red when Madame Cherie shared over the counter that her husband had an enlarged testicle. But Lille responded with tender compassion and sent her home with an extra éclair to tweak Monsieur Cherie's good humor. She winked at me and said, "Gabrielle, it is an honor when people entrust you with the frayed threads of their lives. I weave them into my own fabric, and my tapestry is more sacred for it."

I admired how Lille tended to her flock, never giving up on a single soul, not even the brutish ones. All who crossed her path received an angel's blessing.

The bakery became my sanctuary now, and I started to relax a bit, happy to be tied into my starched cotton apron and up to my elbows in flour. There was never a lull in the traffic; instead it seemed that the lines got even longer. In the midst of the chaos, Lille would look up from the cash register and say, "Bonjour, Madame Leroy. Have you met Gabrielle? She is our new apprentice." Or she would shout out to whoever was waiting in line, "We have a new *pâtisserie artiste en residence*! Join us in the tea salon today between one and three to taste Gabrielle's *tarte du jour*."

Up went signs outside the bakery every morning announcing my *pâtisserie du jour* and Lille's special tea to accompany it. We even got a mention by a food critic in *Le Journal*: "*Levain Bakery, vous promener un gouter du paradis sur terre*." My chocolate torte was becoming quite famous in the neighborhood. Clever Lille. The subtle "angel lessons" were coming at me from every direction.

At the counter one day she whispered, "You know, Gabrielle, the Levain Bakery is a place of miracles. I see them every single day." And she just laughed at my skeptical reaction and wagged her finger at my doubtful face. When I thought of miracles, I remembered the line at Sacred Heart stretching beyond our stone gates each Good Friday. The sick in body and spirit made the pilgrimage to the convent for a holy anointing by the priest and the sisters. All came desperately hoping for an Easter miracle. What they did not know was that for weeks I, lowly Gabrielle, had been the one charged with preparing the oil in the iron pot normally reserved for melting chocolate. My reward was reprieve from singing at matins. After Sister Louise ran off with Monsieur Dubois, the butcher, I had to pick and press the roses for their fragrance and healing properties. I also finely chopped rosemary from the kitchen potager and soaked it in holy water brought each year from Lourdes. I suddenly envisioned the old wooden paddle I had used to stir all the ingredients into the rich olive oil in an old wine barrel.

There was certainly nothing miraculous about that oil that I could see. Those poor pilgrims came every year, hope blazing in their eyes. It made me spitting angry. I watched them walk out our gates without a glimmer of a miracle. Monsieur Pape's depressed son still hanged himself, Madame Blanche succumbed to the growth under her right arm, and dear, precious little Louis never had a chance when that truck barreled through the village and struck him. Where were the miracles then? That stinking oil—it was ridiculous to believe in it.

Lille brushed her hand against my cheek so that I would look up from my work. How did she know my thoughts?

"Gabrielle, Sacred Heart was a crucible for the miraculous. Surely you saw that. The faithful found healing there every year. You infused that oil with your love, and healing was made possible. I believe you do not understand what true healing looks like here on earth. You only see the body. Healing occurs when the soul takes a step closer to the Divine. And you helped that happen."

No, I thought, Lille was misled. There was certainly nothing magical about that oil. For if there was, then I would be sitting beside Sister Karis right now kneading dough. Healing would have meant she would be here with me now. Instead I lived with the pain of her absence piercing my heart every day. Lille did not know that I had faithfully prepared my own batch of holy oil and had anointed Sister Karis's forehead, and caressed her arms and feet with it each evening by candlelight. I even beat my chest, fasted and unleashed a fury of pleas to Whoever was listening, but I felt her slipping away from me just the same. I still released the dirt upon her grave.

"Gabrielle, we were so proud of you," Lille said. "You proved that you could surrender your heart completely to another in the way you tenderly cared for Karis. That is how we knew you were ready. Healing, my dear one, transcends the body. The body is fragile but the soul is eternal. Healing occurs when the spirit recognizes that it is clothed in the flesh for only a fraction of time. A gracious time to freely choose love and experience love. The soul continues on, my dear. And, I must add, in quite a beautiful way."

"But Lille, death is horrible. People we love suffer and then leave us."

"You are right. The Dark Deep mounts a formidable stand with the weapon of death. But death hasn't a fighting chance against love. Love cuts the noose of the death strangler from about the neck of the spirit. Healing is fulfilled, the story continues on. When humans remember their own divinity, they experience a glimmer of life beyond the veil. Fragile bodies and difficult life experiences are only part of their stories."

Lille must have sensed she was losing me with her litany of positivity. I was proving a most ornery and truculent student.

"Gabrielle, are you familiar with the phrase 'on the wings of angels'?"

I nodded a stubborn no when of course I knew the phrase well. It was what Sister Karis always said when she heard someone had died. "Bless Madame's journey this evening on the wings of an angel." I figured it was just another one of her many quirky anecdotes.

Lille then took a postcard out of her purse and laid it proudly down on the tile counter. I knew it well. We had sold those postcards to tourists at Sacred Heart, along with candles, medals and prayer cards. The postcard was a replica of the painting of a host of angels that hung over the main altar at Sacred Heart.

Lille said, "Sister Karis said you loved this painting, especially the middle angel. Remember the mysterious winged being with the unusual eyes? You thought you could see something behind those eyes when you were a child, didn't you?"

My mouth dropped, my cheeks flamed in embarrassment. I remembered Sister Josephine catching me climbing the marble altar and touching those angelic eyes. They were magical doors opening just for me. I imagined I could travel through them to some place like in a dream.

Lille began to tell me a story.

"There was once a young girl who was gifted with visions like you. Her mother had already passed through the Holy Door, and she had been left with her father. At a very young age, this girl was plagued with startling visions. Some came in dreams while she slept next to her young sister, and then others tormented her while she was in the market, or even in the pew of her church. In the beginning, Genevieve would scream out when they came upon her, for they revealed frightful, terrible information. She could see a person on his or her last day on earth, and then she would watch them being carried away by winged figures, angels. At first she did not tell anyone. But one day the butcher's son had a seizure and passed out. His mother wailed that he was dead. And the young girl quickly responded, 'No, this is not his time.' And Genevieve was right. The boy woke up and lived another thirty years before a final seizure took him.

"Many in the town began to whisper that she had the eyes of a sorcerer. After one particular vision, the girl felt compelled to touch a baby with a raging fever. The fever left the infant, and her parents joyously spread the word that Genevieve had healed their daughter. The village erupted, hailing a true miracle. But Genevieve had known it was simply not the day the girl was to be called back through the Holy Door. People started traveling from all around for her to lay hands upon them, certain she could physically heal them. The village flourished. On several occasions, the girl appeared to go into an ecstatic state. It was as if her spirit was drawn from her body, and she traveled to another place. She told her little sister that she followed the angels to the Door but had not yet been invited inside.

"Father Goriot, the local priest, followed her around in hopes that she would bless him with a glimpse through the holy door described in the Book of Revelation by St. John. The village became a popular stop on the pilgrim's road. The hunger for miracles made people do crazy things. One woman, whose son was terribly sick, toppled Genevieve over for a clipping of her hair. Another hid beneath the table where she was sharing a meal with her family and collected her crumbs. Her father became alarmed when an entrepreneurial gentleman stole and sold the soiled water from her bath in miniature Venetian glass bottles. Anything to stave off death. Sadly, they were missing the message.

"The growing desperation for the miraculous took a dark turn. Those who did not experience physical healing from her touch became angry. But she was powerless to change the appointed day of their passing. She tried to comfort them by speaking of the beautiful journey through the Door. Telling them to live fully in every breath, not to waste a single inhale until the appointed day when the final bell would toll. But that only made people more angry. Fear does that. It reveals the worst in humanity.

"As she got older, her visions became more intense, lasting longer. She could now open the Door and glimpse the mysterious world beyond. Genevieve yearned to step through that Door herself. One snowy winter night, she was visited by one of the winged figures. This strange annunciation dream did not frighten her. She had been waiting for this day, the day the angel Raphael would take her further into the Mysteries. Now she saw the vision of herself peeking through the shimmering veil. A magical scene it was, the day of her death; she received her own glowing wings and became one of heaven's own. It would be her own father whom she would escort through the Door her first time as an angel from the Order of Raphael."

Lille stopped telling the story and took my hands into hers.

"Gabrielle, that young girl was my mother. I come from the line of Raphael. We are charged as healers here on earth, and when the day has been counted in the Book of Life, we have the honor of accompanying souls through the Door. Our line was created from the beginning to be celestial escorts, returning precious creation to the Creator.

"I am telling you my story to end your fear of death. You will never be able to fully experience life on this side and accomplish your mission here on earth until you make peace with the presence of death. There comes an appointed time in each journey, angel and mortal, when the road ends on this side, despite your best efforts. And the wings of angels, my esteemed line, will lift the soul and carry it on a beautiful, magical passage through the Door. There is nothing on earth that compares to the moment the spirit steps back into the lighted presence of the Holy One. But here, while we remain hemmed in by time and space, we may offer healing glimmers of the life eternal. And that, Gabrielle, is the joyful job of an angel."

CHAPTER 13

It never ceases to amaze when one looks up into the dark canvas of night and locates their first star, then another, and another, until they shout with glee, stretching their arms heavenward to trace the constellation of lights across the sky. It is a relief to be liberated from the darkness. Sister Karis once told me, "The glittering pattern you see up in the dark sky is the Creator's divine sequence of hope." There is an invisible architecture, drawn with lines of wonder, mercy and miracles laid out across the fabric of creation. But it requires faith to see it. In secret, all of creation yearns to believe there is more to the grand story than meets the mortal eye. To believe that what their heart intuits, is true—to believe in hope.

As a postulant of the angel bakery, I was training to become more astronomer than baker, bravely looking up into the dark night, locating one star at a time, until I could piece together my own constellation of hope. A hope in more than the correct measurements for a plump round of dough. A hope in that which I could not see. A living hope that I could share.

My tiny room at 11, rue de Bourbon was on the top floor of what would have been the servants' quarters when the townhouse was built in the late eighteenth century. The narrow hallway opened doors to eight tiny elfin bedrooms. Mine had a plain wooden desk, a single iron cot covered in a tattersall quilt and an antiquated, brass crooked-arm lamp for reading. I could peek through a small round mullioned window and see the Eiffel Tower in the distance and a section of Notre Dame's front left elevation.

Most mornings I awoke to the sounds of Bernard's violin. And the view never disappointed, even with the disturbing yet fascinating presence of all the ugly stone gargoyles in the eaves. We'd had two of these monsters perched on the chapel's north face at Sacred Heart. They were blackened by time and weather, but they had not lost their ability to taunt the ravens and mesmerize the passersby. Sister Josephine thought the gargoyles came alive when demons threatened the sacred peace of the chapel. She admired them for their ugly beauty. I thought she was crazy.

On this particular morning, the French proletariat had taken to the streets to protest the government's new taxes. The retailers were wary of the power of a mob, so most businesses closed for the day. I was grateful for a reprieve from my usual schedule. But Lille could not keep away. I turned from the window and there she was, grinning with her café au lait in hand.

"Gabrielle, those gargoyles remind us of the presence of evil in the world. We need angels, guardians, and, yes, even the living gargoyles to protect creation from the Darkness. I encourage you to be like that one over there, the big, scary eagle perched on the flying buttress of Our Lady. You see, he has the strength to slay dragons. By looking into the radiance of the sun, his power is continually restored. That remains the secret here on earth, too. When you fall into darkness, look for the light. If not, you will be lost and will only find despair."

Lille casually laid upon my pillow a cream envelope with my name written in beautiful script. And then she disappeared as quickly as she had come. My father's initials were etched in gold on the bottom right corner of the note. The letter felt heavy like a stone resting in the palm of my hand. I looked around the room, sure somehow that Sister Karis had joined me. Her scent of camellias was unmistakable. Then I plunged into the unknown. I read the letter. It was my father's voice I heard. How could this be possible? I stopped and read the words aloud, but it was still his voice in my head. I had no memory of my father, and yet I intimately knew his voice.

> Dear Gabrielle,
> My greatest test was leaving you in the arms of Sister Karis. As you are the hope for the line of Gabriel, your safety overcame my desire to be with you in the flesh. But know that I am always near you. I hope you feel that

now. As you will come to understand, the Winged must experience full humanity to earn our wings. Often that comes with great sacrifice. To love is always to place another before oneself. We must be mortals for a while to understand our divinity. And often that requires suffering, both personally and for those whom we love. It teaches us how to live by faith, to stand before death unafraid. You have been entrusted to Lille, Sophie and Pierre, as they are your Guardians. And Baabar will prove to be your greatest Protector. They are like me, from beyond the Holy Door. Let them guide you, I implore you, *mon coeur*.

You are ready now, or you would not be reading my letter. The road ahead will require courage. You will be tested just as every human being on earth is. But you will never be alone, I promise. Deliver the message of Gabriel, my daughter. The world needs to hear it. I have faith in you. I will wait with patience for the day you cross through the Door and we are together again, and you will understand the whole Truth. Until then, look for the signs. They are many. Remember, you have the eyes to see, and the heart to believe.

—Your Papa

I read his words over and over again, if only to hear his wondrous voice. It was Baabar who awakened me with his deep voice and unmistakable scent of mint and honey. It was still dark, but I could hear the street cleaners sweeping the trash from the day before into the watery canals that ran parallel to the cobblestone streets.

"Gabrielle, it is time we escort you deeper into the Mysteries."

He handed me a coat that was surely Sophie's, because it was splattered with paint, and then he turned me to face him, tenderness in his eyes. He took the azure woolen scarf from around his neck, carefully tied it about mine. "Don't be afraid. I am here for you," he said.

We walked the six flights of stairs down to the courtyard and stepped out onto the street. The ancient gas lamp on the corner joined the rising sun to light our way. We crossed the bridge and followed along the left edge of Notre Dame. I felt safe striding next to him. His large, dark figure was powerful, and yet I knew his real strength was a gentleness that would smooth down the fabric of my spirit. Baabar led me through a pair of massive iron gates, crested with gilded lion-head medallions reflecting gold in the early morning gray. The journey continued up several flights of worn, uneven stone steps until we were halted by two more ferocious marble lions, collared by the royal fleur-de-lis seal. They imperiously guarded the entry.

Baabar announced, "This was once the royal palace for King Louis IX of France. The holy chapel was created in the center of his palace to serve as an architectural reliquary for the sacred relics of Christendom—the Crown of Thorns and a piece of the true Holy Cross."

The building was a delicate piece of lace crocheted out of stone and colored glass. The flying buttresses seemed to flutter like wings, and the steeple tickled the near side of heaven. We entered the lower chapel, which was very dark except for the illumination of a virtual sea of candles. It took my eyes a moment to adjust. The walls were painted in azure, crimson and deep vermilion, with the lion and fleur-de-lis motif dominating in gold. The candlelight softened the architectural columns, buttresses and arches. Up above, the ceiling was a blanket of cerulean blue with thousands of painted golden stars. All of it was magical but no match for what I would see as I climbed the spiral stone steps up to the main chapel. Through the quatrefoil stained-glass windows, I could see the sun beginning to gloriously assert itself.

Somehow at that moment, I knew my life would never be the same. Lille and Sophie were kneeling on the scarlet carpet, hands lifted to the sky, singing in a language I had never heard before. The first morning light began to stream through the magnificent orifices. The entire chapel came alive. Pierre was suddenly at my side. I could feel the pillar of Baabar still close behind me, buttressing my anxious spirit. In the blink of an eye, each figure was attired in a luminous robe of light, and pulsating auras of light appeared around their heads. Pierre next took my hand.

"Gabrielle, the Mysteries will no longer remain hidden to you. It is time you understood the truth of who we are, and who you are."

I was led to the ornate altar, adorned in a multitude of flickering candles. Baabar removed my coat, and I too became clothed in shimmering light. Pierre lifted his hands high and began to chant. His ordination would forever change who I was in this world. And thus he began:

"Before there was day or night, heaven or earth, the Holy One created the morning stars, perfectly radiant, and the most pure reflection of the Creator. We, the angelic, were present at the creation of the world in all its glory and grandeur. We also were present as the Holy One tenderly formed the first human and created for him the rising of the sun for the day and the moon and sequined stars to illuminate the night. The beginning was a magical time of creativity, promise and, most importantly, love. Love is the Holy One's blessed signature upon all of creation. All bear its secret tattoo.

"Hidden within the architecture of flesh and bone, the Holy One included alongside the heart and mind, a soul, a living piece of the Divine. You could say something of heaven was planted inside of every created being. Mortals were also awarded the ambitious gift of freedom—to live and love as they chose. They were to be beautiful wayfarers on earth, fitted with love as their inner compass. Life was to be an adventure until the road found its way back again to its holy beginning. Sadly, the story began to veer dangerously close to the edges of the Dark Deep. Many of the divinely made beings became intoxicated by their own beauty and power. They turned away from the Light of the Holy One, confident they could go it alone. The Darkness took advantage, and with cunning, began to steal them from Glory.

"Love was taken for granted. Forgotten. The human spirit was seduced away from their own holiness. Humankind found itself defenseless against suffering apart from God, and many lost their way in darkness. Mortals forgot or chose to ignore the divine Light living within them. Belief in the mystery, the wonder and the life beyond the Holy Door became nothing more than spun tales for naïve children.

"And thus begins our story. We are the morning stars, angels sent through the Door to guide humanity back into the Light. The boundary between the visible and the invisible is drawn only by the faith of the one on the journey. The holy veil is sheer to the one willing to trust and look beyond, even venture through it. But most remain blinded to the mysteries. If they only knew, there is not a creature on earth who hasn't felt the delicate brush of our wings.

"To become one of the Winged, you must first pass the test of the Holy One. You, like each one of us, have been sent to earth to experience the fragility and darkness of the human story. You too must fully understand the joys and the sorrows of being human and yet still choose the Light. You must believe in the eternal mysteries and deliver the message that love always triumphs. It is the miracle of Creation."

Sophie stepped forward, her outside self no longer flesh but radiant pure light. She was beautiful, almost blinding.

"There have been significant moments in the history of the material world when humanity has exhibited more courage and truly believed in us. And we opened their spiritual eyes to the mystery. We have been called saints, prophets, guardians, angels, apostles and even saviors. Remember the ultimate love of Christus. Others were Abraham, Moses, Muhammad and Buddha. They each were fully committed, some willing to sacrifice all to redeem humanity, some sent to show mortals how to look inside and find peace, and then there were those charged with repelling the Darkness. There is and will always be a battle for the human soul. And now it is your turn to take your place among us. You have been sent as one of Gabriel's messengers, a new Light for this time and this place."

I began to sway. It was as if vertigo had taken hold of me in body and spirit. The room began to spin and I reached for Baabar, blinking frantically, trying to refocus. Thankfully, his big strong hands came under my arms and held me upright. Lille, Jobe and Sophie joined Pierre in a gleaming circle of light around me. Their otherworldly eyes glittered into mine and lifted me off the ground. Sparkles of light danced off the walls, pews and altar. I yearned to go deeper into its source. I was mesmerized, fearful and yet, oddly, it was familiar, as if I had been there before. Baabar's lips were moving, but I was lost in the electricity of the moment, deaf to his tender words. Lille's arm reached around my waist, and we floated together, her eyes transfixing mine. I did not want it to stop, this experience of absolute peace to never end. I was peeking through the Door to my home, the place of Love's perfection.

It was Pierre who abruptly shut the Door. He raised his right hand, and all responded by tilting their heads down in the posture of prayer. It was over, and I felt a depletion of energy immediately. Lille quickly came to my rescue as I began to fall.

"Gabrielle, today you were granted an outward sign of who we are. One day your own angel eyes will reveal the heavens too. In the meantime, you must trust us as your Guardians."

Had Lille just called Babaar, Sophie, Pierre and herself, even me, *angels?* I knew by heart the place in the liturgy where the priest would call for the host of heavenly angels to descend on the altar and join humanity in the worship of God. But I honestly never once considered there were actual angels with real wings of light among us. Such a romantic and sentimental notion, the flowing robes, the gold-edged wings and the cherub faces. But angels coming in the form of humans? Lille, maybe. But Baabar certainly did not look like one of Raphael's saccharine putti. He was dark, ominous and Muslim. Then I thought, *If I were ever to conjure up my own guardian angel, I would want only him.*

Lille broke into my wandering thoughts. "Gabrielle, this is shocking, I know. It was the same for each one of us. Just as the beloved Christus, the Son of Light, experienced the joys and the trials of humanity, we too take on the flesh for a time in order to help souls who have lost their way. Humanity is never left alone. Nor are you. There is always the possibility of redemption, always stars in the dark night. Our wings sustain this hope in the world. We are often called to travel to the very edge of the Dark Deep to rescue a lost soul. The Divine One refuses to give up on anyone."

Pierre stood up with a determined expression on his usually placid face. "Gabrielle, there are many who are desperate for your special gift of light. You must use your sacred eyes. I have watched you in the bakery and know what happens when you look into the patrons' eyes. You are adept at ignoring your visions, but if you are to become one of us, you must have the courage to focus your sight for another. You're a Light-bearer. Life here on earth can be tragic. There are things that happen on this side of heaven that literally rip the seams of the spirit. And that is why we whisper to a hurting world that there is more, so much more. You can touch their souls with holy intuition. Proclaim to them that death is not the end. Love is salvation."

I was so frightened by what had just happened. Or did it happen? I wished it could be like one of Sister Karis's old fairy tales. You could be transfixed for a moment, believing the story to be true. But then the story was over and you were relieved to be back to reality. Then I thought, *I want to believe we are not left alone here on earth, that angels are looking after us, helping us along the way.* My hands trembled as I pinched the flesh on my inner wrist. Yes, I was here, and something dramatic and life-changing had really just occurred.

Pierre hugged me. His voice was tender.

"I assure you this is no sleight of hand for your amusement. You were chosen and sent by the Holy One through two angels of the highest rank. There is much expectation for you as one from the line of Gabriel. Many have come before you, charged with dispelling the Darkness. But the Holy One will never make you do anything you do not choose freely. You have the freedom to go on living just as you are. A fine baker, I must say. Or you may elect to become a Light in this broken world. It is up to you."

Sophie stepped forward with a scroll and presented it to me. I untied the blue satin ribbon. Inside was one of Sophie's hand-painted invitations. On the front was the beautiful spreading tree with the twinkling golden leaves that I had seen in her apartment. It was engraved in a beautiful calligraphy with my angelic name inked in gold in the center. I was invited to a dinner in my honor.

"Gabrielle, we would like to introduce you to our holy community. Maybe seeing others like yourself will aid in your decision making. I promise there will be delicious food, beautiful music and an opportunity to share our story further with you."

I felt as if a train had exploded out of the Gare Saint-Lazare train station, destination unknown, and I was barely hanging on by the scarf Baabar had tied about my neck. My heart was beating at mach speed. Lille snapped her fingers, "*On y va, tout de suite*. We must leave before the guards come." Each touched his or her heart in the angelic sign and offered it to me. I awkwardly touched my own heart and lifted my hand to each in the group. Back on the street, Lille, Sophie and Pierre immediately blended into the crush of French men and women scurrying to the metro, the newspaper stand or the café, all oblivious to the supernatural brushing against them.

The old monk from the day before was sweeping the front steps of Notre Dame. He shyly, almost reverently, flashed me a knowing smile, then casually touched his heart. There were a couple of nuns in their familiar wimples and habits opening the side doors for the first mass of the day. They bowed their heads in my direction as I crossed the square. I turned to look up into Baabar's eyes, trying to see something in them that would help make sense of what had just taken place.

He stopped, "Gabrielle, we are the blessed ones, created to serve the Holy One and creation. Surely the dreams and visions made you question yourself. If not that, what about the eyes? What did you think the first time you saw such radiance in Sister Karis's eyes in the garden?"

Sister Karis had claimed her eyes were sensitive to the sun. I never said anything, but once when she did not know I was watching, she did look directly into the sun, and something strange occurred. The light lit her up, her whole being consumed in its rays, as if she was set on fire. The secret had always been right there before me.

I could pack my bag, take the noon train back to Sacred Heart and easily lose myself in the routine of its bakery. I'd even now welcome the annoying discipline of the sisters! Or…I could step into the wonder and believe in what had just happened. One star at a time? How could I walk away? Please, Valentina, Papa, Sister Karis, guide me now.

On cue, Baabar lifted my quivering chin. "Gabrielle, your eyes were powerfully glittering back there. Pierre was speaking the truth. We can all see it. You were set apart for holy things. Now you must see it. You have the chance to bring Light into the world. I am honored to be your Protector, whatever you choose to do."

Baabar would prove to be more than just my Protector. He would be my Ebenezer, a beautifully chiseled marker on the pilgrim's road, pointing me in the direction I must go.

Every angel is the key to a different endless ocean of knowledge, which has no beginning and no end. In every ocean there is a complete universe with its own unique creation. The diver into these oceans is the Archangel Gabriel.

— KORAN 4:166 —

CHAPTER 14

The next day I found a note from Lille pinned to the oven. It read, "Gaby, you are in charge of the bakery today while we make the last arrangements for the party this evening. Prepare the usual six trays of croissants, seven of pain au chocolats, a dozen tartes of your choosing—I left you fresh rhubarb and a carton of cherries from the market in the cooler—and whatever else tickles your fancy for the *pâtisserie du jour*. Flip the sign after the morning rush, and we look forward to your presence this evening at half past seven. Jobe is there to assist you. Don't forget, it's your special night!"

In any other circumstance, I would have been crawling with hives at the thought of running the Levain Bakery on my own. Even though it was my dream to have my own bakery, I still had much to learn. But on this day, all I could focus on was the fierce duel taking place within me. And I wasn't sure yet who I wanted to win. Clearly, a life ordered by reason, articulated in sharp lines and neat black and white squares, would be a much safer bet. It required courage to surrender one's life to that which could not be neatly proven by mortal eye. They call that a leap. Karis claimed she had no need to touch the holes in Christus's hands or side, for she knew every living creation bore a piece of the Divine. I remember her saying, "Our life is not our own. Thankfully, the heart knows to Whom it belongs."

The morning chaos in the bakery hit a crescendo. I burned the first round of croissants, and one of our most persnickety regulars, Madame Charpentier, pointed out for the world to hear that I had shamefully left the chocolate out of her pain au chocolats. Thankfully, Jobe assumed the helm at the ovens while I manned the counter. Secretly, I searched the eyes of the patrons of the bakery, curious now about my gifts. Serving brioche and café crèmes, I began to test my powers of holy sight. Jobe pointed to an older gentleman, seated with his cap on his knee, smiling in the corner by the teacart for no apparent reason. Jobe took this opportunity to impart his own angel wisdom. He spoke directly to my spirit with only the blink of his eyes.

"Gabrielle, he is a dreamer. Dreamers believe in a world that cannot be seen by mortal eye but only known by their intuitive hearts. They breathe in hope and see in the most ordinary things—the extraordinary. Despite suffering on this side, the dreamers spend their lives looking for miracles, big and small. There are also the wind chasers. They spend their lives chasing the wind, hoping they will find something to ground them. They look everywhere, but never inside themselves. And sadly, they never experience the peace freely given by the Holy One. And then there are the stones. These poor lost souls have buried themselves in the dark riverbed of life. They have stopped in place. Frozen in fear. They no longer dream or try to chase the wind. Instead they hover at the edge of darkness, and by their choosing, create their own hell on earth.

"You will touch all three of these wayfaring spirits crossing your path here. That is, if you choose *our* way. A glimmer of Light from one such as you can change them, sending their lives in an entirely new direction. Love does not disappoint."

Jobe turned off the big oven and touched his heart, then lightly tapped mine.

"I bid you adieu. I have a party to attend tonight honoring an angel from the esteemed line of Gabriel." He parted with a wink and knowing smile.

After a hectic day in the bakery, I stumbled wearily up the stairs to my room, catching a glimpse of myself in the hall mirror. My hair was twisted in a messy knot, my apron covered in flour and pastry cream. I was a tangled mess. Then I spied the dress hanging on the brass knob of my door, a beautiful shimmering sheath of pink silk, the delicate color of the inside of an Andalusian rose. On the floor below the dress was a pair of gold sandals looped with pale green taffeta ribbons. Curiosity spurred a burst of new energy. I hurriedly bathed and washed my hair with Baabar's gift of scented argan oil. I splashed myself in camellia water in honor of Sister Karis, hoping she would be with me somehow tonight.

Baabar found me staring at a stranger in the cracked hall mirror. I was mesmerized. The long dark waves of my hair behaved for once and fell gracefully to my bare shoulders. My eyes were dark, traced with a mysterious gold thread that cast a soft glow across my entire face. My cheeks flushed a high color. Who was this creature standing before me?

A deep chuckle rumbled up from Baabar. "You seem surprised by your own beauty. No hiding behind the baker's cap and apron tonight!"

Then he handed me a small, beautifully wrapped box tied with a lavender ribbon.

"Your Protector wishes to bestow upon his protectee a gift on the evening of her angel's agape feast. This was my mother's, who was also a very beautiful and gifted woman, full of the compassion I see in you as well. Open it now. I hope you will like it."

I was not accustomed to receiving gifts, especially not one like this. At *le Noël*, the sisters would exchange little handmade tokens of their affection. One year I collected branches from around the garden and placed them in the hollowed center of a cut trunk of an old oak tree. Then I made ornaments for each of the sisters and hung them with colored ribbons. The sisters were so pleased on Christmas morning. But this gifting was different. This was much more than a token. I slowly untied the ribbon and carefully removed the beautiful wrapping paper from the box. Inside I found a pendant necklace. It was a simple gold chain, threaded with moonstones and a single red ruby heart. I had never seen such a lovely thing in my life.

"We call this an amulet in my country. Some believe it has power to meld two hearts into one. In my village, people came to our house for my mother to bless their lives with her sacred heart." Pausing, he announced, "Gabrielle, like my mother, you too are a healer of hearts. You just don't understand how to use your gift yet."

Baabar carefully fastened the necklace around my neck. I touched the sacred heart with my thumb and forefinger, a talisman of my new life.

Baabar was so regal, dressed in his father's djellaba, an embroidered, hooded robe that fell in graceful royal-blue folds to the floor. He is honored as an inspired marabout in the Afro-Arab districts of Paris. Traditionally, a marabout is a scholar or holy teacher of the Koran. But Lille said they were also believed to possess special powers of clairvoyance and healing gifts with their amulets. Many claiming to be marabouts in Paris today have become quite popular as *"docteurs d'amour."* The younger generation seeks them out in the markets for magical amulets, African love blessings and tattoos of the protective eye. Baabar was different. He had come from one of the most distinguished family trees of marabouts in Western Africa. A city in Morocco was even named after his family, Sidi Waliy Baabar.

The patriarchs of his family in Morocco were highly regarded Muslim religious leaders, revered elders of their village, sought after for their wisdom and special gifts. My Protector had been groomed to follow in their footsteps until his father was mysteriously poisoned. Then Baabar was abruptly taken from his mother and sequestered in the home of his devious uncle, Rehemoth Sidi Daoudi. There Baabar came face to face with the Dark Deep for the first time. He was forced to learn the evil art of destructive amulet making, introduced to sorcery and taught to reject his pure gifts of illumination. Baabar's uncle had become a bitter man, seduced by the Darkness and jealous of the young Baabar. Word spread of Rehemoth's plot to murder his talented nephew, and the family responded quickly, sending him away again under the cover of night following the African diaspora to Europe. His father's old Turkish rug bag was packed with a black-velvet vest embroidered in holy scripture, two linen dishdashas, his grandfather's Koran and several tapestries hand-stitched by the women of his village. Because of his well-known family, he was royally welcomed into the twelfth arrondissement of Paris. Though expected to be *le grand marabout*, Baabar realized that he had really been called to Paris for his spiritual gifts, far exceeding love potions and fortune telling.

We set out for the fête, walking through the medieval quarter of the city. Baabar stopped at a quaint jewel box of a flower shop on the rue de Grenelle, *La Fleuriste*. Baabar pointed through the window to Madame Laurier. Hands gesticulating, she fluttered out to greet us with a gift in hand.

"Sophie let me have a peek at the exquisite fabric for your dress. I hope you like what I have made for you."

I opened the lavender-and-silver-papered box to find an exquisite halo of delicate white flowers. Their perfume was intoxicating. Madame Laurier reverently placed it gently upon my head and whispered, "The gardenias are in honor of your mother." I looked into her eyes, where I found only kindness.

Baabar and I next crossed the Place Saint-Sulpice square to the Church of Saint-Sulpice. He suggested we take a moment and go in.

"Gabrielle, I believe there is someone here who has been waiting a long time to meet you here."

The church was dark and so still except for the flickering candles on the high altar. An old woman with a hood hiding her profile stepped from the shadows bearing a single candle. We silently followed her into the Chapel of Holy Angels, known for its lovely murals painted by the artist Delacroix. The strange woman raspingly began to speak.

"For many years, Delacroix was criticized for painting scenes of angels in battle. Humans feel much safer seeing cherubs in white robes, golden halos and feathery wings. But the wise artist knew that in the shadows of reality, a fierce battle rages between the forces of Light and Darkness. You should be very proud of your father. He gave his life for the Light."

My head jerked up at the mention of my papa. I turned to question this old crone. She would not let me see her face. The fingers on her hands were gnarled and grotesque. Then she turned, and I saw the disfigurement of her face. I gasped at her ugliness; she was a living gargoyle.

"Don't let my face frighten you. A price dearly paid for underestimating the Darkness. My name is Hannah, and your father gave his life to save my own. I am not blessed yet to call myself one of your kind. But I have a faith that enables me to help the cause of goodness. Your father found me on the street, broken, selling my body, at the sacrifice of my dignity. I no longer believed I had anything else to offer to the world. Your papa coaxed the light that still flickered deep within me to shine. And that is why I have waited for you. I promised him that I would endure long enough to make sure you were entrusted with his special things."

Hannah limped to the side wall and removed a stone. She took out a velvet purse, inside a most unusual key, and a crystal box with a ring inside.

"Your father told me you would need these if you accepted your mission."

I tucked the key safely in my pocket and then took out the ring and placed it on my third finger. It fit perfectly, a scrolled silver band set with a translucent stone.

"Gabrielle, this ring is a beacon in the darkness, reminding you that you are never alone. It shimmers when in the presence of an angel. Inside is engraved: I am with you always. Generations of the line of Gabriel have worn this ring."

I didn't know what to say. I could see in her rheumy eyes that she wanted me to be like my father. I leaned in closer and gave Hannah an unexpected parting kiss on the cheek. She recoiled, trying to protect me from touching her repugnance. I wrapped my arms more tightly around her. I could feel her fragile spirit searching me over, yearning to feel my father's presence. An energy rose between us, and she stepped away.

"You are your father's daughter. Be strong. The world needs you now." And then she was gone, as if having never been there.

Baabar and I departed in silence. I played my fingers over the stone of the ring, hoping to feel some connection to my father.

"Gabrielle, point your finger with the ring in my direction," Baabar said.

It suddenly illuminated in front of me. I smiled, pleased and emboldened by my father's legacy gift.

Arm in arm, Baabar and I continued up the hill to find Pierre waiting at the iron gates of the Jardin du Luxembourg. The garden was a botanical tapestry, embroidered with flowers of every color, size and perfume. Fruit and almond trees lined the parterres of green. Pierre jubilantly greeted me with a kiss, cheek to cheek.

"Gabrielle, you look so much like Valentina tonight. Her spirit will be with you. You will see."

He led us over to the Medici Fountain, and we all stopped to admire the impressive stone angel whose wings stretched wide over the tourmaline waters. I stepped to the edge and saw my image in the pool. But then other faces appeared in the water too. Faces I did not recognize. People who weren't there. I looked to my left and to my right, but it was only me peering into the well of wishes.

Pierre whispered, "They have come to bid you well. They are angels who have returned home after completing their mortal mission on earth. Many from both sides of the veil want to help you meet your destiny."

A moment of reflection and of mourning my old life, and then I crossed the pebbled path bordering the palace. The ring was glowing on my hand. Ahead, torches flamed on either side of the entrance to the L'Orangerie. My heart began to race, and Baabar put his reassuring hand under my elbow. Pierre explained that the L'Orangerie had once been a winter conservatory for the royal family's treasured orange and lime trees. The building boasted six grand steel windows curved like archers' bows fifteen feet in the air. They were painted jade green to complement the curling green leaves that peeked out from their opened panes. Billowing white linen curtains hid the secret party waiting inside.

Lille greeted us first. She was dressed magnificently in satin, the color of a silver moon, her neckline edged in sparkling crystals. Her blond hair was adorned with rosebuds around the crown of her head and secured with a sapphire pin. Her blue eyes were full of excitement.

Two gentlemen in black evening suits and white ties opened the creamy curtains to reveal a magical room full of trees clad in twinkling lights. Dangling from their branches were many gold discs, hundreds of them, as if a treasure chest of golden florins had spilled from their arms. As these twisted to and fro, they reflected a surreal golden glow across the room.

A giddy Sophie in a ruby-red gown locked arms with me and pointed to the dome above, with its magnificent frescoed ceiling of cherubim. In plaster, angels descended from heaven, wings swooping above our heads. They appeared to the eye so real that I reached up to touch a wing.

Sophie giggled. "The ceiling was painted several hundred years ago by one of our kind. The artist was Josephine Lautrec, the daughter of one of the ladies-in-waiting to Marie de' Medici. As the story goes, Marie found young Josie feverishly painting beside the wishing fountain where you stopped tonight. She was so impressed by her drawings of angels that she commissioned her to reproduce them in life-size scale for this ceiling."

Sophie led me deeper into this room of enchantment. The center of the gallery was anchored by a very long table covered in a damask cloth of purest white. Candles were everywhere in blown-glass vases of every known and maybe unknown color. The room was set to seat a choir of 77, yet I saw no one in the room but us. Suddenly a mysterious wind stirred, and the curtains around the room lifted. The golden discs began to gyrate on the tree branches, creating otherworldly music. I gasped. Angels began to step into the light, their eyes glittering. A multitude of them, all singing in the same language that I had heard in the chapel before, piercing me now, painfully but exquisitely. These voices were breaking me open, and I had no power or desire to stop them. The strange beings moved toward me, formed a circle, and their exultant singing became louder. I wanted to translate the words, to understand what was happening. All I knew was that I didn't want it to stop, ever.

A glow rose from these lighted spirits. They were wondrous floating lanterns on a dark sea. One at a time, each stepped forward greeting me.

I admired my ring and its sudden gleaming brilliance. Pierre announced their angelic names and the number of years each had been clothed in human flesh. I stood in awe as I peered into each set of supernatural eyes. Did I see the edge of a wing? Surely I am dreaming.

Pierre raised his hand, and the room went supremely still. Sophie joined us in the center of the circle and took my hand. "Gabrielle, I would like to introduce you to the Communion of Angels in Paris. Our kind are scattered in secret constellations across the world. We are all angels, testaments to the wonder and mystery of creation. We were created before time and space to aid humanity and reveal the eternal world of the Spirit. Tonight you heard our native language for the first time. It is your first language. In time, you will remember it again. This evening is a celebration for all of us. We have waited with much anticipation for your arrival. We pay homage now to your light coming down to earth."

There was thunderous clapping, cheering, as the wondrous sea of hands lifted in unison to the night sky. And then through the window I saw it—a star. But no ordinary star. A supernova. And the party erupted in cheers.

Lille took my hand and pulled me in close to her.

"Gabrielle, this star was created in your honor on the day of your birth. You are part of the divine constellation of hope."

I thought then, *How does one respond to such love?*

Thankfully, Pierre invited the guests to take their seats. I quickly collapsed into my chair beside him. Baabar was on my other side. I was grateful that my gentle giant was with me. The centerpiece on the table was signature Sophie, a noble living tree with its branches covered in golden leaves. I would soon learn that this magical tree was the symbol for our particular conclave of angels. Across time, the angelic have used certain symbols or seals to announce our secret presence. Centuries ago, during the time of Christus, the fish was discreetly emblazoned like graffiti on walls for those with the spiritual eyes to see.

Pierre said, "There are always signs of our presence in the world if one has the iris of faith to see them."

Baabar stood to read a blessing written especially for me.

"My dear angels, seraphim, spirits, powers and principalities, and those visible and invisible from the esteemed line of Gabriel, I bow in humility and gratitude for my role as Protector of Gabrielle. We come this evening to welcome her into the mysteries. May Gabrielle never be frightened by earthly life, knowing she is guarded by many wings here on earth, until the day she returns through the Door, her mortal journey divinely called to an end. May she have the courage to follow those who have come before and bring light into the darkness of this world. May this food, music and company celebrate her beautiful spirit this evening. We bow in gratitude for her Light."

In conclusion, Baabar raised his arms to the sky, and the entire room stood and joined in the recitation of their Angelic Creed. I could not understand the words, and yet I knew intimately they were a great expression of love. Lille translated for me.

"We, the wonderfully made, beautifully hemmed in before and behind with sacred threads of light, are created to serve the human race, enlightened and empowered by the Holy Spirit. With humility, we take on the flesh so that we become like them in every way yet may rise above on our wings of love to remind them again of their spark of divinity. We honor the unique differences and beliefs of each of creation, knowing they incarnate the creative genius of the Holy One. We offer tender mercy when their paths become difficult. We help them trust in the great truth that love wins out against the darkness of this world always. Finally, we bring humans through death and joyfully bear their souls up on our wings to return to their Creator."

I was struck by the devotion of these shining creatures. Was I really one of them? These servants bearing faith, hope and love as their divining stones? My immediate reaction was that I was not worthy to be one of them. I had made too many mistakes. My pride was more often my compass than love. I cringed at my selfishness and lack of patience with the people in the bakery. I was surely not quick to forgive, and sometimes secretly harbored doubts there even was a God. And if there was, a bitter taste sometimes roiled up in my mouth. I became angry that this God could allow such suffering and hurt in the world. Surely I was not cut from this angelic cloth?

Lille sat down next to me. "Gabrielle, I hear your thoughts. Each one of us struggles with weakness. We are not God, just his chosen helpers. The darkness of this imperfect world is quite successful in confusing the spirit. It takes discipline for your purest part, your undying soul, to speak for you in the world. It must be your beacon of light in all the darkness. The Holy One will guide you if you allow it." My face must have shown my dismay. She laughed and said, "But right now, the only thing you must focus on is this delicious meal."

A parade of happy young men and women entered the candlelit room, large covered silver trays above their heads. They lifted the engraved tops to reveal alabaster enameled ramekins. I knew immediately what we would be having for dinner. I could smell the lemon and thyme wafting up to my nose from a perfectly roasted *poulet* resting upon a mound of creamy potatoes, accompanied by truffle-dusted haricot verts. Delicious. The au jus dripped from my chin and revealed a smile of pure joy.

Lille giggled, "Karis said this was your favorite meal. I believe she would make this for you every year to celebrate your birthday. Tonight we too will celebrate a birth: Your birth into angeldom and esteemed place as one of Gabriel's angels."

During dinner there was a continuous stream of guests presented at my table to welcome me. Some knew my mother and father. I was surprised to recognize many of them, ones who had crossed my path on evening walks around the Île Saint-Louis, or had shown me good humor over the bakery counter. There was Bernard, the street performer, who always gave me that certain knowing, playful smile. I recognized the monk from Notre Dame who had presented me with the coin. There was Monsieur Gabon from the coffee shop next to the Levain Bakery, who faithfully greeted me each morning with a kind *salut* and a perfect espresso to commence my day. I saw Doctor Blanc, who had kindly attended to me when I came down with the flu, Madame Laurier from the flower shop, who had created my beautiful diadem of flowers for this evening, and Pip, my faithful taxi driver. Even the gargoyle woman from the church was in attendance. I could not believe they all had been living right alongside me and yet were clearly so much more than I had imagined. Each angel wore a boutonniere attached to a vellum card with his or her human name written on it and, next to it, an angelic name in beautiful script of gold leaf.

Sophie danced and twirled over in her glittering gown.

"Gabrielle, I see the funny look on your face. I ask you, how can we aid the human story, understand joy and sorrow, if we do not become like them? The Holy One was so wise to send us to live in the fragility of flesh and bone; taste the salt of real tears; endure the pain of loss and disappointment; revel in the taste of one of your chocolate tortes; persevere through unpredictability; and endure the fear of the unknown. It is difficult, *oui,* being human. We get to see and feel firsthand why creation needs Divine help on this side. None can go it alone, even an angel. Even *we* need something larger than ourselves, the presence of the Holy One—to illuminate our paths. Now enjoy the dessert. A moelleux au chocolat to die for!"

Pierre then rose from the table and made his way to the piano, which was also covered in twinkling lights.

"Gabrielle, I composed this song the day you were born on the pilgrims' road to Santiago. It was played in the church where you were consecrated as one of us."

As he began to play, I knew he was telling me a story, *my story*. As the notes fairy-dusted the top of my head, I was brought to a center of longing for love, a reality that was much larger than I had known, felt or seen in my human frame. It was a love beyond this world—wilder, deeper. It had the power to crack me open to my very beginning, a place where my spirit was unburdened by the realities of life and death. The music took me across an invisible boundary to a sanctuary of pure joy. When the surreal song ended, I sank back to reality, but it was a new reality this time. I knew I was an angel. A Light-bearer for this time and in this place.

Lille hugged me and whispered, "Yes, you are, my dear."

For the first time, I acknowledged the light flickering inside of me.

With a parting kiss on each cheek and a wink, Lille turned back to me. "I shall expect to see you in your apron and baker's cap tomorrow at the usual time. *A tout l'heure, ma chérie.*"

I was still floating on the notes of Pierre's song, as if in a dream. Pierre squeezed my hand in parting.

"How many lives are waiting to be touched by the light of Gabriel? You see them every day in the bakery, you pass them on the street, each with a story, full of dreams, fears and suffering. It is time you make your earthly life count for something, for someone, for many."

As he turned to follow Lille out into the garden, he looked back at me with a wink of pure mischief and said, "Could you feel them here tonight? Some in attendance this evening, we could not see. I smelled the scent of camellias. I believe a certain gentleman with a spectacular mustache was twirling a Peruvian beauty around the dance floor. Valentina and Josef are looking out for you too. You'll see."

The evening was like a dream. Baabar scattered the darkness, protecting me as we walked home. But it was only a matter of time before I too would have to learn the cunning ways of the Dark Deep. The Raven was biding its time. Soon it would make its move and test my Light.

PART FIVE

The Message of Gabriel

That is all an angel is: an idea of God.

— MEISTER ECKHART —

CHAPTER 15

I became something of a celebrity baker on the Île Saint-Louis. Many made the pilgrimage to the Levain Bakery for my *tarte du jours*, macaroons, pastries and chocolate confections, each a bit of culinary art inspired by a story, a dream or a memory from my unusual childhood. A bakery favorite was my interpretation of the traditional French *religieuse,* better known as "the nun." It was my special tribute to Sister Karis. Dear Karis had donned the simple black and white wimple and habit for me. Now I knew how much she had loved color and her Bernard. I filled the first pastry bun, for her head, with a rose-scented buttercream, then placed it on a pastry-bun body filled with pure dark chocolate. I imagined her childish grin and the twinkle of approval in her kind, crinkly eyes.

There was no one like Karis for me, but I was given a sweet serendipity in her sister Sophie. She too laughed a great deal, and her bright-red hair broadcast the energy and generosity that percolated within. She did not take life too seriously. No sweating the small things. Just as in her paintings, Sophie reached for a grander experience of living. Whether it was a perfect cappuccino after a walk along the Seine, a good day's work on a canvas or a belly laugh shared with Lille, you could count on Sophie to find the joy in every moment.

One evening I surprised Sophie with a new pastry created in her honor. It looked like the traditional *moelleux au chocolat*. But this was no ordinary chocolate cake. It had the surprise of a red-hot chili pepper at its center. I named it *Le Pétard*, "the firecracker," a perfect tribute. She loved it.

Sophie and I began a teatime ritual on Sunday afternoons when the bakery was closed. I would bring the dessert and she would surprise me with a new herbal tea. Her friend Tsing Tao had a teashop in the Marais quartier and reserved his most special leaves for Sophie. I brought my sketchbook and she happily offered recipe suggestions. We even painted on a canvas together in her studio. It was her idea to paint the old gargoyles since I now counted them as friends. I'll never forget her sage advice.

"Gaby, look for beauty even in the ugliest of this world. Just like those stone gargoyles, we must protect the sacred in life."

Most Sundays I found her standing on the paint-splattered wooden stool in front of a seven-foot tall canvas hanging by invisible wire lines from the rafters. Her paintings were alive, splashes of vibrant oil color. Sophie's art touched so many. I think it was the hue of love that delighted everyone. Her art had the power to transport you somewhere magical. Sophie always blended imagination and mystery with reality. Her explosive abstracts rocked every boundary yet bridged every division. When I told her my thoughts on her art, she replied.

"That's how love works. It transcends the material world and embraces the inner spirit. Love does not see Buddhist, Christian, Hindu, Muslim, Jew, man, woman, black, white, sexual orientation, poor, rich, sick or healthy. It sees human and embraces all."

Trained at l'École des Beaux-Arts, Sophie was discovered by the famous art critic Jean-Claude Lenore, who penned her work "heaven sent." The irony. Her first show, "Angels Among Us," was held in the Église de Saint-Germain-des-Prés, the oldest church in Paris. It was a series of angels so real that some believed the beautiful creatures fluttered off the canvas at night to dance with the moon. Her real mission was to offer a glimpse beyond, a peek through the Veil.

I especially admired her series *Magical Doors*. The first time I viewed one of the symbolic seven doors, I actually reached for the shiny gold door knob, thinking I could step right through the opening. Each unique door was a surprise and beckoned the viewer to take a step bravely forward. One door was leafed in gold and covered in a beautifully carved relief. Another was splattered with a variety of hues and mixed-media graffiti in celebration of our multicultural world. I especially loved the door covered in panes of colored glass. It was as if you were looking through a kaleidoscope. But the last door caught me off guard. Its paint was peeling off, and its hinges were rusted. This door was plainly beaten down, a reference to the hard knocks of this life. And yet, as in the others, I could just see through its cracked opening to a promised land, the same view as the others had had.

Sophie said, "We each have access to the Door, some more imposing and polished, some more worn and beaten from living. But all can open to reveal the sacred country of the Holy One. You must find a way of your own to herald the message that love transcends this life, help humans to believe there is more than what they can see here."

Pinned to Sophie's easel were St. John's words, "And lo, in heaven an open Door." All want to believe this to be true, that an open door awaits us. Heaven. Where is it? Can I remember the place of my beginning, all beginning? No one wants a good story to end, or to suffer through a painful story with no hope of redemption. We have no memories, snapshots, or mementos from the other side, the place of our beginning. Some claim heaven is of our own making. As is hell. They suggest we already live in Eden, and that a perfect earth is possible. If only we would make peace, feed all the hungry, clothe the naked and love instead of hate here and now. On my doubting Thomas days, I believed heaven as nothing more than a figment of a generous imagination, or an opiate to soothe the pain of this world's hard reality. Clearly, go to any hospital—there is no escaping death. It appears the end of the story, and that scares the hell out of even the most callused. Peeking through the Doors in Sophie's paintings hinted at a different reality. Her colors, so bold and fearless, captured a light from a source unknown.

"I have to tap my feet when people dismiss the place from which we all began, the home of the Spirit," Sophie said. "But it does require courage to believe in that which you cannot see. And yet I assure you that the Holy One does not create and then discard the masterpiece."

I had no words for Sophie in the beginning. I would smile, kiss her cheek to cheek, and then run for cover, the bakery, where I could blissfully make sense of the world. There were natural laws found in the kitchen that grounded me in a salt-and-pepper reality. I knew that by combining exact measurements of flour, water, yeast and salt, I would have a perfect round of dough, one I could smell, taste and mold in my hands. I knew that if I placed that dough in the oven on a set temperature and for a certain allotted time, the dough would rise and become bread to nourish another. An ongoing tug of war always raged between one's intellect and one's heart.

Sophie said, "At some point, human and even angel must welcome the mystery, journey inside to the place of the soul and set free the wondrous spirit. For the eternal spirit knows the Truth and will one day find its way back home. You'll see."

CHAPTER 16

No opportunity would be forfeited to impart angel wisdom. Sophie, Lille, Pierre—all of the lighted beings—encouraged me to look at the world and my purpose in it with an expanded view. An angel's view. I could not escape the invisible wings. After my introduction into their secret community, I felt, intimately, all their eyes watching me, waiting to see if and how I would deliver the message of Gabriel. Pierre began working with me to further uncover my gift of visions. Strangely, they were coming more frequently now, with an intensity I could not ignore. Instead of blinking them away, Pierre encouraged me to look directly into the eyes, to see the person's whole, intimate interior.

He said, "Gabrielle, you meet patrons at the counter of the bakery, and you can see with your spiritual eyes the invisible heaviness that weighs them down. The Holy One will help you spread your wings around them, proclaim the Message of Love, and encourage them to live closer to the blessed lives dreamed for them. The Dark Deep is clever, using the hardships of earthly life to imprison the precious soul. Imagine the bird in the ivory cage that sees the possibilities, even dreams of the world outside the cage, but cannot find a way to freedom. His door is locked. Just so, humans are caged by fears, regrets, resentments and guilt. Like our little canary, human souls eventually forget that they were ever created to soar. Breathe hope again into the cage."

The bustling bakery was filled each day with human life, stories full of joys and sorrows, and I was instructed to inhabit them now. I had no idea the suffering, anxiety and hopelessness well hidden behind the eyes of so many.

Through my visions, I was privy to the things in life that had weakened these spirits. I could see both agony and the joy engraved upon their souls. With Pierre's guidance, my gifts continued to grow. If I emptied thoughts of myself, I could focus. Looking into someone's eyes became a journey through a maze. Hypnotizing the person for just a moment, I could find my way around the turns and bends of their stories. Often I would have to step over scaffolding, built up over many years, protection from the pain. But those structures also kept out the joy. Life's disappointments, mistakes, invisible wounds and lost dreams, all kept the spirit away from the Light and dangerously closer to the edge of the Deep.

Sometimes the visions affected me physically. I experienced a painful jolt, like being shocked by a live electrical wire sparking out from their eyes. It was hard to disengage. He or she would walk out the door of the bakery with a loaf of bread but not out of my mind. For days I carried their knotted stories around with me, my own spirit twisted by the ache of humanity.

In the beginning, I was such an infantile angel; not even a syllable of Gabriel's message could cross my lips. My mortal insecurity rendered me mute, I guess. I didn't believe enough in my gifts or powers as heir to the angel Gabriel. Then it all changed on the day a mother and son came into the bakery for a bag of cinnamon *palmiers.*

Adding a few extra cookies to the wax-paper sack, I looked up into her eyes—hollow, the skin around them dark, papery thin and deeply lined. A sudden vision brought me into an alarming, fluorescent-lit hospital room. Her son, much younger, was attached to a series of wires and tubes. A dark-magenta liquid was dripping from a clear plastic bag into his veins. The fear for his life was raw in her eyes. Blinking, I looked over at her son, finishing the crisp, buttery cookie in two bites, so naive to the anxiety his mother still carried. Her son was here, alive and laughing. And yet the past would not let go of her. The fear of losing this magnificent child, whom she loved so dearly, nearly paralyzed her, keeping her from living fully. Her haunted eyes spoke the truth: Nothing on this side was ever a guarantee.

In that instant, my lips conveyed my first Message of Gabriel. Crazy. A presence took hold of me. Only a whisper. *Can she hear me?* I reached out to touch the mother, and the words tumbled out, soundlessly.

"We must live with what we have right now. Do not take for granted this time, this moment, this love."

The mother returned a nod of gratitude. After they left, Lille wrapped her arms around me in affirmation. "Bravo, my dear. You just delivered your first message. You were spot-on with that frightened mother. Part of living by faith is learning to live with the unpredictability of this world."

Another day I saw into the future through a pair of almond-shaped eyes. A little boy, his mandarin coat buttoned all the way up to his chin, came into the bakery with his father. He could barely see over the counter, so I leaned over and patted his shiny black, perfectly trimmed hair. I knew that he did not live here but was only visiting his grandmother. Madame Lao owned the *tabac* store on the corner that sold cigars, newspapers and Chinese herbs.

When I looked into the little boy's eyes, I saw the angry welts on the backs of his legs, now hidden from the rest of the world by his culottes. I could hear his father's thundering voice and his ominous footsteps as he approached with the bamboo branch, repeating the pain his own father had inflicted on him. The little boy stood in place, submitting stoically again to his fate.

Into the future, I watched as the pattern was to be replayed again and again. The young boy, grown into a big, scary man with the same bamboo branch, releasing anger and fear with every swat across his own son's legs. What would it take to break the cruel cycle? I took the child's hand, squeezed it, and flashed my love to him with the silent words: "You are stronger than them. You will find another way. You will choose love and put down the branch."

The child bowed his head to my message, and when he looked up again, I saw a bit of hope in his eyes. That little boy understood right then that he was not alone. He saw the faint outline of my wings and smiled, knowing that an angel was on his side. Life would be different for him.

I was starting to take baby steps. Nevertheless, I stayed up late most nights, quarreling with the gargoyles after a day's labor in the bakery. Now, it was no longer about the long hours, the hot ovens or the dull ache of my feet. It was my spirit that was suffering. There was too much hurt in the world. How was it that these humble souls could still breathe when the cords of grief, anger, guilt, hurt and fear were choking their spirits? And I felt so incompetent, barely touching their pain carefully concealed behind polite *bonjours* and *merci beaucoups*.

Worse, I began to care for these people, the Levain *réguliers,* on whom I was "practicing" my gifts. Each day the sweet-smelling bakery was filled with their familiar voices: Madame Charpentier, Papa Joe, Violette, the Manoir family and many others. I knew these customers intimately—the peculiar half-shuffle, the bright-tangerine embroidered scarf, the musical lilt of a daily bonjour. I went to Pierre, thrusting my fist in the air like a fishwife, angry that he wasn't teaching me how to help them more. So much more.

"It's too much to bear, to carry such burdens."

In his calm, still voice, Pierre said, "Gabrielle, you cannot simply snap your fingers and make it go away. But you can be present in their lives and engage them with your heart. Learn from your ancestors. Remember what the angel Gabriel said before delivering every one of his messages: 'Do not be afraid. The Lord is with you.' My dear, it's all about Hope."

Pierre claimed these were the growing pains of an angel. I was stretching my newly awakened spirit for another's redemption. It would require courage and sacrifice, he said. I could hear Pierre whispering in my ear, "That is love, my dear one. Freely give the best of yourself for another. It was never promised to be easy. Ah, but what joy there can be."

What Pierre didn't elaborate on was the challenge of reaching these souls, covered in invisible sharp quills for their survival, their protective armor nearly impenetrable to Gabriel's message. For example, Levain's surliest porcupine, Madame Charpentier, proved a most formidable test of my gifts. Her daily shrill was unmistakable. It was more a screeching whine, like I remembered when the bow came down too harshly upon the strings of Sister Carol's violin back at Sacred Heart. As she dug coins from her gargantuan black leather purse, Madame Charpentier delivered her daily litany of grievances: Her bread was stale again, or her pain au chocolat did not have the same amount of chocolate as last week's. On and on she grumbled. In the spring, she ranted that her neighbor Marie's flowers in her window boxes brought the bees into her own window. And on Mondays, one could always count on an especially fevered diatribe of how her daughter-in-law's poor cooking for Sunday lunch gave her terrible indigestion. Nothing suited her, ever.

Lille did her best to appease Madame Charpentier, but each morning brought the next round of irritating complaints. Most had lost patience with Madame Charpentier's harpy personality long ago. But they did not know her painful story, carefully hidden in the rat-tat-tat of daily negativity. Underneath the sharp porcupine's quills was a wounded animal. Madame Charpentier had lost a child—her only daughter. And it had been her fault.

She was supposed to be watching tiny Charlotte at the water's edge. But someone called for her, and she turned her back for mere minutes, and Charlotte was gone. How does a person survive such devastating loss? Such guilt? Madame Charpentier's biting tongue was her only way to exhale.

I decided that the next time Madame Charpentier looked over the glass and said her usual, "Oh, Gabrielle dear, it looks as if someone forgot to keep her eyes on the oven—your *pain au chocolats* are a bit too crisp today," I would hold her attention, get a good look into her eyes. That first vision nearly knocked my feet out from under me. I saw this mother, aged beyond her years, sitting alone at the white marble café table in her cluttered kitchen. Her husband had left her soon after the accident. Her only son resented her. Bitter tears streamed down her face, little Charlotte's school picture clenched in her hand. Her tongue had been sharpened like a knife by ten years of guilt and unfathomable loss.

Taking a chance, I reached out to touch her shoulder one day. "Madame Charpentier, I feel your pain."

Before I could finish delivering the message, she spun around in a fury.

"You are just a stupid, naive *jeune fille,* and not even a good baker at that."

Madame C. did not return to the bakery for weeks. I was convinced I had done more harm than good.

Lille comforted me. "Those are many years of pain she has been lugging around. She needs mercy. Deep mercy. Don't give up. You have the words inside you that she needs to hear. Be patient."

But I feared Pierre, Lille and even my papa had overestimated my gifts. Maybe I was only meant to be a baker—and a poor one at that, it seemed.

CHAPTER 17

Normally I loved my Sundays. It was the only day of the week when I was on my own and not covered in my usual vestments of flour and sugar. It had been a tradition since Monsieur Levain opened in 1793 to designate Sunday as the "baker's Sabbath." The sign above the door read, *"Les Souris Dormons."* The neighborhood children loved to sing a song about the famous mice of the Levain Bakery, who put on their sleeping caps and traveled to the land of Nod every Sunday.

I watched from my window as our neighbors strolled by, dressed in their Sunday finery. Mothers fixed balky sons' bow ties and tied satin ribbons in the braids of their rosy-cheeked *jeune filles*. All dutifully scurried to mass. Afterward the cafés and brasseries overflowed with families, chattering and breaking bread in a shared communion meal, hoping for blessings in the week ahead.

I spent my free day wandering along the Seine and browsing through the markets and *bouquiniste* stalls peddling old books and vintage magazines. Teatime sent me to *La Verre Bleu,* where I enjoyed the people parade and savored a *café crème* or two. My favorite spot, however, was the *Marché aux Fleurs* on the Île de la Cité. Lille and Sophie introduced me to this ancient flower market on one of my early weekends in Paris. And that is how I met my first friend outside the bakery, sweet Violette Masson. We were close in age, and she quickly recognized I could use *une jolie copine*. Hand in hand, giggling like schoolgirls, Violette welcomed me into her community. I looked forward all week to our Sunday promenades through the pavilion of flower stalls, so many green awnings and old brass lanterns, so many twists and turns, like a charmed botanical maze. Booths selling purple orchids, bright-red hibiscus, cacti, even orange trees. It was a living kaleidoscope of vibrant color. Violette even taught me how to arrange my own bouquet creations—a mass of roses, freesia and tulips tied with simple raffia.

A special treat was the *Marché aux Oiseaux*. Every Sunday, the backside of the flower market was transformed into a live bird bazaar where tangerine, indigo and buttery-yellow canaries sang for customers' attention. On one of my first visits, with much encouragement from Violette, I came home with a little green bamboo cage, holding a blue-green and coral cockatoo. I named her Sucre, because for dribbles of sugar water, she would sing for all she was worth.

Lille teased me for turning 11, rue de Bourbon into a veritable zoo. In my first weeks, I collected a bird, a fish and a poodle, all creations the nuns had forbidden in the abbey. Lavender, my curly gray canine companion with a white-fur necktie, was my greatest joy. He slept at the foot of my bed and came along on my Sunday promenades. Lavender received his name from his previous owner, eccentric Madame Leroy, who liked to dye his fur a shade of violet every Easter. She was the talk of the neighborhood, always wearing peculiar English fascinators and accompanied by her outlandish purple dog. They paraded up and down the rue de Bourbon on Easter morning in grand fashion. Sadly, Madame Leroy died choking on a chicken bone; she left no instructions for her loyal lavender dog.

For days after her death, Lavender arrived every morning, just as he had done with Madame Leroy, for her croissant and loaf of sourdough, and a special dog biscuit for him. When I learned the dog was homeless, sleeping under the Pont Marie bridge, I decided I needed a purple dog. He became family but also served as the new sentry at the door of the Levain Bakery, bestowing happy bonjours with his wet nose to all who crossed the threshold. Lavender was special; he too had a clairvoyance, which often aided my angelic efforts. He exhibited this uncanny ability to sniff out a spirit in need. And when the shadow of Darkness loomed, Lavender set up barking and howling.

Even on Sundays, days of human repose, Pierre and Lavender insisted I practice my gifts. There was to be no rest ever for the winged. Pierre proved a demanding professor. He politely chastised, "Gabrielle, on the Sabbath our Christus provided healing, though the Pharisees disapproved. Those healed did not complain. Pick a spot, and watch and wait. You will know when and what you need to do. Every breath is ripe with divine possibility."

I looked forward to Fridays in the bakery because it meant Violette would arrive at half past eleven to pick up her standing order: five baguettes, a dozen mini *quiches aux épinards et champignons* and two *tartes aux abricots*. Violette was in charge of the flower market's end-of-the-week lunch, and I was welcomed to the communion table as well. Every Friday, Jacques, her apprentice, decorated a table with leftover flowers and pulled up mismatched café chairs. Old Madame Tarpin brought her wondrous *chocolat chaud* with a hint of peppers. She claimed the red flesh of her peppers aided digestion and energized everyone for the afternoon's labor. Violette reserved me a special seat at the table next to her. Outside the bakery, the flower market became my special second home.

Violette had inherited her family's flower stall when she was just eighteen. Her mother and father had died in a car crash outside of Toulouse while visiting her brother at university. Charles was studying to become a doctor and had rejected the old market altogether, quick to dismiss the fact that the stall had been in his family for generations. In the house where Violette and her brother grew up, there was a framed deed with the King's fleur-de-lis seal. The Masson family had owned the rights to their flower stall from the very beginning, back to royal days of patronage. Inside the stall, prominently hung, was the supposed sword given by Napoleon III to commemorate the family's 150 years in the *Marché aux Fleurs*.

Loyal to her family, Violette tucked away her childhood dream of designing wedding dresses. Her brother traveled to America to complete a medical fellowship and left Violette to continue the family tradition. At night she sketched dreamy dresses of tulle, lace and organza. By day she created magical floral wedding bouquets. The way Violette individually wrapped the stems of the flowers in multicolored pastel satin ribbons often rivaled the wedding gowns in beauty. Parisian brides flocked to Violette's stall, begging her to do the flowers for their weddings. She famously did the bouquet for the French president's daughter's wedding, having rare ecru and peach tulips flown in from the Keukenhof Gardens in Amsterdam.

Violette fell in love once. I saw it right there in my dear friend's eyes, although kept well hidden behind her generous smile. She knew well the joy and suffering in loving someone with all your heart. His name was Remy, so handsome and full of life and laughter. His family was well-known all over France for their rare, coveted orchids. Remy and Violette had grown up together as children in the market, spending afternoons sharing ice creams, feeding the lovebirds nectar at Monsieur Louis's stall, and chasing the feral cats that roamed the stalls in search of scraps. They were a happy pair—Violette in her braids and ribbons from the flower shop, Remy in his blue-striped overalls and jaunty French denim cap. But as a teenager, Remy could not break from the family curse of drinking early and carousing late into the night. Violette knew the awful price of loving Remy, but still she could not change the direction of her heart. He arrived at the stall one night with a broken fuchsia orchid, waste from the day's sales, and she could smell the stale wine on his breath. But there was that smile, the same crooked smile as when they were kids, and she was lost again. Her body craved his, and she surrendered to her passion. It was quick. He was numbed by the alcohol and had no idea what he had done, what he had been given freely and joyfully by Violette.

Remy would thoughtlessly disappear after that night. This became his pattern. He would return from a binge, clean-shaven with a skip in his step, the broken flower of a "second" and then a third orchid in his hand. And always that smile. And she would surrender again. She lost their baby just when her belly was swollen enough for the vendors to know what had happened and feel her shame. Remy was off on another one of his reckless jaunts without a word.

Once in a while, Violette would stop by the orchid stall and, brushing her fingers across the delicate blooms of a Chartreuse Maiden, nervously ask Remy's younger brother, Leif, if he had any word from him. Leif was the yin to Remy's yang. He also worshipped his older brother, charmed by his easy enjoyment of life. Gentle, quiet Leif had spent his entire adolescence listening to his mother sing the praises of his older brother, while he dutifully washed the leaves of the orchids and coaxed the blooms as if they were his only friends. Every visit from Violette caused his heart to beat faster and a paralysis to freeze his tongue. In the last eight years, he had only nodded at her, maybe a quick bonjour, his eyes always down, inspecting the orchids. When Violette walked away, the sadness so evident in her face, he would curse himself for not speaking of his own love for her. Next time he would invite her in to see the most precious of his orchid family. The one whose petals were a ruby necklace dangling from the neck of its branch. Next time. Always next time.

I would learn a painful lesson in the eyes of Violette and Leif one bright-blue Sabbath Sunday. It would be in their eyes that I would see the Raven for the first time and, sadly, realize my limits. I had no power over free will. Choices are freely made, consequences are doled out, and those left behind must find their way out of the ashes of another's destruction. Nothing is more painful than watching someone you care about in evil's clutch and realizing your hands are tied. In the blink of an eye, one decision, and lives are changed forever.

On this particular Sunday, I found myself in the market square, Lavender merrily marching at my side. I should have known the Darkness was near by the nervous stepping of my canine companion. A pair of beady-eyed ravens greeted us with sinister smiles as we passed through the market gate. The first thing I noticed was Leif. With Remy always stealing the glow of the stage's lights, I had never noticed Leif was handsome in his own right, with an unmistakable kindness in his eyes. He was busy explaining the origin of the white orchid with lavender inseam to a Japanese woman. Next door, Violette was as skittish as a bronco, her mind clearly elsewhere, nervously browsing Madame Goriot's booth.

I heard her ask, "Madame Goriot, why do you have dead plants displayed on the front table?"

"Mademoiselle, those are my Jericho roses. Surely you are familiar with St. Mary's flower?"

I stood to get a better glimpse of the flower they were discussing. It looked like nothing more than a withered tumbleweed. I moved closer to Violette.

Madame Goriot continued.

"The Jericho rose is found in the Sahara desert. When the rains cease, the Jericho rose curls up like a ball of yarn and dies. But what makes this flower so special is that within the ball, its seeds are tucked in safely, waiting. They are quite hardy and can live for many years. Watch this."

I was curious now. Violette kept glancing over her shoulder to see if Leif was free. She feigned interest in Madame Goriot's discourse on the rose. But I was fascinated. Madame Goriot bathed the Jericho rose with water, and in seconds the dried-up ball loosened, stretched and virtually breathed again.

"See how the seeds are set free to bear fruit again? It's one of the miracles of creation. The Jericho rose resurrects right before us."

Violette kissed Madame Goriot cheek to cheek and, smiling, accepted a Jericho rose, now wrapped in a brown paper sack tied in twine. But she was not ready to believe in resurrections. She must bear her cross first. Slipping away to the store next door, she grabbed Leif's arm.

"Have you seen your brother?"

"No, I have not. But somehow I sense he is nearby."

"Leaving the grocery last night, I was sure I saw him hiding behind Le Café du Monde. But when I crossed the street to go to him, he was gone. I am terribly worried."

"I was sure we lost him for good the last time he was here. Maybe this time, together, we can help him pull away from the drug demons—really help him get clean for good. Then he'll want to come back to us. Even work here beside me in the shop. I would let him be in charge."

The vision came to me then, suddenly and painfully. I saw a sculptured Pietà, but now it came to life, a real mother and her dying son. At first I could not make out the face of the boy, only the needle marks, snakebites that crisscrossed up and down the insides of his arms. Then I heard the keening wails of the mother as she held the limp dead body of her son in her arms.

"Remy, my Remy. Come back to me, son. Come back to me."

Remy had welcomed the venom as it entered his veins. It had been his choice, without any regard for those who loved him. He had surrendered to the dark side long ago. Behind the image of a grieving mother and child, I saw a dark shadow, a malevolent specter whose cold eyes sent a sharp chill into my heart. And then the vision dissolved, and the sounds of the market day around me resumed. I was now freezing on this sunny spring day. Lavender was barking wildly. My eyes quickly searched the busy street, hoping I could stop the coming disaster. Then I saw them, the pair of Ravens rising into the suddenly ominous sky. Remy had freely made his choice, and the Darkness had won this day. I prayed for his redemption by the higher power.

Violette had already returned to her shop, busy tying a grosgrain cerulean-blue ribbon around a large bunch of marigolds for a handsome, tall young gentleman whose face was strangely familiar. We startled one another, and my heart jumped. Our eyes locked, but suddenly a loud scream broke my concentration. I looked for Leif. The policeman had just broken the news of Remy's death to Leif and his mother. And then I watched as my friend fell to the ground, the cross too heavy to bear.

The entire market lost its gaiety and took on the shroud of mourning. Many paid their respects to Violette, too, honoring her as the grieving would-be widow. A sunrise memorial service was held for Remy at the great horse fountain in the center of the market. Each member of the market family placed a tiny candle in a paper lantern on the edge of the water. The tears flowed for this senseless loss of a beautiful son.

Leif and Violette reminded me of the Jericho rose before its watering—empty and hopeless. The Friday market lunches fell by the wayside without Violette spearheading them. Leif abandoned the store to his apprentice and set off on a pilgrimage to Malaysia in search of the Gold of Kinabalu, the Rothschild's Slipper, the most elusive orchid in the word. The orchids became his only salvation, all he could depend on. The Rothschild's Slipper was considered by orchid connoisseurs to be the find of a lifetime. It grew on the slopes of Mount Kinabalu, so rare it put forth a bloom only once every fifteen years.

Back in Paris, a heavy blanket of sadness settled over the market. What was once one of the happiest places to walk on a Sunday morning had become colorless, a near cemetery. I learned then that the human story is never written in isolation, the good or the bad chapters. Each is connected intimately to one another. When one suffers, all suffer. And angels shed tears too.

CHAPTER 18

My favorite patron of the Levain Bakery was surely Papa Joe. I had never even thought to look into Papa Joe's eyes. The way his smile curled up all the time, the charming dimple in his left cheek, surely meant all was well with this jolly man. But all was not as it seemed, as Pierre would keenly point out in one of our lessons.

"Never overlook the concealed pain of the human heart," Pierre instructed. "There is not a single human being without need of healing in some contour of their story. Don't be deceived by appearance or the ruse of a steely smile. There could be much pain behind it."

I knew it would be Papa Joe when the bell above the door first tinkled to commence the day. He faithfully arrived each morning for his café au lait with vanilla crème and a *croissant amande.* This time I held his eyes in mine. Papa Joe had lost his wife, Emilie, to cancer two years before. In my vision, I saw him faithfully by her bed as she screamed in the middle of the night, the cancer eating through her bones. She begged her Joe, willing to deal with the devil if only for a moment's reprieve. He kept his faith then, holding on to hope and her beloved hand for what time was left. He even traveled to Lourdes for holy water to bless her tortured body when the end was near.

Papa Joe would never admit that his own body was becoming rigid. Most noticed the changes but figured they were the result of his loving but grueling care of Emilie. First it had been just a facial muscle; then, gradually, the disease traveled, leaving painful stiffness in first one place and then another, until his whole frame would turn to stone. But not his spirit. No, Papa Joe hung on to his faith. He was a dreamer. But it was getting harder now.

I saw him step from his apartment on the rue de Lyon with his cravat tied perfectly and tucked carefully inside his buttoned-up, navy wool blazer. He was always freshly shaven with a hint of the rosemary and orange cologne Emilie had given him. I looked into those brave eyes as I twisted the rose paper around his standard-order croissant. The vision of this dear man's life was struggle and then struggle some more. It was a chore just to lift his head from the pillow at the first cock's crow, and then to carefully drag each leg from under the covers and lower each to the floor. Oh, the agony then to stand, one hand on the bedside, the other grasping the crystal knob of the nearby dresser, his face clenched in pain. The simplest movement was a challenge. I looked at Papa Joe's smile and wondered which was worse—pain of the body or pain of the spirit?

Papa Joe wore his rose-colored glasses. But his eyes told the hard truth of his suffering. I pretended I was straightening his already straight tie, then silently whispered, "She's okay, Papa. Your Emilie is in a lovely room in the clouds waiting for you."

After months as a practicing visionary, I felt the weight of suffering around me. It grew heavier and heavier still. The invisible weight of others' angst was testing the strength of my spirit. I felt weak from all the sorrow and guilt, especially of those I had come to love and admire. Each night I climbed the old stairs to my room, laboring to place one foot in front of the other. I felt lost. How could I help all the hurts? These people I loved so much, like Papa Joe.

One night, after turning off the lamp by my bedside, my dark room suddenly became engulfed in blinding light. There was a voice. My heart heard, "You are part of my Light. I will help you." It was just a whisper at first. But night after night, this otherworldly voice grew louder, my heart thumping within my chest with the message, "Feed my people."

I was already feeding these people. Every day. I woke up before the pigeons; even the gargoyles were still slumbering across the way. I kneaded loaf after loaf of bread. I twisted the dough in the shape of hundreds of crescents. I tucked chunks of chocolate into blankets of buttered dough. I stirred the eggs, crème and butter to make the quiches. I laid the apricots in perfect circles around the edges of the shortbread crust. I was doing nothing *but* feeding the flock.

Baabar found me early one morning crouched in the corner of the bakery, my apron turned up over my head in misery. I was defeated by my inability to act upon all my visions. How could I help carry Violette's grief for her, or ease Papa Joe's pain? Or wash away Madame Charpentier's guilt?

Baabar said, "Gabrielle, what is wrong? I have never seen you like this. Has someone hurt you?"

Baabar, my Protector, was always thinking of me. He arrived earlier to the bakery each morning to prepare the dough for the baguettes so that I could sleep a little longer, and my café crème was always waiting for me on the marble café table. Baabar would not even allow me to lift the broom to sweep the excess flour from the brick floor at the end of the day. Such tender care.

"Baabar, I am doing what Pierre instructed. I am looking deeply into the eyes. The visions are like little needles puncturing holes in the fabric of my spirit. I am not even making a dent in the suffering. Look at Madame Charpentier, Violette, dear Papa Joe."

Baabar took my hands into his. "Remember, we see through the mirror dimly here, yet love has proven its power to see us through. Patience, little angel. Set down your rolling pin and focus on feeding their souls. That is how you must tend to creation, my baker friend. You have the gift of seeing into people's stories. Touch them with as much love as you can, and soon a new path will open. You will see."

That evening, clearly up to her usual mischief, a jaunty Sophie arrived to my room, picnic basket in hand.

"I hear you are in need of a little divine inspiration, *mon amie.* Grab your sweater—we have been invited to a special concert in the park."

Walking to the Jardin du Luxembourg, we passed the stone angel guarding over the old wishing pool. A little girl in flaxen braids, eyes pinched tightly in concentration, tossed a coin over the stone wall's edge into the water, wishing for a pony. I envied her innocence. Brushing my unseen wings over her tiny shoulders in a blessing, I made my own wish: for a world where there was no ache to living, only joy.

As we climbed the stairs to the upper terrasse of the park, a mass of people formed concentric circles, like the rings of Saturn, around an antique Versailles gazebo. I too submitted to the gravitational pull that was drawing each of us to the vortex of otherworldly music streaming out from a massive white grand piano. I could not see it, nor could I see the pianist, but I could hear the exquisite sound.

Children were playing with marbles and dice in the dirt, families were sharing a repast on blue and red-striped flannel blankets, young men and women were resting on the seats of their bicycles, beggars were hunched against trees. I saw Muslim women with brilliantly colored scarves fluttering in the light wind and, of course, young lovers touching and frolicking. There were a pair of neon-orange clad monks kneeling on the edge of the sidewalk, their solemn faces to the ground. I heard French, English, Chinese, Russian, Hebrew, Arabic and Italian spoken. Despite the swelling sea of bodies, there was always room for more to join in. And they did. We were strangers, yet it seemed tonight somehow we were all divinely connected. Something mysterious was calling each one of us to lay down whatever burdens we were carrying and, for just a moment, surrender to the healing music.

I remembered a story Sister Karis shared with me as a child about the tens of thousands of people who gathered in a desert to hear Christus speak. There was no food available except for five loaves of bread and three fish. By a miracle, what seemed insignificant proved more than enough to nourish everyone. The music notes in this place at this moment proved to be our miracle loaves.

As the magic musician played, it was as if we were drawn out of our bodies. Complete silence descended; only those beatific notes. Not a word was spoken, but something was happening. I closed my eyes and a vision took me. I saw thousands of lights dancing above the people. They blended into one another, causing the Light to expand outward. Time slowed to a stop. There were no divisions, just licks of light dancing freely to the music, becoming the music. The monk and the Muslim. The beggar and the rich man. The child and the old woman. All spirits together. I saw their lights expanding before me. There were no hurts, tears, or hurtful barbed divisions. I could no longer distinguish language, race, age, creed, sex or color—only spirits alight. It was a soul feast. I turned and saw a multitude of wings etched in light and glowing together on the edge of the crowd's outer circle.

Sophie whispered in my ear, "This is a *Glimmer*." It is not a dream. What these people are experiencing right now is what the Holy One always hoped for creation. You are seeing a glimmer of creation at its best, where each spirit is refined and purified, and joined to others. Remember, the

Holy One does not look upon the outward appearance but only the heart. Now you may see as the Holy One sees. Each spirit easily, joyfully, bows to the sacred in another. All souls fed. The world made right by the power of love. Now there is only forgiveness, mercy, compassion and hope. Tonight is a glimpse of paradise; spirits are alight, they commune freely, each drawn together by divine love. You see, it is possible sometimes, here and now too. What do you think dear Christus was preaching about? He left his Golden Rule and promise of love's power. We must honor the Holy One, too, and help incarnate love's reality here and now."

I opened my eyes. The music had stopped. I watched as the pair of monks kissed the ground and turned to leave. I looked over to the beggar, who noticed a half-eaten sandwich left on the ground and smiled in relief, whispering a blessing for the day's bread. The innocent children gathered their shiny marbles, the remains of family picnics were tucked back into the woven-reed baskets, the crumbs became little gifts for the pigeons waiting patiently in the elm trees above. The piano was covered in black-felt cloth for another day.

At the garden's massive gates, Sophie turned back briefly. "Gabrielle, that was *presque paradis*, my friend. Tonight you saw the potential of creation as the Divine envisioned. Beautiful pieces of Light. Look beyond the external existence to the spirit. Invite heaven to break through. Every soul yearns to hear the message of Gabriel."

Sophie gave me a parting kiss on the cheek and a saucy wink. Speechless, I watched as she transformed into a figment of light before me and ascended, shimmering, into the night.

CHAPTER 19

New resolve. An angel on a mission, determined to feed every spirit that crossed my path with hope. I could not change what had happened to Madame Charpentier's daughter, bring Emilie back to Papa Joe or protect Remy from the evil drug raven. But I could blow on the flickering flame of every soul that crossed my path and fight to dispel the darkness. The time had come to accept the mission, to duel with the Dark Deep.

Something was unleashed inside of me. My heart expanded, and I thought I felt the tiniest rustle of wings as I threw myself into the task of feeding bodies and souls. My first order of business was Madame Charpentier. I was going to feed that poor woman's soul if it was the last thing I did. I made a white chocolate mille-feuille, a pièce de résistance. I carefully folded the puff pastry in circles over and over again, whispering prayers and filling each layer with dark chocolate Chantilly cream and succulent red raspberries. On the top, I made an angel cutout with crystal sugar, a symbol of who I truly was. This had to work.

Madame Charpentier didn't miss an opportunity to announce to whomever in the neighborhood would listen that she was boycotting the Levain Bakery. As she put it, "due to the new management." However, the busybody just could not stay away. The bakery was the center, the touchstone, for the whole neighborhood. Hiding behind her ridiculous oversized black sunglasses and garish feathered red hat, she entered the bakery, claiming her new *boulangerie* down the street was closed. Before she could order her sourdough *boule* and *pain aux raisins*, I stepped from behind the counter and presented my gift.

"You inspired this creation, Madame Charpentier. We have missed you these last months. You are a treasured member of our family here at the Levain Bakery. From now on, everyone will know this pastry as *Le Charpe*. I'll hope to see you in the morning for your regular order."

I inwardly smiled at the stunned look on her face. She took my beautifully wrapped *cadeau* and left without a word. I closed my eyes and experienced a future vision as Madame Charpentier carefully set the gift upon the kitchen table. For the longest time, she just stared at the gold cardboard box tied in our pink satin ribbons. It had been a long time since anyone had given her a gift, if only a pastry to be eaten. She just wouldn't allow it. I saw her inner light now struggling to flicker. For just a moment, she laid down her guilt and grief and allowed herself a measure of mercy. I don't think anyone had ever seen Madame Charpentier's smile. It was beautiful. The return of a tiny glow of her spirit showed me that I had indeed fed her. The next day, she arrived with mostly kind words all around. This would be a journey, but I knew now she would make it. Today, somehow, she made a courageous step toward living again, even allowing herself a taste of joy.

Always smiling, Papa Joe proudly and painfully walked into the bakery next. I looked up into the sky, begging to take on some of his pain. Our youthful bodies perform seamlessly until the day they reveal their fragility. How dependent we become on our fleeting bodies, ignoring our spirits for far too long. I searched through Sister Karis's bible of recipes for anything that might heal my dear friend. I remembered that Sister Karis touted cherries for their medicinal powers. It was Baabar who suggested the Sour Cherry Pirouette Tart. I set about making the delicate, flaky almond shortbread crust and filled it with a velvety vanilla cream. As I placed each cherry in a design around the edge of the crust, I sent up a healing prayer that Papa Joe would be able to open the door of his body's cage and fly free of pain. Lastly, I sprinkled chopped pistachios across the top and wrapped the tart in red cellophane paper with a perky raffia bow. I hoped it would offer some kind of reprieve, a breath of peace for this suffering man.

When Papa Joe arrived the next morning, I invited him behind the counter to visit my kitchen. His eyes lit up as though Picasso had just invited him into his atelier. He loved all the big ovens. On the white-marble counter, he found his gift. Such a child's delight on his face. Baabar brought in a chair from the bakery, and I served him a café crème with his dessert. A vision came quickly to me as I watched him close his eyes, savoring the first bite. I saw Papa Joe as a young man, rippling strong, no lines of strain on his face. His eyes were alight for a beautiful woman in a white dress pirouetting into his brawny arms. Here was the real Joe, stripped of his pain and suffering, only his happy spirit to identify him. I blinked and the vision was gone. Instead I heard old Papa Joe's boisterous laugh: "You treat me as King Louis royalty, *ma chérie*. If only my Emilie could be here to enjoy this too."

I took the corner of my linen apron, dotted the crème away from under his nose and whispered wordlessly in his ear.

"Maybe she is, Joe."

The next day, Madame Charpentier burst through the crowd and announced the terrible news. Papa Joe had laid his head upon the pillow that evening, a knowing smile on his worn face, and peacefully died in his sleep. I was sick until the vision came—it was a date. I watched as Papa Joe stepped into an elegant room in the clouds to find his Emilie wearing that white dress and a mischievous smile. Two spirits together again. And the story continues on.

The grief still came. I thought the cherries would heal him. Maybe I would have more time with him, more time to love our dear Papa Joe. Baabar took my hand into his and led me back into the kitchen.

"I was too late!" I cried. "How could you all have trusted me, a silly girl who only knows how to roll dough on a baker's table, with the wings of Gabriel? I have lost Papa Joe for all of us."

Baabar gently lifted my chin. His dark eyes looked tenderly into mine.

"Gabrielle, it was your love and whispered prayers that escorted Papa Joe to the door of his earthly cage. It was his time. You nourished his spirit for the journey ahead. He is fully healed now. Last night in his dreams, he saw the vision that you experienced here in the bakery. You blessed him so he could peacefully surrender to the path beyond. You pointed him toward the mystery. It takes courage for humans to face death. Unlike us, they fear what comes next. They hang on with an iron tenacity to life here and now. You lightened Papa Joe's spirit so he could fly. What more could the Holy One ask of you? You loved Papa Joe with your whole being."

The next couple of days were filled with planning a celebration of Papa Joe's life. The neighborhood was invited to a party in the garden. Sophie made a beautiful collage of photos of Papa Joe's life. I laughed at the one of him playing the violin and kicking his feet up, with his Emilie smiling in the foreground. Pierre arranged a piece on the piano in his honor that perfectly captured Papa's Joe's lively personality. Violette gathered flowers from the garden and entwined them with ribbons in the shape of a heart to lay upon his grave. I contributed a tray of *puits d'amour*. They are called "wells of love"—simple choux pastry on the outside, but bite into the center, and you are gifted with a creamy vanilla custard that melts in your mouth, leaving a smile on your face. This was Papa Joe for me.

Several weeks after the funeral, Sophie stopped me on my way to the market. "You are making quite a name for yourself. And I am not speaking of your tarte au citron, with those perfect meringue clouds on top, but your *other* gifts. You are tending to souls quite well. I feel I must warn you now to pay attention, because the Dark Deep will have eyes on you. The Raven will come for you, challenge your light."

All I could do was nod. I didn't understand, and I had little time to concern myself with this mysterious darkness, especially after I looked into the eyes of Madame Manoir. For months I had watched Lille gathering the unsold bread on Fridays and any of the leftover quiches or tartes and carefully preparing a box for little Louis Manoir to pick up each week on his way home from school. His mother, Madame Manoir—or Serene to all who knew her—was a beautiful woman with five precious boys. She was known to dress each one in a navy-blue, hand-tailored sailor suit on Easter morning, and to pin a rose boutonniere on the lapels. They were her *petit* princes.

Serene's malaise had started harmlessly with her forgetting the beans on the stovetop or the baguettes warming in the oven for dinner. The family ribbed her for the series of burned pots as they took turns on Saturday morning with the bristle scrub. Then it was the occasions where she would draw a blank on names of familiar people in the neighborhood. Serene would apologize effusively, citing poor sleep or the yoke of motherhood. Her husband, Olivier, protected her and slowly began taking on many of her household duties, fearing she might hurt herself.

The lives of the Manoir family changed dramatically when Serene did not return home from the market one Saturday. Olivier found her in the Tuileries gardens, helping a little boy direct his boat on the water. She was calling him Alain, the name of her middle son. But it was not her son. Olivier wept like a baby. He was losing the woman he loved. She looked so innocent in her spring floral dress with the sash tied to the side, and yet her mind was betraying her, betraying their family. Most days she would sit in the window seat, looking out on the tourists lining up for scoops of ice cream from *Maison Berthillon*. Often she would excitedly wave down to the street as if she knew the strangers.

The daughter of Monsieur Costes, a student at the Sorbonne, offered to sit with Serene during the day, and often not a word was exchanged. Serene was gone, lost to a place from which her children and dear husband could not rescue her.

Sadly, I knew something was wrong when she arrived in the bakery one afternoon in her housecoat and slippers. Her ear was noticeably bleeding where she had pulled the pearl earring, a gift on her wedding day, straight down through the fleshy lobe. She stepped up to the counter like a child, overwhelmed by the selection of cakes, tarts and pastries. It was too much. She began to whimper.

"I cannot choose. There are too many. Can you help me?"

Her eyes transmitted her pain and vulnerability. The vision reached in and grabbed my spirit by the apron strings. I saw a child's birthday party, Sam's ninth. Serene wore a beautiful vintage ruffled-lace apron tied around her waist, and she was stirring chocolate batter with a wooden spoon, all the while saying prayers for her precious towheaded birthday boy. The joy in her ministrations revealed a mother delighting in her son. Blinking, I quickly wrapped an apple turnover with cinnamon glaze, stepped from the counter, snatched away my apron and asked if I could walk her home.

That night I made the dark chocolate sponge cake layered with crème Chantilly and chocolate mousse, exactly as she had made for Sam's ninth birthday. I finished the cake in the morning with ribbons of white chocolate on top. After work I placed my creation in one of the green cardboard Levain cake boxes and made my way to the Manoir house. When I arrived, the family was sitting around the table enjoying a bowl of potato soup and chunks of French bread. Olivier was talking to their sons about school. But Serene fidgeted at the table, clearly struggling to follow the conversation. It pained me to see her desperately trying to hold on to the life she was no longer a part of. She was sitting at a table among strangers.

Olivier welcomed me in and opened my gift. Everyone squealed in delight over the chocolate cake. Tears welling, Olivier jumped up to give me his chair. Next Louis brought out Serene's fine china and placed the cake in the center of the table. No one but me could see the light flickering weakly behind Serene's eyes. And then she spoke.

"Sam, do you remember that cake I made for you on your ninth birthday? I had a devil of a time with the chocolate icing. What a day that was. The red, white and blue kite with the longest tail was your favorite gift."

As she lifted the fork to her mouth, I watched as the light flickered out. And she was gone again.

I reached for my coat, and Olivier followed me to the door. "Thank you, Gabrielle, even if it was for just a moment. To hear my Serene remember a happy time. I miss her so much."

Gabriel's message spilled out before I even knew what was happening. "Olivier, there will be a time when you will have your Serene again. I promise."

As I stepped onto the street, the clouds decided to loosen their belts, and now the rain tickled the top of my head. I said a prayer.

"Holy One, give them a time, a place, where Serene will look into Olivier's eyes and remember again."

CHAPTER 20

The next Friday afternoon, Baabar invited me on a field trip. He called it supplemental education. But I knew it was just his way of finally introducing me to his people living in the African district of the eighteenth arrondissement.

"Gaby, your gifts are needed outside the bakery as well. There are so many of my people who are in desperate need of the Light."

I was honored to accompany this prince to visit his expatriate Moroccan kingdom now located in the *banlieues* of Paris. I knew Baabar, humble as he was, commanded much respect from his African brothers and sisters. They claimed him as a prophet, a healer, some said even a savior. Baabar worked tirelessly locating work, apartments and medical care for them.

The eyes on the metro were so curious about this imposing Arab man, who was comfortably holding hands with a young white woman. I was clearly an outsider coming into this world.

Stepping off the metro, I was immediately seized by the savory smell of roasted lamb and a cacophony of Arab dialects. Bearded men with brightly colored kufis were in heated conversations, their hands constantly adjusting the linen fabric of their dishdashas, their restless sandaled feet drawing circles in the dirt. Stalls of hawking food vendors twisted like a train down the block. I was sure Baabar had taken me on a magic carpet ride to another country. One vendor after another touted the glory of their *tagine du jour* of lamb, chicken, prunes, preserved lemons, figs and apricots, all displayed on saffron beds of basmati.

Baabar stopped at Al Jabar's stall and offered me a pastilla, a Moroccan pastry filled with goat cheese and sprinkled with cinnamon. We continued down the street, and I heard the shouting of two older, heavily bearded men, traditionally attired, with mint teas before them in the Maroush Café. Next I saw a beautiful, dark African woman wearing a flowing sarong, her ears heavily adorned with several large gold hoop earrings. She stood majestically by her shop's display of brightly colored *babouches*. The assortment of African slippers was magical with its array of sequins and fine beading. I watched as she artfully rearranged her silk hijab head scarves into a colorful fan upon the table. In the stall beside her was an ancient, brown-wrinkled woman, arms lined with bracelets, a dark purple abaya covering her flowing silver hair. Almost disdainfully, she motioned for me to come and inspect her selection of painted tea sets and hookahs.

I could feel Baabar's pride for his people and his culture. "When General Bonaparte brought the Rosetta Stone back from one of his triumphant military campaigns, he brought with it the Maghreb, and the French fascination with Arab and African culture. Today there are hundreds of thousands of Algerians, Tunisians and Moroccans, all trying to make a life in Paris and the surrounding *banlieues*."

The people bowed in greeting to Baabar, some from the Arab grocery store, then more from an African CD shop and, lastly, a crowd in a bustling café, whose delicious aromas tempted me to order plates of the couscous with sizzling lamb kebabs.

But an angry crowd was forming ahead. Baabar took my hand and pulled me close to him. We turned the block and were faced with another group of punk youth screaming Arabic slurs at Baabar. I assumed they were because of me. The smoldering resentments, even Baabar could not temper.

We arrived at a gritty building, the dark windows seemed to peer down at me with reproach. Baabar opened the scuffed, black metal door to the smell of decay. Broken glass was everywhere, a dangerous mosaic to mark our path forward. I heard the frantic screams of a young child. The dangling light bulb hanging from the peeling ceiling was long dead, so we picked our way carefully down a dim hallway. The stench of burnt grease and discarded sardines wafted from the door of the last apartment at the end of the hall. Baabar knocked, and an old woman, Naima, cracked the door, keeping the chain lock until she saw who it was, and when she did, she immediately smiled. Her savior had returned.

We stepped inside, and I was stunned by the many squatting bodies squeezed into too tight a space. At first I thought maybe they were all here to share a meal together. But the cots leaning against the walls told a different story. This was everybody's home. There were three generations of North Africans pinched together on a faded, ragged Tabriz rug.

I could feel the dark almond-shaped eyes assessing me.

Baabar turned to me, his eyes filled with admiration.

"Gabrielle, this is the Mamomar family, the Louana family and the Rabouna family. They came from Morocco, two villages over from mine, three years ago and wait now for government housing. Only two of the men have found jobs. The baby, Laila, there in her mother's arms, is sick. Her parents brought her to Paris, hoping that doctors could help her. She has difficulty breathing as she was born with only one healthy lung."

Baabar placed the large sack he'd brought in the center of the rug and began to distribute his gifts. There were several loaves of bread, toilet paper, candles, a couple of blankets, two whole raw chickens, necks and all, from Gaspard's butcher shop, and a dozen of my fruit and savory tarts. Gratitude filled the tiny space.

The obvious matriarch of the group, Naima pointed her cane toward the kitchen and called in Arabic to one of the teenage boys to fetch her the turquoise glass bottle in the cupboard. She motioned for me to come to her. Baabar quickly supported her as she awkwardly stood. With much import, she opened the mysterious bottle and poured some of its contents into her hand, then touched my forehead in blessing, saying several phrases in Arabic. The holy water dripped down the slope of my nose and rested on my bottom lip. The sweet citrus fragrance was a gift to my olfactory senses.

Naima next unfolded a white linen handkerchief and proceeded to bathe my hands in the perfumed water. Baabar whispered, "This is orange-blossom water from our country, and it is her way of welcoming you to her home and into her family."

I thanked Naima and turned around to the others, instinctively bowing. A vision came at that moment. It told a bleak tale. Every natural law said this many people should not be crowded into this little space. Baabar channeled my thoughts.

"Gabrielle, they came here seeking a better life for their families. The human spirit will go to such limits for those they love. One will give up everything, even his own life, for another."

A handsome young male stepped out from the shadows and started yelling at Baabar in Arabic. I could not understand his angry words, but I could taste the venom in them. Baabar placed his arm around the boy's shoulder and brought him in for a brotherly embrace.

"This is Hakiim," Baabar said. "He is eager for violence, so easy he thinks to solve problems. He wants to arm us and fight for a better life. For the dignity of his people. He wants to fight for little Laila, his sister, who is dying."

Hakiim had such an innocent face, but his eyes were so full of bitterness. I could see that it was not in his true nature to fight. Laila's mother was softly whimpering on a three-legged, dilapidated sofa, the baby tucked inside her wool burka. I wanted to help, to heal this baby whose light was now a mere flicker. I looked into Hakiim's flashing eyes. The vision frightened me. Hakiim was being pulled in two directions. Baabar took hold of the boy's right arm; an eerie darkness enveloped his left. It became a shape, and I knew it was something devious and evil. The last thing I saw was Baabar, weak and yet drawing on every reserve to fight the Darkness and transmit his Light. I blinked and looked over at my dear friend. He bowed his head to me.

Baabar spoke like a true prophet. "The battle is coming. And one must offer his own life to save the many. Sometimes it is the only way for salvation."

We exchanged good-byes. Baabar touched Hakiim one last time on the shoulder. Naima held my hand and squeezed it. She said something to me in Arabic. Baabar translated. "Naima said she will pray for you on your journey. She sees your light. She believes you can save them."

We returned home in silence. I wanted to make things right for Laila, Hakiim, Naima and especially Baabar. I took out my sketchbook and began to draw the face of baby Laila. I imagined that if I could capture her spirit on paper, I could save her. Her mother would not cry anymore. Hakiim would shed his anger like burnt skin. He would go to school and grow up to be a noble man.

I awoke the next morning to find the face of Laila unrecognizable on the page. My tears had blurred the lines; her little spirit was now distorted on the page. Lille bustled into my room with coffee and sat on my bed as my tears released in a fury. I could not stop talking.

"There was sweet Laila, struggling for every breath. And her mother quietly desperate behind her burka. Oh, and Hakiim, who should naturally have a kind, gentle face but…the anger, the bitterness, familiar weapons of the Deep, now battled for charge of his soul. And then Naima blessed me with this orange-blossom water. And…"

Lille held me in her arms.

"Gabrielle, it is okay. We are promised that each story will find redemption at its divinely appointed time. Have faith."

But I feared the look in Hakiim's eyes. They told a different story. His face was hardened as if all the tears had dried up within him, leaving only burning salt upon his spirit. And that salt was about to dance with the devil.

Clearly, I could no longer scoff at the presence of evil in this world. As much as I wanted to believe that all was good, it simply was not the truth. I remembered then what the gargoyle woman had said to me in the church.

"Angels must be warriors willing to give their lives for the Light to prevail."

PART SIX

Alchemy of Chocolate

I send Love's name into the world with wings.

— THOMAS MERTON —

CHAPTER 21

We all, humans and angels alike, experience the transcendence of the world when we offer up to the universe true love in any form. Although some have tried—and will continue to try—to sabotage what was meant for good, love is unconquerable. The Holy One will never cease introducing love into the world. Sometimes its shimmering thread surprises you when you least expect it. For me, that luminous thread would have a name—Luc Bessier.

Pierre and Lille happened to be away, traveling on another one of their mysterious trips. Sophie was working at a furious pace to finish her paintings for the art show, "Through the Holy Door." When Baabar was not in the bakery, he was with his people in the French Maghreb, where there recently had been an incident on the rue de Maupier. Two Arab youth were shot and killed by a French policeman, who mistakenly believed they were breaking into a store. The fuse was lit, and before long, the flame would make its way down the coil. Baabar tirelessly preached peace and patience, while Hakiim secretly followed a different leader, a bearded fanatic who commanded increasing numbers of minions over to the Dark side.

And so on the providential evening of the ninth of July, with the Guardians away, my story took a turn—really a swerve. I met my destiny. It was Bastille Day, and I was invited by the mayor to create a chariot of desserts for his annual fete aboard the Bateau Mouche. The entire week I had worked at turning Paris's landmarks into edible masterpieces of pastry, sweet Chantilly crème and many hundreds of macaroons. I was especially proud of my meringue Sacre Coeur and my Notre Dame built stone by stone with cut macaroons. I even included the gargoyles on the flying buttresses in dark chocolate. But my architectural creations did not compare to the contributions of Luc Bessier, the mysterious chocolatier and owner of the Petite Alma Chocolate Shop. His Eiffel Tower of dark chocolate and a Rodin's "The Thinker" in white chocolate were pure magic.

I was certainly familiar with the name Luc Bessier. All Parisians were. Chocolatiers were quite the celebrities, and Luc did not disappoint. Lille had a Paris Match magazine article in her office about this renegade chocolatier. In a leather jacket, lounging on the back of his razor-sharp Ducati motorcycle in front of the Petit Alma Chocolate Shop, he was steely perfection. Unconventional childhood, it said, with parents who were either missionaries, nomads or gypsies. The journalist, clearly caught under his spell, penned him as mysterious, unpredictable, with mythic green eyes and dark, like cacao beans, hair.

But this wasn't the real Luc Bessier. A lifetime ago, he had been a gifted pediatric surgeon, the scalpel his instrument long before the sculptor's chisel. The best of his kind, said to have miracle hands. His specialty had been excising dangerous tumors—not ordinary, run-of-the-mill tumors. His calling had always been the children. The ones whose cheeks were supposed to be rosy, arms meant to be throwing the winning baseball or legs dancing perfect pirouettes in pink leotards. Luc had fought to save the innocent, to give them the chance to live and love. Death was always close, and these battles had challenged everything Luc held true.

Luc had understood his calling during his final pediatric rotation of medical school. One particular case would forever change him. There was no name for the corpse, only number 301b. Not a single hair was on her body. The chemo had made sure of that. There were scars up and down her arms and just above her heart, where doctors had gone to battle against the dark enemy that had greedily eaten away at her flesh. Etched in faded purple marker on the inside of 301b's wrist were the words "I have dreams." Luc made a promise that day to 301b: He would fight to give kids the right to dream.

It was never for the notoriety that Luc spent endless hours in the lab, wrote papers on treatment options, performed hundreds of surgeries a year, or slept countless nights on cots outside his little patients' rooms. He wanted to be the one there when they called out in pain. The parents of his children trusted him in their darkest hour. They called him their angel. And he was. For a while.

Before every surgery, Luc could be found kneeling in the chapel in the hospital. He prayed for mercy for the child and asked for a blessing upon his hands to heal. Then he would close his eyes and envision all the possibilities of whom the child could grow up to be one day. He would dream their dreams. After surgery, the little girl or boy would say, "Dr. Luc, what did you see in my dreams?" And Luc would say, "Mon petit, I saw you flying an airplane." Or "Jean-Pierre, I heard you playing Beethoven's Fifth at the Palais Garnier to the applause of thousands." Or "Rachel, you are destined to become a better doctor than me." For Luc, it had always been about giving a child the chance to make his or her life count for something.

The nurses claimed that in surgery Luc's eyes were sometimes closed. Something else seemed to guide his hands inside the child's body. Once a green young resident assisting in the operating room claimed he saw a strange light radiating from Luc's fingers like electricity. The man fainted, and it was never mentioned again. Where most doctors would close up, frightened by the magnitude of the disease, Luc would bid his nurse to put in another Chopin track and carry on into the night. He was fearless—but more importantly, full of faith that his Creator would make things right for the child. Wasn't there some natural law against kids dying before even falling in love? There had to be.

Luc had many successes. There was the new vaccine, his discovery of antibodies taken from rats, and always more innovative drugs that eased the side effects of chemotherapy. One would say he was victor over the enemy forces by the record number of children's happy faces that wallpapered the walls of his office. But no one saw the shoebox of pictures on a closet shelf in his apartment. Every week on Sunday, he would spread them out, the faces of the ones he hadn't been able to save. Little by little, his faith was chiseled away by the voices of every mother and father who had said goodbye to a child too soon. Helplessness grew as these lost children haunted him, their faces branded like invisible tattoos across his grieving spirit.

Petite Alma changed everything. She burst into his office with a joy unlike any he had ever seen. She wasn't afraid. She dreamed big and made him do the same. In that little nine-year-old body, there was more wisdom than could ever be found in all the awards and degrees prominently displayed on his office wall. Petite Alma loved chocolate better than anything. She could tell you what was inside a truffle and a ganache, and how you made German chocolate cake German. When she was too sick to eat the chocolate she loved, she had her mother, Pauline, buy boxes of it for everyone else at the hospital. Green and nauseated, Alma was determined to still enjoy chocolate in the smiles and sighs of delight in others.

One late night toward the end, Alma's mother lay exhausted on a cot outside her daughter's room. Luc took the midnight shift. Alma could not fool Luc like she did her mother. The immense pain seized her every breath. Luc climbed up on her bed and massaged her swollen legs as she drew pictures of the fancy chocolate shop she dreamed of owning one day.

She whispered, "Chocolate always makes people feel better."

Alma was the reason Luc saw the Raven for the first time. Alma tried to reassure him.

"Doc, I'll be all right. You'll see."

What irony. A child had more faith than he, the famous almighty doctor. She pointed to the wings in the corner of her room near the end. He saw them too. Luc cursed the mysterious presence floating above Alma's tortured body.

"Damn you to hell for not saving her!" he screamed. At that moment the Darkness descended on him. A grotesque raven flapped its wings as the Light left the hospital room. Then Luc was utterly alone.

Alma took her last breath surrounded by all those who loved her as well as a glimmering host of angels. But that meant little to Luc. He laid down his scalpel and his faith and walked out of the operating room that day, never looking back.

Luc turned with a scary vengeance against the Creator whom he had once admired, prayed to, trusted and deeply loved. He would no longer honor the One who could create such beauty only to abandon it. And this included his parents. For how could they believe and serve such a cruel Master? Faith came at too heavy a price. Luc became a dark soul, living dangerously close to the edge of the Deep. With nothing to believe in, angel and mortal alike become terribly dangerous in the world. A dark Raven's dream.

After Alma's funeral, Luc packed his bag, purchased a camera and wandered the globe aimlessly for months, snapping pictures of all the cruelty and destruction in the world. He blew up the pictures, held them up to the Holy One and, through gritted teeth, growled, "Here's another one for you. I will not let you forget a single one of these faces for as long as I live.

They were your creation, and you betrayed them. You allowed them to be defeated by the very world you created for them."

A year after Alma's passing, Luc began receiving postcards from Alma's mother. Each was a picture Alma had drawn of her magic chocolate shop. Pauline's notes simply read, "It's time we started making her life count for something. We owe her courage that. Let's make chocolate."

Pauline had known exactly what to say.

Luc returned to Paris after the third card from Pauline. She had already found the perfect place on the Île Saint-Louis for the Petite Alma Chocolate Shop. Luc tried to change her mind, even finding better storefronts in other *quartiers* of Paris, but Pauline was sure this was where Alma would have wanted it. Stangely, a woman named Lille, the owner of the Levain Bakery down the street, had made Pauline an offer she simply could not refuse. Luc hated the irony. But Pauline was sure she had heard Alma's unmistakable giggle in front of the store. She signed on the dotted line that very day. Of course Luc gave in, and an unexpected path opened.

On any day of the week, a line of children and adults circled the block, all excited to enter the magical chocolate shop. Heavy crimson drapes, like the grand velvet curtains on a theatrical stage protected the entrance and stirred curiosity. Patrons slipped through them to discover the magic waiting inside. Per Alma's request, each guest received a special *bisous,* a chocolate kiss, before leaving tied with a little note that read, "*Love more.*" The Petite Alma signature dark-brown box tied with a bright-pink satin ribbon became famous. Tourists and Parisians alike made special pilgrimages to the shop for one of those alluring boxes, full of chocolate promises to make life better one moment at a time.

On this particular Bastille Day, the Petite Alma Chocolate Shop had been invited to create the grand finale for the mayor's celebration, an Eiffel Tower, fifteen feet tall, of pure dark chocolate twinkling with tiny white chocolate lights, just like the real one.

Luc approached me as I was finishing the last touches on my macaroon Notre Dame. I immediately recognized him from the day in the flower market when Remy died. Those unforgettable green eyes with flecks of gold in them. He feigned interest in the flavors of my macaroons. Blushing and fussing at straightening the white linen tablecloth around my sculpture, I rattled off pistachio cherry, elderberry, dark chocolate with a red-pepper swirl and, my personal favorite, coconut and honey. He said nothing. I looked up into his mysterious eyes and was perplexed by what I saw. They reminded me of an eclipse of the moon, utter darkness. I saw so little light reflected in his eyes. Then he looked at me in the strangest way, as though he too recognized something familiar or rather disturbing in my eyes.

Coldly, as if disappointed in his discovery, he said, "I see you are with the Levain Bakery."

It was bitter chocolate on the tongue, the way he said it. Before I could respond, he disappeared. I was left with an electric current sparking in the air between us. I curtly called after him, "You may call me Gabrielle, thank you."

Looking back, I should have seen the signs. A red-hot chili pepper had turned up in my roux. Lille mysteriously materialized on the boat beside me. Had she not just been in Africa? She grabbed my elbow and hastily pulled me away to leave.

As we crossed the bridge onto the cobbled landing, Lille shocked me. "You must stay away from him. He is callous to our ways. He no longer believes in our gifts. He is in the clutches of the Raven."

But there he was again, suddenly standing under the broken streetlamp, hidden in the dark shadows. But I could see those green eyes, unmistakable; whether lighted or not, they were the most beautiful I had ever seen. Lille was dragging me now. But his eyes drew me in, and I wanted to look deeper. What had happened to make his eyes so full of pain and a disgust that unsettled me? Where had his light gone?

I spun around to find Lille in her most beautiful glowing state, commanding in a pool of light. She was radiant and now engaged in a duel, the Light just edging out the Darkness. She kept me close within her beaming circle of illumined protection. Clearly Lille was sending a message. When I turned back to the streetlamp, he was gone. Lille was no longer a beacon but was trembling.

The next day in the bakery, I looked up from wrapping two quiche Lorraines for Madame Leroir and met those same strange, beautiful eyes. Luc explained that his partner, Pauline, was ill and had sent him for Lille's famous healing *potage* soup and a fresh-baked *bâtard*. But I sensed he had come for me, as well. I had not slept the night before. Tossing and turning, every thought returned to him. And how I felt when he looked at me. There was an unexplainable connection. Almost as if we were cut from the same cloth.

Coming up behind me, Lille pinched my arm. "Turn away from his eyes. You can't save him. You'll only get hurt trying. Remember who you are and what you have been charged to do. A dance with the devil will only find you at the scary edge of the Deep."

Luc's voice was low, so masculine, intoxicating. Did he have any idea how his energy was affecting me? I was falling hard under his spell. That rakish, dark hair that undulated in smooth waves just below his starched white collar, his ruddy cheeks and, again, those mesmerizing green eyes. He pointed to the last pain au chocolat in the case. I had never seen Lille so taut.

She came around the counter and, through gritted teeth, seethed, "You made your choice. Now please go." Surprisingly, he just nodded and left.

Lille was uncomfortable in his presence, I could tell, and yet there was a strange, longing familiarity. I was most surprised by the look in her face when she had touched him. I would swear it had caused her real, physical pain. That night, as I made the last turn up the spiral steps to my room, Lille stopped me.

"Gabrielle, he will try to turn you from the Light."

I just nodded and opened my door. Before I closed it, I was sure I heard her whisper, "He is one of the Fallen." But when I turned to question her, she was gone.

The following week, I arrived at the bakery to find the most beautiful arrangement of roses carved from pure white chocolate, and a card that read, "Felicitations from Petite Alma." The Levain Bakery was abuzz as to my mystery admirer. Lille knew, though.

After a long day creating mini madeleines dipped in a cherry-chocolate glaze, I hung my apron, unable any longer to resist Luc and the magnetism of his green eyes. My excuse of an evening promenade was not bought by Lille. We both knew I was heading straight for the Petite Alma Chocolate Shop. Like it or not, the Spirit was at work now.

On the street, Lille called after me, "A world without angels is a world without hope."

Her warning was lost on me. I was busy unbinding my hair so that it would be free, a thick curling mass down my back. With flushed cheeks and a quick step, I eagerly leaped into the exciting unknown.

CHAPTER 22

The Petite Alma Chocolate Shop was tucked on the corner of rue des Rêves and rue de la Terre. The awning above the storefront was a ribbon of whimsical script clearly taking inspiration from a child. Pauline had commissioned a calligrapher to replicate her daughter's handwriting and used one of Alma's own drawings to inspire the shop's magical spirit. Inside there were rich truffles of every flavor, smooth ganache and decadent chocolate bars stacked on top of each other like bars of gold in their foil wrappers. Warm chocolate crème spilled from a magnificent waterfall fountain in the center of the shop. All part of petite Alma's dream.

Pauline smiled at me from the counter, "I wondered if you would come. When Luc curiously mentioned your name from the Levain Bakery, well, I just had to meet the new 'star' of the Levain Bakery. Lille certainly has high hopes for you."

I turned and there he was. I blushed furiously, heart beating wildly, giddy over just the sight of him. A beautiful but confusing vision. He asked me something, but I was speechless, hypnotized by his presence. Looking into his face, I tried using Pierre's training, but despite my best efforts, I could not penetrate his mystical green depths. Something was blocking his light and my ability to see the story of his spirit. My cheeks were on fire. I was sure my whole body must have been glowing. I could hear Pauline giggling from behind the counter.

I stammered, weak at the knees, "I just wanted to thank you...um...for my bouquet. It was from you, I assume?" He didn't even flinch. With the same blankness of his eyes in his voice, he responded.

"Actually, it was Pauline. She must always play foolish matchmaker. I must have mentioned something about you after the Bastille event. And she cannot help herself. Since you are here, take a look around Alma's Chocolate Shop. Try whatever you'd like."

I nodded, embarrassed by my impetuous visit, the tongue-tied act of a silly schoolgirl. He stepped behind the counter, intently focused on the day's receipts, but I was sure his eyes were on me.

A vault of chocolate, creatively displayed in glass cases, perfumed the room. From Karis, I knew a little about the history of chocolate. The pharmacist for Louis XVI and Marie Antoinette experimented with the medicinal properties of cocoa and discovered that it was also an amazing aphrodisiac. The entire royal court at Versailles fell under its spell, and many a love dalliance took its inspiration from a cocoa-dusted truffle or a dark chocolate ganache. Today the chocolatier is revered as highly as any Michelin three-starred chef. Not surprisingly, the Petite Alma Chocolate Shop was awarded the prestigious Medallion D'Or the first year it opened.

There is an alchemy to working with chocolate. It requires just the right heating and just the right cooling for the cocoa butter to crystallize and become malleable for the sculptor's hand—much like a love affair. Sister Karis and I created hundreds of chocolate *lapins* and Easter bells together. We melted down both white and dark chocolate to a pure liquid, then carefully poured the mixture into the abbey's ancient three-dimensional metal molds. Karis squealed with delight when she discovered the rusted tin mold for our signature bunny, long buried in a crate with old kitchen utensils, at the village *foire à la brocante*. I enjoyed the important task of taste-testing the first bunny every Easter.

Sister Karis admonished, "Now, Gaby, check to make sure the chocolate has a shiny finish, a pleasurable fragrance and that it snaps in your mouth at the first bite. It must provide a taste that draws your spirit out to play."

In spite of himself, Luc had become a master chocolatier, and his shop was the place of sugary dreams. A whimsical chandelier of crystal stars and crescent moons twinkled above. It cast a sparkling light across the entire room. Everywhere I turned, there was a chocolate confection tempting me. Alma had left strict instructions that the patrons of her chocolate shop must be allowed to taste the chocolate before committing their purse. She said, "There is nothing worse than nibbling on a truffle only to find it wasn't your favorite caramel but rather the surprise of a red-hot chili pepper!"

The shop promised a magical experience. Time turned a blind eye to allow the spirit a reprieve from whatever in life was threatening to weight it down. Joy was found in pure chocolate. You could see it in the flushed cheeks and bright eyes of even the most curmudgeonly. Inside the chocolate shop, everyone knew a child's delight again. Petite Alma had indeed left her mark here.

Pauline directed my attention to the impressive pyramid of truffles. Row upon row of perfect, succulent, bite-size nuggets of smooth chocolate ganache poured over lumps of caramel, hazelnut crème, champagne or lavender, and even a hot chili pepper for the brave. I admired Pauline, who was busy arranging a large platter of mini chocolate tarts. My mouth watered at the rich shortbread crusts with generous dollops of velvety hazelnut crème. She looked up and winked at me, then dared me to try one of the white chocolate pralines rolled in hazelnuts on the counter.

"Don't be bashful. You must try something. It's the only rule of the shop!"

We shared a giggle at a little towheaded boy, barely able to see over the counter, who fearlessly swiped his chubby index finger in a crystal bowl filled to the rim with dark chocolate mousse. No schoolteacher reprimands for him. Petite Alma would have loved it, Pauline said.

Next came a gold-timmed tray with perfect molten chocolate cakes dusted in gold, with matching gold teaspoons ready to discover the rich caramel waiting inside. I couldn't help myself. After one bite, I too became a devoted vassal in petite Alma's happy kingdom.

With a feline grin, Pauline piped up proudly.

"Did Luc mention my ten-layer chocolate sponge cake, soaked in amaretto and mocha cream and topped with a raspberry-chocolate ganache won this year's Medallion D'Or?"

Pauline had become a master chocolatier as well. Alma's chocolate shop had saved her life. Later she would confide that she had heard a voice. She had assumed it was petite Alma's but couldn't be sure. Regardless, the voice had penetrated her sobs and whispered that she had a choice to make. She could lie down or rise up and honor her daughter's life.

Luc found me admiring the back wall lined with an amazing collection of chocolate sculptures. There were replicas of Rodin's "The Kiss," several mini Eiffel Towers and even a Victorian dark chocolate birdcage holding a pair of perfect, white chocolate doves.

"It was Pauline's idea to pay tribute in chocolate to the French artists we both admire," Luc said.

I picked up an elegant black box with a miniature of a Toulouse-Lautrec painting on the cover.

"This one is the Lautrec. In the spirit of the Moulin Rouge, we created a rich chocolate-layer cake with a crème brûlée filling. For St. Valentine's Day, Pauline created the Fragonard, a puffed pastry full of rose-flower cream and a raspberry compote, lightly resting on a buttery white chocolate sable crust. My favorite remains the Picasso, a modern sculpture of black and white chocolate cubes filled with maraschino cherries."

Luc moved closer to me. I couldn't breathe, much less move away, even if I had wanted to. Both of us felt the mysterious energy surging between us. Luc lifted up a silver tray in my direction and said, "Would you like to sample this week's chocolate macaroon? It is filled with a coffee buttercream and rolled in pistachio nuts."

His fingers brushed against my cheek as he lifted the cookie to my mouth. I could not focus on the perfect harmony of flavors bursting in my mouth for his warm breath tickling my ear.

Luc misunderstood my silence.

"You don't like it. We clearly haven't mastered the macaroon yet, like you have. I will try white chocolate with a hint of lime for next week."

I blushed. "Oh, no, it's sublime."

For a moment I had his eyes locked into mine. Pierre would have been proud. But then Luc jerked away. He was angry, as if he knew what I was trying to do. He started to leave, but Pauline stopped him at the door.

"Luc, Gabrielle is still new to the city. Invite her for an evening stroll. The weather is perfect tonight."

His genuine affection for Pauline chastened his temper, and he briskly but reluctantly ushered me out the door.

That evening would be the first of many secret, enchanted walks together around Paris. We both knew something was happening, but neither of us would speak of it. Our celestial audience, however, was keen to watch every step of our fast and furious courtship. Only they knew the consequences of our union.

CHAPTER 23

One must never underestimate the mysterious workings of Creation. Life, all the joys and the sorrows, provide the keys to open door after door until finally, one day, we reach the end and the beginning all at once. Then the whole story makes perfect sense. Within the boundaries of the visible and the invisible of creation, we live, we lose, we learn, we hurt, we grow, we sacrifice. Only to realize with the final key of Death turning in the lock that it had always been and would always be about Love. Nothing else mattered.

Unbeknownst to me now, I was falling in love for the first time. It would be my greatest and hardest test on earth, to love another with my whole being. Luc became my docent, the city his living museum. He waited for me at the streetlamp on the corner between the bakery and the chocolate shop, always bearing *un gouter*, a special chocolate treat from Petite Alma. He said very little at first, a few comments here and there about his beloved city. We walked almost nightly, and I learned every *quartier* of Paris—the museums, the gardens, the place for a perfect bowl of onion soup, another for steak frites. I was introduced to classical concerts in hidden chapels and poetry readings hosted in natural amphitheaters of bending chestnut trees. I took daring rides on the back of his roaring motorbike, exploring the city under the moon's gaze. Every feminine nerve in my body was awakened.

Secretive about my outings with Luc, I was especially careful to keep them from Lille. How naive. Had I forgotten whom I was living amongst at

11, rue de Bourbon? They knew what was happening but remained silent. Pierre had instructed the winged community, "Remain in the shadows." It was a risk he felt he had to allow me, allow both of us. He reminded them, "The only way Gabrielle will become a great Light-bearer is if she experiences the darkness and then reclaims the light within herself."

But Lille had other plans. One Saturday afternoon, Luc and I were watching a close game of pétanque in the Tuileries gardens. Two grand old pères were arguing in rapid-fire French. One flung his ragged cap to the dusty ground in protest, while the other kicked up the dust with his clunky boots. Each was determined his silver boule was the closest to the cochonnet. Luc had chosen the spot because it was next to the oldest glacier establishment in Paris. I was enjoying my last bite of peach and violet ice cream, while Luc taste-tested his third scoop of chocolate, ever seeking a clue to Napoleon III's secret recipe.

I saw Lille first. She was trying for undercover but failing miserably in her tortoise shell-buttoned maroon trench coat. There was no disguising her radiance. And then, poof...she was gone in the blink of an eye. It was not the first time I would catch her watching us. I knew Luc felt her presence too. Once I caught him glaring directly at her. That war-ready stare sent chills down my spine. He was angry and cold, unmoved by the deep sadness I saw in Lille's eyes. When questioned, Luc abruptly changed the subject, pointing to a family of plump, greedy pigeons squabbling over a tossed stale baguette. I let it go, laughing, not wanting to upset him or damage what was burgeoning between us. I wanted to pull him into me, but he remained guarded, far away, as if his doors were shut and bolted to any glimmer of my love. Something was going on between Luc and Lille, but neither was willing to divulge the relationship. And I refused to do anything that might tilt my happy axis. My new life had become like a treasured necklace—each walk with this mysterious man added another pearl to the sacred strand.

Our weekend roundabouts through the French open-air markets were my favorite, I loved all the lively exchanges of recipes, boxes of *fraises de bois*, vines of ripe cherry tomatoes, and mounds of exotic spices, olives and pungent cheeses. Luc knew every vendor on the rue Mouffetard, one of the more colorful street bazaars in Paris. We walked the cobbled street, picking up cheeses, plums, a jar of olives, a baguette—anything to inspire a picnic in the park nearby. Troubadours could always be counted on to serenade us at the bottom of the rue Mouff, along with a colorful band of dancing gypsies. Following tradition, we never left the market without joining the troupe. The tapping of the tambourine, the sweet plucking of the violin and the sweet voice of young Michelle, led us to the Cafe Rouler for a pastis. My senses took over and I forgot everything else.

Luc's favorite haunt was La Closerie des Etoiles. It soon became my favorite spot in Paris too. The café was tucked inside an enchanting courtyard behind an ivy-encrusted wall. One entered through a nearby hidden rusted iron gate. Tiny white lights twinkled from a pair of almond trees flanking a bubbling central limestone horse fountain. The elegant waiters, dressed formally in crisp white shirts, tailored black vests and perfectly tied bow ties, served us elegantly. The tables were mostly reserved for *les regulieres,* and Luc was one of La Closerie's best. Sitting close together, in our usual tufted burgundy leather booth in the back, we ordered two, sometimes three, kir royales, content just to be together. Conversation was easy. Not so easy now was keeping our hands off of each other. If even our fingers touched, I felt it all the way down to my toes. The definition of bliss.

Benoit, the maître d', and his jolly brother, Louis, played jazz on the piano late most nights. Tuesdays, they were accompanied by the seductive, raspy voice of Angelique, an old-school, blowzy cabaret singer. Luc said the café had always been a refuge for artists, writers and musicians. Benoit was known for turning a blind eye when their pockets pulled empty. The walls were covered with memorabilia from the colorful clientele—a framed handkerchief with a lipstick stain and Gauguin's initials in the corner, a pencil sketch of one of the legendary garden soirees by Renoir, and a malodorous poem barely legible, scratched out on an ivory linen napkin by Sartre. This last read: *"You have stolen my face from me; you know it and I no longer do."* I loved it all.

When the café emptied, Benoit and some of the older waiters pulled up chairs, poured their own toddies and petitioned Luc to spin a tale. It was the only time I saw Luc let his guard down. He was full of interesting anecdotes of Parisians come and gone. He could add storyteller to his repertoire. One night he told a tale about a little-known artillery officer named Napoleon Bonaparte, who kneeled on the church steps of the Église Saint-Martin with a bouquet of lilies ninety-nine Sundays in a row until the widow Josephine agreed to marry him. Next came the story of the young artist Picasso, who lived for one straight year in a cold, dilapidated building down the street, subsisting on bread and absinthe, while he painted the famous "Guernica." But never did Luc tell his own story. He remained a mystery. I had no visions with him. Luc was protecting me from something. Maybe himself?

Walking one afternoon down the narrow, cobbled rue Saint-Rustique in Montmartre, Luc took my hand into his. But this time was different. I felt him loosening the hinges of his armor, allowing himself to feel something. My heart flipped, and I no longer heard the cajols of the portrait artists. Nor did I imagine the whispering breath of the ghosts of Toulouse-Lautrec, Dalí or Van Gogh in the rarefied air, clinking their glasses in absinthe toasts. No words were exchanged. Just a look. That was enough. An electric current charged through our bodies with the touch of our fingers. I yearned for his body against mine. And yet it was my spirit that was most anxious to unite with his.

Caught up in the moment, I stumbled. In one graceful move, Luc scooped me up and brought me into him. I buried myself into the safety of his chest. He whispered into my ear, "I have you." We stood like that, so tightly pressed together for a long time. I refused to move; I was finally where I was meant to be…until I ruined everything. I asked about his family. A harmless question. I wanted to know where he had come from. I wanted to tell him where I had come from, tell him about Sister Karis and Sacred Heart. But more than anything, I needed to *see* the man beneath the brooding *machisme*, the quicksilver motorcycle and the chocolate accolades. I quickly learned my lesson. Luc called the evening to an abrupt close. I did not see him again for days.

My angel intuition saw the darkness smoldering beneath Luc's exquisite surface. I should have been suspicious from the beginning when I could not see into his eyes. He would blink, hide them beneath his cap's brim or quickly turn away from my gaze. My gifts of illumination were impervious to his will. He refused to let me travel into his eyes and learn his story. The moment he sensed I was breaching his stronghold, he pulled up the drawbridge and disappeared.

Luc floated in and out of my sphere. I would not see him for days, even weeks. Just when I had convinced myself he was gone, an amour of my imagination, I would step out onto the street to find that shy smile and his hand waiting to take mine once again.

One evening in late October Luc casually suggested we stop by his apartment after a bistro dinner in the Marais. I was elated. We stepped into an ancient elevator, an art deco glass windowpane with a black swan as its center and a brass accordion door to enclose us. There was a small leather seat with a worn strap to hold onto when the tiny compartment lurched and settled onto each floor. With barely enough room for the two of us, the aroma of cocoa in his clothing drew me happily into his chest.

The elevator door jolted open at the top floor, an attic transformed into an ocular dream. The view over the Seine bewitched with the Louvre outlined in a tangerine glow as the sun took its final curtsy of the day. Six tall arched windows spanned the room. With a bronze lever, the center window could be folded out, allowing in the low hum of the city below. I heard the horn of the Bateau Mouche, signaling its departure from the Quai Voltaire.

High, exposed beams and pickled, broad-planked floors gave a handsome character to the lofted room. My heart was racing now in anticipation. I imagined the look on Mother Superior's face had she known what I was thinking. The room was partitioned by a beautiful chocolate-brown brocade curtain with a coat of arms embroidered in silver and royal blue at its midpoint. The far side of the room held a small kitchenette and directly across was a magnificently carved oak bed, with a desk and chair nearby. The rest of the space was open for Luc's studio. I saw a much-used pottery wheel, and next to it a large rustic wooden table covered with torn canvases and a myriad of carving tools.

Luc spoke, "I create models in potter's clay here and then replicate them in chocolate at the shop."

On a drying shelf beside the table was a Grecian urn; beside it, a realistic model World War II bomber, and beyond, a beautiful blooming rose in a majolica-style vase. Luc was an artist.

Luc invited me to try my hand at sculpting. He told me to close my eyes and feel the clay. The nerve cells in my body twitched in a pleasant frenzy each time his chest pressed against my back. Lost, I barely heard him whisper, "Don't move."

I had stopped breathing. Suddenly his hand brushed the curls away from my neck, and he gently kissed the tender skin behind my left ear. Then his lips made their way down the curve of my neck. With his fingers, he traced a line from there to my heart. So very slowly, too slowly, he unbuttoned and peeled off my thin sweater to expose more terrain for his skilled lips. I clinched my thighs when he next held my suddenly swollen breasts with a sculptor's admiration. His hands traveled lower, and I wished they would press through me to my center. He exhaled and kissed me long and hard. Our first real kiss. I invited him in, wanting every part of him. I was floating. I closed my eyes, ready to happily surrender my all to him.

Suddenly he jerked back.

"Gaby, you are bleeding."

Flushed with passion, I dazedly looked at his face, not understanding. Knocking over the stool, he jumped to attention. I glanced down. My hand was gripping the blade end of the sculptor's knife. I never felt it.

Luc yelled, "This is my fault! I have hurt you. Just as they knew I would."

He was horrified at the blood spurting over our once promising, beautiful star. Before I knew what was happening, Luc had tied a makeshift tourniquet around my arm to stop the bleeding. Next, he pulled out a black leather satchel from an unseen nearby cabinet. I watched, dumbfounded, as he brought out antiseptic and a sterile surgical kit, then proceeded to tend my wound. What was more amazing was his new demeanor. Cool, calm, professional and competent. When he was done, he bowed his head. This was the real Luc. I witnessed the unmistakable flicker of light in his eyes for the first time as his gifted hands were at work. Once I was bandaged, he gently put my sweater over my shoulders and had me back on the elevator, rattling off doctor speak: Elevate your arm, take two aspirin every six hours, the bakery is off limits for seventy-two hours."

I barely heard a word. I was in a trance of disbelief.

As the elevator doors closed, I peered through the stained-glass window and saw the truth. It had been a long time since he had used his hands for what they were meant to do. Sadly, the Darkness descended in the space between us, killing the new light. The elevator lurched and threw me back onto the bench. A chill came over me, and I was frightened. Luc sent me away with barely a nod goodbye.

Luc disappeared after that night. Weeks and months passed without a word. My disappointment was palpable. You could even taste it in my lifeless *pâtisseries du jour*. No richness to speak of. But my hand healed beautifully with the faintest hairline scar to remind me of what had happened that night. Pierre and Lille never said a word. Instead they took my melancholy as the perfect opportunity to increase the vigor of my lessons. Broken heart or not, the line of Gabriel still rested on my shoulders.

PART SEVEN

In the Patois of Angels

I will no longer hide you from the Mystery.

— BOOK of TOBIT —

CHAPTER 24

Two weeks after Luc disappeared, Pierre surprised me in the kitchen and petitioned Lille to steal me away from the bakery for the afternoon. He led me across the courtyard to a hidden door beneath the marble staircase, then unlocked it with the golden key that always hung from the chain of his pocket watch. Inside was a copper lantern suddenly aflame, and down into the darkness we went. A cold wind rose up like an apparition to greet us.

"Pierre, are you sure we should be coming down here?"

The steps circled down round and round. Pierre happily lectured as we progressed.

"You are one of the seven Luminaries sent from the Land of the Blessed to carry out the divine plan in the Vale of Tears."

"The Vale of Tears, Pierre?"

"Yes. The archangel Mik'hail named earth the Vale of Tears because he had never experienced the groan of humanity or tasted the salty dew secreted from their eyes. He took all of humanity's grief into himself, and he too wept for the first time. You see, there are no tears in heaven. It was Mik'hail who requested leave of the Holy One to go to earth, sword in hand, to defeat the culprit of human tears. And that is how the choir of Luminaries came into being. Angels took up the cause of humanity.

"The Holy One tapped eight angels, each with his or her own unique abilities, and charged them to guard the human story. There has never been a time on earth that has not included the presence of angels. The archangel Mik'hail was released from his post in the garden, protecting the Tree of

Life, to become the first angel commissioned to aid humanity. Sadly, his first battle was with one of our own. The beautiful Lucifer was seduced by his own powers the moment he took on flesh. He saw earth as a kingdom to rival heaven. His kingdom. Lucifer lost his way and was finally defeated and eternally banished to the Dark Deep. Now there are only seven Luminaries, each with a host of angels at his or her command. The lines of Mik'hail, Raphael, Auriel, Barachiel, Sariel, Jophiel and Gabriel all are working here and now on behalf of the Holy One.

"There is a hierarchy in the angelic court. An angel rises by his or her commitment to the human story. An angel may also fall, Gabrielle. The task of serving the Holy One and uplifting humanity can be a difficult one. Many times humans reject the holy Light. We all know well the power found in fear, arrogance, and pain. But the Holy One has the power for redemption, even for wayward angels. The Guardians encourage angels, like you, to rise and serve. You have mastered your gift of holy sight. I am proud of you. Today, we will expand your angelic training."

We reached another door, and Pierre took out a second oversize key, which was silver and twisted in an intricate scroll design. He opened the next arched door, and I saw a glowing light ahead. I found myself in a grand library, mahogany bookcases in rows of six, each separated by a Corinthian marble column. The impressive library was the sacred conservatoire for every word ever written by humans and angels on the subject of angelology. This was as far as mortals were allowed. A third disappearing door was hidden inside the last bookcase. Pierre took an ancient leather-bound book from the shelf. Inside was a key carved from the branch of an olive tree. He turned it gently in the lock, and the door opened to the most delicious secret yet. Who could have imagined this was below the bakery.

Pierre crowed, "Voilà! Welcome to the Chamber of Angels."

Levitating above was Jobe, lighting candles with his finger in a magnificent crystal chandelier hanging from the swooping corbel-vaulted ceiling. An ethereal glow gradually spread over the entire room, its size matching the entire building aboveground. The light entered every fiber, cell and atom present. Every edge was smoothed, and my spirit was instantly nourished.

"Gabrielle, receive the Light. Angels thrive on pure light. The light in the Vale is fractured, because it is constantly challenged by the Darkness. But in this special place, we are able to connect with the Almighty source. We come down here to be energized by the pure light, to be reborn again and again. It is the only way we can fully give of ourselves to the world. If not, like humans, the earthly world will diminish us. We must fill ourselves here so that we may gift others with this Light."

I had never considered my own light reserves and the need to replenish them. I see now why Sophie took me to the concert in the park. She was trying to restore my light. I had given the best of myself to Madame Charpentier, Papa Joe, Violette, Serene and especially Luc. And I was in need of a light renewal of my own now.

Pierre showed me how to pull my shoulders back and spread my fragile wings, to open my heart, free to receive the pure light. Intuitively I knew I would need extra reserves for the road ahead. The Raven was biding his time. The Guardians would do their best to prepare me, but ultimately it was my fight. The Light battling the Darkness. Belief against unbelief. The soul overcoming the body. Love swallowing fear. It would all come down to sacrifice. True love requires it.

I heard the music now, and my feet lifted off the ground. I no longer had to fight earth's gravity. I was free. My spirit floated around the room, hesitant at first, and then delighted in how natural it was to fly. For a little while, I could let go of the world and just live in the light. Once my spirit had returned to its full glow, Pierre waved for me to join him at the table in the center of the room.

"This table was made long ago from an olive tree that grew in the center of the temple garden in Jerusalem. On the day that Christus took his last earthly breath, the tree was struck by lightning and split in two. The tree was dead. The world went silent and dark. But within three days, a green shoot came forth. The Darkness had underestimated the power of Love. Humanity is never left in darkness for long."

The magnificent table stretched almost the length of the room and was set with seven ornate chairs, each with a different name and symbol carved in ivory at the curve of its back. Pierre touched a chair and said the angel's name and symbol.

"Mik'hail, the warrior, the flaming sword; Sariel, the healer, the olive branch; Barachiel, the protector, the lightning bolt; Raphael, heaven's escort, the winged chariot."

He paused.

"This is Lille's family chair. Hers is the line of Raphael, blessed long ago with the honor of carrying the soul of Moses home, finally bringing him into the eternal land of milk and honey."

Pierre touched the chair of Auriel, with the lighted arrow. I knew it was his because his glasses were hanging over the chair's arm. His fingers traced over the well-worn grooves around the scalloped edge of the chair's back. He said, "My line was tapped for our gifts of Light transfer and guardianship."

Pierre then pointed over to the chair of Jophiel, the angel of wisdom, symbolized by the all-knowing eye. And Jobe winked at me and said, "I'll be watching over you always!"

Pierre motioned for me to come to him. He pulled out a chair for me. Here was the seat of Gabriel, with the symbol of a golden trumpet, for the Holy One's herald of Love.

"You are the divine messenger, entrusted with the words taken directly from the lips of the Holy One. They have the power to wipe clean the soul, obliterate transgressions and anoint with mercy, forgiveness and love. Your messages redeem. It is written that one from the line of Gabriel will blow the trumpet to signal the final jubilee. He or she will call all to return to the Land of the Blessed. But until that day, the line of Gabriel brings the message of hope to the Vale."

I traced my fingers along the edge of the golden trumpet. Curious, I turned to Pierre.

"What messages have others revealed before me?"

Pierre took a seat and invited me to do the same. I fit in the seat perfectly. It was as if the chair had been carved just for me.

"A message is spoken for a certain time and place. It may be a prophecy, a portent, an annunciation or simple words of mercy and hope. In a time of great unrest, Gabriel revealed to Daniel the promise of a Savior. It was also Gabriel who whispered the holy words of the Koran into the ear of Muhammad to inspire a new way forward. My favorite remains Gabriel's announcement to Mary that she would bear a Savior. She too would learn both the trials and the rewards of being one of God's angels. And those are just some of the ones that humans thought worthy to record. Your line has been delivering inspired messages since the beginning, for millenniums. If only humans would have the ears to hear them. Come, I have something to show you."

Jobe took me under his wing and we floated together to a Louis XVI *cabinet de curiosités* at the back of the room. Inside there were seven glass shelves, each holding a unique treasure box.

Pierre pointed to the chain around my neck. "It is time to put to use the key your papa left you."

I removed the chain with the key and now-glowing ring from around my neck and handed it to Pierre. Since the old woman in the chapel had entrusted me with papa's things, I had worn them close to my heart. It was revelatory and reassuring how the ring glowed in the presence of angels.

Pierre lifted out a silver box, its top inset with pearls and inlaid with seven golden trumpets. I used my father's key and unlocked it. Inside was a book, but no ordinary book. The images and words were literally moving across the cover.

I gasped. "What is this? A living book?"

"Indeed. This book tells the history of the line of Gabriel across time and space. Also, your own personal story is unfolding right here before us."

I turned the pages in wonder. My perceived reality was no longer clear. Billowing clouds moved across the first page. A constellation of stars in the shape of a trumpet twinkled on another page. They were so real I could pluck them from the page. Then an opalescent moon waxed from crescent to gibbous and, finally, to a full butter moon right before my eyes. I turned the page and an image appeared too surreal to believe. It was a creature with many wings created out of different wavelengths of light. It lifted off the page as quickly as it had appeared, and then disappeared. There were golden symbols, beautifully calligraphed and now pulsating with brilliant light. I looked closer at the scurrying script, but the language was unfamiliar.

"Pierre, is this an ancient dialect? I cannot read the words."

"No, Gabrielle, it is the celestial language, the tongue of angels, the very language spoken by the Holy One to bring creation into being."

"I don't understand. I can only see sparks of light."

"They are illuminations. We angels are the purest of creation. Due to our close proximity to the Holy One, we receive the greatest amount of divine light. Our eyes, wings, movements and even emotions manifest as pure light."

"I don't understand."

"That is because you have forgotten how to communicate with your spirit. You have allowed the earthly world to teach you its language. You are out of practice with your native tongue. But it will come. Inside this holy book is the story of every single angel from the line of Gabriel. It is your genealogical tree, the written history of your kind—I mean angels, of course. It is here that you too will leave your story for those next in line."

"Is there a code? How do I translate the symbols into words?" I was curious about all the Gabriels who had come before me, hoping they would clarify my own destiny.

Pierre responded, "No code. Close your eyes, open your heart and be patient. This is the next step to your full maturity as an angel. The symbols will make sense to the divine within you. You, my love, must remember your first language again. Humans see through a mirror dimly on this side of creation. They have lost all sense of the wonder and mystery of their Creator. They no longer understand their own value. You must remember again who you are, Gabrielle. You bear a spark of the Holy One inside you, and that is power. You must learn to tap into the source, learn again how to speak from your soul. The mirror will allow you to see only by the measure of your faith."

But the book remained impenetrable. I felt my humanity painfully. I felt my poor faith even more.

"Gabrielle, calm yourself. Rome wasn't built in a day. A word of caution in the meantime: The Vale of Tears does everything in its power to discourage."

"What will I find in the book?"

"Divine providence. Wisdom. Sacred stories that prove God is indeed still working in all things for good."

"Have you read them?"

"No, this book is written for the Line of Gabriel. You are now the next guardian of Gabriel's story. You are responsible for understanding its meaning and your role in continuing it forward. Humans cannot see the mystery with their eyes, and yet even in their fragility, if they quiet their lives enough, their spirits sense something more. They too yearn for the wondrous, and yet they haven't the language to communicate about it. But the language is engraved upon the soul of all creation, not just the angelic. One must garner the courage to allow the spirit a voice."

"I don't know how to begin."

"Gabrielle, start from a place of love."

He stopped abruptly. I saw him in his eyes. Luc's face. There was no hiding my heart. Pierre knew my truth.

My Guardian nodded in genuine consolation and then continued, "Love is the only perfect truth in the Vale of Tears. Without it, all live a meager existence, far from what was divinely intended. Sadly, there are those who forfeit their stories to the ever-present Darkness."

I could feel my shoulders cinch up toward my ears. Was he talking about Luc?

"Remember the angel Mik'hail with the flaming sword? He is out there cutting through the Darkness at every turn. I have seen Baabar do this for you. Don't give up. You are not alone. We are all here to help. Love bridges the gap between the Land of the Blessed and the Vale of Tears. One day there will be no more tears. Only milk and honey and the eternal olive tree. That is the sacred promise."

I placed my finger in the grooves of the carved tree on the back of the Gabriel chair. Its branches boasted gold leaves exactly like the ones on Sophie's wall. But there were also tarred leaves, and I wondered why.

Pierre read my thoughts. "Sadly, they represent members of your line who chose the dark path. They didn't trust that love was enough to see them through. They gave up."

I noticed underneath one of the black leaves the name of my grandfather branded into the wood.

"Where are they now?"

"They live in the Darkness, by their own choice. A place absent of love, hope and light." I thought of Luc.

"Is it forever?"

"That is not for me to know. I can only trust that the Holy One retains the power to redeem even the ones with the darkest hearts. I believe a day will come when all will kneel before the Creator and accept his Love."

Pierre stood up from the table and clapped his hands three times. This reminded me of Monsieur Lautrec, my teacher at my old grammar school, who would do the same after a less-than-stellar round of conjugating verbs. I sensed that Pierre worried his pupil was missing the point. He rolled up his sleeves, determined to get down to the marrow.

"Gabrielle, you will never find what you are looking for in this imperfect world. You must look inside and connect with the Light. Only then will you understand who you are and what you were created to be."

I noticed a leaf on his tree, neither gold nor tarred black. It was a faint shadow.

"Pierre, what about this one?"

"It represents an undecided soul. Something has dimmed his light and yet he has not fully surrendered to the darkness. He lives in this in-between, going through the motions, reaching out for anything and nothing. This angel is too afraid to look inside for fear of what he might find. He places a great strain on the rest of our line. And yet, if I give up hope for him, I might as well disavow the Holy One's power. So I press forward, one foot in front of the other, trusting in the Light to redeem."

Pierre muscled a smile but forgot I could *see* the pain hidden in his eyes too. Angels do indeed weep, and he was hurting for his shadow of a leaf on a tree, secretly praying that love would find a way with one of his very own.

CHAPTER 25

Over the next weeks, the *Angel Holy Book* drew me to its secret chamber, and yet I remained deaf to its message. Jobe, the gatekeeper, hovered always nearby, curiously invested in my awakening. One afternoon I found the sacred texts of Jews, Christians, Buddhists and Muslims waiting for me on the library table, all red-lined for angelic appearances and their revelations to the world. I read where the angel Jibraaiyl, from the line of Gabriel, whispered the Koran verse by verse to Muhammad over twenty-two earthly years. His words announced a wondrous invasion of holiness into the world. I was surprised to learn that the Buddhists called our kind bodhisattvas. They believe we helped to free souls from attachments to this world, especially fear. There were also accounts of angels carrying out divine judgment on earth. King David, the city of Sodom and King Herod were just a few who felt the fire from our wings of wrath.

I preferred reading about the heroics of my kind, such as the freeing of the great Daniel not once but twice—first in the fiery furnace and then in the lion's den. I read that heaven rained tears of joy across the parched earth in honor of the faithful man found in Abraham. There was not a day righteous Abraham lived without the protective shelter of our wings. And then fearless Moses, who encountered angels throughout his life in flaming bushes and seas that parted for him. The Divine surrounded him always. But the greatest for me was when the angel Gabriel revealed to the virgin Mary that she was with child. What an honor to announce a Savior to be born, who would change the world. I felt my wings twitching as I read the accounts. These texts from different times, cultures and belief systems all had one thing in common: The presence of angels proved that the divine hand was upon every breath of this world.

One night Jobe arrived at my door with a mysterious blue-leather journal wrapped in wrinkled linen, along with a tray carrying a pottery bowl of cherries and a chipped earthen mug of *chocolat chaud*. A gentle and erudite monk had written the journal and claimed that a radiant white creature visited him nightly in his dreams throughout his life. Each time, she left him an enigmatic message etched across the insides of his eyelids. At the bottom of each page in the journal, the monk had drawn the remembered symbols from his dreams. They were the same ones from the mysterious *Angel Holy Book*. Jobe had marked a page with a red ribbon for me. The monk had written the message near the end of his life. He had lamented his spiritual blindness and stubborn pride that had kept him from deciphering the symbols.

Jobe had enclosed a message for me: "Knock and the door will be opened. Ask and you shall receive."

I feared I was as blind as the monk, expecting to decipher the puzzle in human terms. Every time I crossed paths with Jobe, he just tapped his chest, the place of the heart, and flashed a knowing smile. Weeks turned into months, and I came no closer to decoding the *Angel Holy Book*. The Book refused to open its secrets to me, and on top of that, I also suffered terribly from no word of Luc. My existence became a labyrinth of my own design, and I was running into one dead end after another.

After an exceptionally hot day at the ovens, I decided to take a stroll, knowing my feet would predictably lead me to the Petite Alma Chocolate Shop as they always did. Pauline was in the window preparing *un cadeau* of chocolate éclairs. She waved for me to come inside.

Fussing with tying the rose ribbons on the chocolate gift, she said to me without looking up, "Gabrielle, I have seen you walk past this store nearly every evening since he left us. I wish I could tell you he was here. But I can't. Luc does this; he disappears. He did the same thing after Alma died. I had hoped you would be his reason to stay. But he is determined to run from anything good in his life."

With a weak à bientôt and a strangled sob, I stepped back out onto the street, only to be met by the unnerving cawing of a host of black ravens, their oily black feathers flapping and beady eyes taunting me. "Watch yourself. The Dark is coming," they seemed to be saying.

Baabar suddenly appeared at my side. He was protecting me from the darkness once again. His arms of steel surrounded me. In his deepest, most commanding voice, Baabar said, "You are floundering, my love. Let me help you. You are looking everywhere but inside." And he touched my heart.

Tearfully, I cried out, "Baabar, where do I turn? I'm lost."

Baabar lifted my face to his.

"Return to the Beginning."

"The beginning?" I asked.

"Yes, to the One who first separated Light from Darkness. Allah, the Ineffable, the Great I Am, the Source, God, the Holy of Holies, the Savior. The name makes little difference. You will find the peace you seek, the answers, the way forward by kneeling before the One who gave you breath, wings and your light."

Late that same night, when everyone was sleeping, I put on my robe and crept down to the Chamber. Then I did something I had always been slightly suspicious of—I prayed. I had watched the sisters of Sacred Heart kneel, bowing their heads in submission on the cobblestoned abbey floor in complete surrender. They had trusted in what they could not see. And they had appeared to find answers. It couldn't hurt to try.

As I kneeled, there were no words, just tears, total vulnerability. The heaviness of life caught me as in a net. I was fighting to keep a positive view of the world, but I was losing. I prayed for help. Then from nowhere and everywhere at once, I heard the still, small voice.

"You were never meant to do it alone, Gabrielle. The earthly world will not provide the answers you seek. I have been waiting for you to approach me, my child."

I stammered, "H-Holy One, Whoever you are, Wherever you are, I beg you. Show me the way."

Only silence.

In the days that followed, I committed to whispering prayers while rolling out dough, sweeping the front steps of the bakery, walking around the neighborhood—everywhere and in all things. I prayed for peace, knowledge, healing, heaven, angels, milk and honey. I prayed for love, especially Luc's. My life was transformed into one long, living prayer.

Baabar just smiled. "Pray without ceasing. That's a fine way to knock at the door."

It was Monday, July 3, a day much like any other day in the bakery. Madame Charpentier came in with a litany of compliments—yes, compliments.

"Gabrielle, your *pain aux raisins* is divine. My daughter-in-law, Colette, announced that I am to have a granddaughter this spring." I was sincerely happy for her. It was time that she knew joy again.

It was Madame Charpentier who commented first on the mysterious wind brewing outside.

"A wind like this means the heavens have something to say," she importantly prophesized.

I hurried down to the Chamber of Angels, to the Book. The pages were turning with a fury, finally stopping on number 777. I touched each symbol on the page with my finger, much like a child learning to read for the first time. A strange sound escaped my lips. It felt funny on my tongue. I placed my finger on another symbol, and again my tongue twisted and curled to release another sound. The new language was lyrical. The strange sounds linked hands to form words, phrases. I could hardly contain my excitement. First, I heard my papa's voice telling the story of my birth. Next I heard my mother's voice describe the glow that had surrounded her on the day I was conceived. She shared many secrets and taught me new words of love. I understood for the first time whom I was created to be. I was imprinted with the gift of visions from my father and the ability to heal from my mother. The letters spoke of my mother's travels and healings with plants and herbs and the mysterious swirl of waters. My father was the *enlightened* one. Inside his earthly church, a place of lit candles, stained glass, whispered prayers and sweet incense, he had offered a home to the lost. Souls traveled long distances to be anointed by the Light in his holy liturgies.

Applause startled me. I turned around to find Baabar, Sophie, Lille, Jobe and Pierre, each clothed in brilliance.

"Gabrielle, you did it!"

I understood what Sophie had said, but it wasn't in human-speak. She was communicating to me in the holy language of angels.

I hungrily returned to the Book. My chest opened and my heart leaped across the pages. The *Angel Holy Book* was alive for me.

I bowed my head in gratitude, understanding for the first time my gifts, my responsibility as a light-bearer. I knew my days were already numbered in the mind of the Creator. There was a beginning and an ending to my story here on earth, and I had neither the power nor the desire to change that. I now had to make every moment, every breath, count. In sublime peace, I knew one day another seeker, like myself, would come to the *Angel Holy Book* and look to my story for answers too. Maybe even a child of my own. My life of light was my way forward. And I was ready.

None of this changed my longing for Luc, but I would never allow the Darkness to win ground or souls on my watch now. If I felt despair in the labyrinth of my earthly existence, I knew I could look inside for the Light. I was committed to being one of the best in the line of Gabriel.

Who could have known that this promise would be tested so soon?

PART EIGHT

Enlightment

Angels are spiritual creatures who glorify God without ceasing and serve his saving plans for all creatures.

— ST. THOMAS AQUINAS —

CHAPTER 26

Where there is Light, there is always Darkness. It is the irrevocable truth here on earth. It is no easy feat to lift up the Light when one is surrounded on all sides by Darkness. And the Deep never lets up. It presses on the heart, challenges its muscularity and greedily feasts on what was meant for good. Angels know there is no escaping the fragility of life on earth. Even Christus wept for humanity. Loss is loss. Hurt is hurt. Pain does not discriminate—age, gender, race or creed have no exceptions. Or the winged ones, for that matter. All of creation weeps into itself, every cell connected to one another fighting to endure. But an angel's gift is to know and share that there is more to the story than can be seen. It is no accident that in every documented encounter with an angel, the first words are, "Do not be afraid."

Pierre organized a dinner to celebrate my homecoming, as he called it.

"Gabrielle, you have been journeying long in a foreign land, speaking a different dialect, drinking from a well that has done little to quench your parched spirit's thirst. But you have found your way back to us. You have remembered who you are. What power you have now. We must celebrate. Tonight you will sit among the angels, in the Chair of Gabriel."

Feeling light as air, I put on a flowing dress of lilac, trimmed in sky-blue satin, and accessorized with Gabriel's key and Baabar's ruby heart. I returned to the Chamber of Angels to find the long table dressed in an elaborately crocheted white tablecloth. A large crystal vase of violets, peonies and hyacinths was surrounded by a scattering of verbena-scented votive candles.

The meal was a communion offering from each of the angels. Baabar had prepared brochettes of roasted Moroccan chicken in a mint and honey glaze, artfully skewered on rosemary branches. He bowed formally after his presentation. Everyone then clapped when Pierre ceremoniously placed a beautiful Limoges platter in the center of the table. He carefully cut through the bubble of foil to reveal a whole fish nearly swimming in his secret sauce of thyme, olives, lemons and tomatoes. Next Sophie complemented those dishes with a fragrant risotto of chanterelle mushrooms, spring onions and ribbons of Parmesan. Not to be outdone, Lille presented a long, hearty farmer's loaf from the bakery stuffed with generous chunks of garlic, rosemary and fontina. Lastly, Pauline had graciously sent the pièce de résistance. It was an exquisite *gateaux truffe.* The night was a true feast for angels.

The dinner was served on Sophie's collection of faience plates, each with a hand-painted design in the center. She said they were made by her artist friend, an angel in Moustiers-Saint-Marie. Looking down, I noticed my plate had the image of an owl perched on a branch. I thought of *le monsieur owl,* who had made his home in the abbey's largest oak tree back at Sacred Heart. As a child, I imagined him as my sage protector and friend.

There were no more secrets. I was one of them now. I could speak their language. Lille discussed neighbors around the bakery in need of care. Pierre reviewed upcoming trips to visit other Winged clans like ours, even suggesting I could accompany him to the healing springs in Hungary, a favorite haunt of my mother's. Sophie announced her art show opening the following week. All seemed curiously right with the world. The pendulum was in balance.

But not for long. The hourglass was nearly finished. Jobe suddenly pulled Pierre away from the party. When he returned to the table, his face was somber.

"I have just received word that little Laila took her last earthly breath. Baabar, you know what to do. Safe travels, my friend."

Baabar nodded at Pierre and turned to me, his eyes penetrating. "Gabrielle, I know this is your special day, but I believe you are needed in the Maghreb tonight."

I arose quickly from the table. Pierre took my arm. "Happiness only lasts for a time, my dear, but so does sadness. Deliver Gabriel's Message."

In my room, quickly changing into appropriate mourning clothes, I briefly stopped before the mirror. I felt the Darkness swirling around my shoulders, planting the seeds of anger, doubt and fear. Kneeling, I opened my heart and prayed for strength.

The angel Gabriel then vowed as I went into the night, "I will step into the darkness, but not without taking the light with me."

Baabar and I stepped off the metro at the *Barbès-Rochechouart* stop. An Arab woman swathed in a royal-blue caftan beckoned us to her stall, stacked high with tagine pots and brightly colored mats for the hammam. I smiled and said, *"Pas du jour."* Baabar stepped forward, and immediately she bowed her head, knowing why he was here. It seemed everyone in the Maghreb knew why he had come. The very air was steeped in grief for the little girl. The woman offered Baabar a jar of precious ointment for the anointing. "Bless her journey for me," she said. He bowed in gratitude.

The lady motioned for me to come closer. She procured a string of prayer beads from her pocket and pressed them into my hand. "I see in your eyes, little one, the spirit of a healer. Do not be afraid. Today you will deliver a message of hope." When she touched me, I felt a quick passage of energy. Her strong spirit had encouraged mine forward.

I was unfamiliar with Muslim burial customs. Before we entered the apartment building, Baabar explained, "There is nothing more difficult on this side than to lose a child. You will be met by stoic faces, but behind the black veils, the tears will never cease. Today they received a blow from which most never recover. A mother has suffered a mortal wound to her heart. Nothing earthly can heal that kind of loss. You must strip away your human self and allow the Holy One to use your pure light to console her."

As we walked the two flights of stairs up to the apartment, I wanted to run. Why did it have to be this way? Again Baabar's strength scattered the darkness for me. Naima opened the door. One look told the awful story of despair, anger and hopelessness. They fell across me in a shroud.

Baabar whispered, "You may grieve later. Right now, your angel wings are to surround this family. Bring out your light. The message of hope is yours to give. Quickly, Gabrielle."

Dingy sheets had been hung from the tops of the windows to ensure the room was truly shrouded. Candles lined the floor, marking a path to the back room. Naima motioned for me to follow. Baabar touched my hand and said, "It is an honor to be included among the women who will prepare Laila's body for the journey."

I lost all consciousness of time and space. I was given a silver bowl filled with warm, scented water and a swath of white linen cloth. I watched as the women tenderly bathed Laila's little frame. Under a canopy of candlelight and the soft hum of Muslim hymns, the very air in the room grew strangely tender. All for sweet Laila. I lifted her tiny hand, dipped my cloth in the orange-blossom water and began to wash each tiny finger. I turned the palm of her hand over and allowed it to rest in mine. The water turned brackish from my tears; they did the anointing now.

Into the jar of scented ointment, we each dipped our fingers, then gently rubbed them over her innocent flesh. Laila's mother, Rheina, whispered into her baby's ear, "Little one, look for your papa. He will be waiting for you at the gate. You will know him by his kind eyes." And then she kissed her forehead one last time. A starched and perfumed kafan was next carefully folded over Laila. The women joined in whispering final prayers before they released the beautiful child to Baabar for the journey home.

A scream broke the holy silence, cutting through me like a scythe. A mother's keening for her child, who was gone. Nothing could ever be the same again, nor should it be. I imagined other mothers across the planet beating their chests, stomping the ground and spewing curses up to the clouds for this unnatural parting. I had to do something. I closed my eyes, placing one hand on Laila and the other covering the eyes of her mother. A light formed on my fingertips, and I saw the miracle. Laila's shimmering spirit lifted into the air. Smiling, she reached down and removed my hand from her mother's eyes. Rheina looked up into the light. Her daughter was more beautiful and alive than she had ever seen her. A peace washed over her, and she collapsed into my arms. I looked over at Naima. I knew she had witnessed the vision. She had been invited into my secret, the secret of my Light.

Baabar came to the door, solemnly approached the bed and lifted the lifeless body into his herculean arms. This physical body would be buried in a consecrated field outside of Paris. The property was owned by the mosque, land provided as a sacred burial for those far from their native home. I noticed a heavy pottery jar on the table filled with an ocher-colored dirt. Naima drew a handful of the golden dust and signaled for everyone else to follow.

She whispered, "Every immigrant family living in Paris has a jar just like this one. If they cannot be buried in the ground from which they came, then they take with them the soil that gave them life."

At the service, while the imam gave the Janazah prayer, Laila's mother scattered the dirt from her homeland over the dismal opening in the bed of earth. The imam raised up his hands and exclaimed, "From the earth you came; into it you shall return again. But your spirit will rise and soar. And we will see you again, little Laila."

I returned home on the metro without Baabar. He said he must take a trip away for a while. Baabar asked Hakiim to escort me safely back to 11, Rue de Bourbon. Now a stranger, Hakiim sat across from me on the train, never once looking up from his hands. I watched as he clenched them together so tightly, ensuring that whatever he held inside could no longer breathe. It was hope that Hakiim was smothering.

When the train stopped at the Cité metro stop, Hakiim bid me farewell on the platform and quickly jumped right back on the train. The doors shut, but I glimpsed the enemy staring back at me. The skin of his face was pulled tight, the mask of a villain, and I gasped when I saw the dark specter hovering over Hakiim. But it was too late. The train pulled away like a snake, slithering with a calculated stealth—straight into the Darkness.

CHAPTER 27

I did not want to meet the new day without Laila. The pigeons cooed, and the gargoyles kept their stone stares. I imagined they grieved alongside me. I pulled the covers angrily over my face, imagining what it would feel like to die, the dark earth packed hard over my face and body. I did not hear Lille float in, nor did I smell her scent of camellias. But morning had arrived, and a glimmer of hope returned with Lille. I kicked the covers away.

"Gabrielle, dear, Laila is with Baabar. They set off on the journey as soon as he knew you were safe. She's stepping through the Door as we speak. She is finally breathing free, and what a happy day for Baabar. I remember when I carried Valentina, your dear mother, through the Door. Her spirit was positively sparkling with her love for you."

But I thought, *What good did that do for those of us left behind?*

Lille took my face in her hands. "You know it is only the flesh that is beholden to time, not the spirit. Death lasts less than the length of a breath in the earthly story."

I bowed my head and knew she was right, but the pain in my heart remained. I envied the power held between the two outstretched arms of Time. Its razor-sharp limbs moved in a calculated dance with the moon and sun, never once burdened by emotion. Time never flinched, held its breath or stopped in place when life proved cruel; rather, it soldiered on. I wished to untangle myself from its brusque clutches. I was weary of watching its invisible strings pull and tug until there was nothing dignified left. Only defeat. It seemed we were all beholden, slaves to the inexorable rhythm of

Time. That made me angry, mostly because I too had to bow to its reign. I feared Lille underestimated the frightening reality of death for humanity. One could not escape its looming shadow. Had she forgotten that Christus had sweat blood at the knowledge that his last breath was near? Mortal eyes are able to see only their denouement sealed with a handful of Moroccan dirt. A switch flips from on to off in an instant. The final page is turned. "The End" is written in a grand flourish, and the human book is placed on the shelf of someone else's memory, until that too is buried away.

Lille looked at me with dismay. "You forget, Gaby. We need time to heal, time to grow, time to love—time, sweet angel, to serve. I warned you the flesh was never meant to win the duel with Time. It was only created to be a temporary vessel for pieces of the Light. In the end, it's Time's arms of mercy that release the spirit to return home. Laila is there now. Home. Now, meet me in the bakery, *tout de suite*. We must carry on."

I pulled on my white linen pants, rolled them up just above my ankles, and threw on a red-striped sailor shirt and comfy leather moccasins. I repeated the words "Carry on" as I twisted my hair in a long braid and defiantly tied a red ribbon around the curl on the end. Ultimately, that was all anyone could do— Carry on. For there is a reality beyond this reality. That is the promise. I knew it to be true in the deepest place of my being, in the same way I knew I was an angel. I took a breath of relief then, tied on my newly starched Levain apron, and planned the day's baking.

Instead of entering the bakery through the courtyard, I liked to exit the grand doors of 11, rue de Bourbon and access the bakery from the main street. I claimed it was for Lavender, so he could socialize with Heloise, the grand dame poodle of the neighborhood. But secretly, I hoped Luc would be waiting for me under the streetlamp on the corner, just like before. What foolishness! Instead, I was always only met by Jean Charles, setting up his easel and paints on the bridge for *plein air*. Luc had left in a dark cloud of mystery—no explanations, no apologies, no contact. It had been eight months, twenty-three days, five hours and eleven minutes since I had last seen him. Now I only heard him calling for me in my dreams.

But this day was to be different. Beneath the glow of the streetlamp, I saw him. Black leather jacket and revved silver-bullet motorbike. I nearly fainted. I heard Sophie's voice behind me. "Looks like the prodigal son has finally returned home."

No pride restrained me; I ran directly into his arms. He whispered in my ear, "I've come for you."

I nodded in a trance.

In the time it took Lille to untie her apron and rush into the street, I was gone. I tucked my hands into the pockets of Luc's leather jacket and leaned forward into his familiar, hard-muscled back as we soared across the bridge.

No words were spoken. His body communicated all I needed to know. His now long, dark curls peeked out seductively from his helmet and tickled my cheek. We swerved in and out of the city's morning traffic and hit the highway, leaving Paris to dance with the day—a perfect day.

I lost all concept of time or responsibility. Dangerously liberated, I whispered to the wind, "Time, you may know the count of my days here on earth, but you will never decide for me how I shall spend them."

We were headed to the Val de Loire, in the direction of Orleans, famous for its *châteaux* and once the decadent hunting retreat for the royal courts. I remembered a tourist poster that hung in Monsieur Lapin's butcher shop back home. It had colorful pictures of the famous castles in the area, and Monsieur Lapin's son, Michel, could name each one. There was one I loved, Chenonceau, a gift from King Henry II to his mistress, Diane de Poitiers. The architecture was designed like a jewel box, built over a river and meant to house the king's most precious treasure. She must have been quite a mademoiselle. Young Michel joked that the randy king was often spied fishing out the window of his *toilette*. I giggled again at the thought.

Luc roared off the highway and turned onto a dirt road. Verdant forest surrounded us on all sides. Sentinels of plane trees stood at attention for the long-lost liege's return. We sped over a river, where two young boys in short pants were tossing a line from their stick fishing poles. Churning the gravel, we made another quick turn through an opening in the hedge onto a private drive. Speeding by, I nearly missed the wooden sign, "*Les Rêveurs,*" nailed on a grandfather oak tree. Two crumbling stone columns, clad in suits of ivy and sporting gas lanterns for top hats, pointed us down an ancient French *allée* of chestnut trees. Under the graceful arc of branches, the fallen leaves fluttered from our quick passing. The path was dappled in shapes of jade. It seemed we had left the world behind.

The avenue of trees opened onto a pebbled courtyard, anchored in the distance by a charming old manor house. Its architecture was brawny yet had a delicacy to its spirit that beckoned romance. The perfectly blocked white-limestone facade boasted a Juliet balcony with a thick layer of blooming jasmine spilling over its edge. The house had a mysterious narrative to tell.

As I looked up into its broad face, I hoped it would share a little something about its prince.

Luc helped me off the bike. A welcoming party of wagging tails circled at our feet. The trinity of Brittany spaniels was ecstatic at the arrival of their master.

Luc said, "May I introduce you to Truffe, Chagall and Oliver." Clearly the favorite, Oliver brushed against my legs, sniffed at my feet, then offered me wet-nosed kisses of approval. Glancing up, I saw someone peeking from behind the front window drapes, and I waved to her.

"Oh, that is Fleurie. She runs the place. Come in, and I will make introductions. I'm sure she has spent the morning preparing a special lunch for you. She has the picture of the wedding cake you created for Monsieur de Valbrey's daughter pinned on the pantry cupboard."

I was flattered and childishly pleased she knew who I was.

Luc was noticeably different here. At ease. Tucking my hand in the crook of his arm, I asked, "Does this place belong to you?"

"Yes, I grew up here."

"Does your family live here too?"

"No, I am on my own now." And with that he released my hand. Confused, I followed Luc up the curving stone steps into the foyer, where on either side of the French doors, two large jardinieres of weeping cherry trees spilled forth with pink buds like a glorious fountain. We stepped together into the gallery, which was framed on both sides by flowing cream drapes, each pulled back with twisted gold cords. The parquet floor ahead was dramatic, with a sunbeam design, cleverly embedded at intervals through the length of the room, the sun rising with every step. The thick plastered walls were an ivory hue, with a gilt molding rimming the ceiling like a halo of shimmering light.

The house challenged its inanimate boundaries of stone and mortar, and pulsated with life. My skin took on a new radiance in the warm light of this wondrous space. Or maybe it was from the love I felt for Luc. Regardless, I felt real happiness in the house's welcoming embrace.

Fleurie appeared as if she had read my mind, and she announced to Luc's dismay, "Love can make anything come alive, dear. Bonjour, mademoiselle. I am Fleurie, and I am pleased to welcome you to *Les Rêveurs.*"

She scurried away down the hallway with the dogs at her heels, shouting back, "Le déjeuner will be ready *tout de suite!*"

Enlightment

I caught a glimpse of myself in the French trumeau mirror on the way into the salon. My hair was now twisted in a very messy braid, curls loose everywhere, and my cheeks were flushed ruby. But my eyes told the truth; I was in love. Surely he could see it. Life was fragile. I had learned that all too well with the passing of Laila. There was no stopping the arms of Time. We were allotted only a certain number of breaths on this side. And I was determined to saturate them with love.

Luc was already in the salon, where I found him happily conversing with a lovely white parakeet with a viridian diamond on her back. She was chattering from a bamboo cage in the window with a grand view of the camellia garden. The bird and Luc were old friends.

The walls of the large salon were painted a Renoir watery blue, and the ceiling above was a frescoed wonder of clouds. At one end of the room was a fireplace large enough to step into. As it was summer, the opening was filled with a large silver vase of peacock feathers in a broad fan arrangement.

An abstract sculpture of angel wings in stark blue-gray steel stood on a pedestal in the corner. But it was the painting above the fireplace that caught my attention. The colors swirled on the canvas with a curious energy. In the center was a commanding purple tree, a red heart carved in its massive trunk, and leaves of gold appeared to flutter to life on the branches. I was certain the artist was Sophie. And the tree—our secret crest. But why here? There were too many secrets floating between us. It was time I knew the truth about Luc…and he deserved to know the truth about me, too.

Luc turned me toward him, holding my hands in his. We both dug our toes in to steady ourselves from the electricity sparking in the air between us.

"I brought you here because I could feel your pain from that little girl's passing. I cannot explain it; I am connected to you somehow. From that first day in the flower market, a door opened inside of me. And you entered in. When I close my eyes, I feel you. That first day at the Petite Alma Chocolate Shop, when you were eating Pauline's truffle, your joy nearly knocked me off my feet. The night you cut your finger in my studio, I felt your pain in my own hand. But last night was something else, more profound. I felt the grief in your heart. I knew I had to go to you. I cannot bear to see you suffer. My heart cannot take it."

I didn't know what to say. Inside, my world was spinning. I started running through a recipe for chocolate mousse, listing the ingredients;

three eggs, one cup heavy cream, two tablespoons espresso, four—or was it five?—ounces bittersweet chocolate. Anything to remain standing.

Luc laughed. "I hear you, Gaby. I wish it were as simple as a recipe for *mousse au chocolat.*"

I grabbed for the chair to keep from falling. Everything wasn't as it seemed. Who was I in love with? He knew my thoughts?

"I haven't been completely honest with you, Gabrielle. And I am sorry for that. I was trying to protect you from myself. I am no longer in the Light as you are. I too was charged with special gifts. But I walked away from them long ago, never to return. That day I saw you in the flower market, I didn't know you were one of them. I only knew that we were connected somehow. But that morning in the bakery, I realized you were the one they had talked about since I was a child. I saw the way Lille protected you. Which also meant that our paths were always destined to cross."

My mind was racing. But before I could ask him any questions, Fleurie interrupted us. "Luc, son, you know I am patient, but your lunch is growing cold in the garden."

We walked hand in hand together deeper into the house, down a long vaulted hallway punctuated with grand iron lanterns. The walls displayed a typical collection of black and white framed family photographs, but unlike any I had ever seen before. The eyes—even in black and white—the eyes were lit from the inside. But it was the last picture that clutched my heart. It was Luc. His eyes—they frightened me. They weren't as black as the Raven's, nor were they luminous like mine. Sadness projected from them, bringing me to tears. I cringed at the missing light in his exquisite eyes. My throat constricted and I gasped. There was no shying away from the truth. Everyone had known it but me. And yet, hadn't I known it all along? I was in love with one of the fallen.

I joined him in the garden. There was a charming café table set for two. Fleurie clucked and cooed over us. The air was perfumed by a riot of peonies, white roses and mint arranged casually in a silver pitcher. The table was set on crisp white linen with an heirloom collection of porcelain *Sèvres*. Cobalt-blue plates trimmed in gold, crystal glasses and antique silver seemed more fitting for a lord and lady than a humble baker and a mysterious chocolatier—two angels...sadly, on opposite sides of the fight.

Luc poured a chilled Rose d'Anjou from the estate's vineyard. Fleurie placed a bowl of Spring pea and basil soup before me, topping it with a generous dollop of crème fraîche. A plate of buttermilk-dill heart-shaped biscuits arrived, accompanied by a ramekin of her homemade strawberry preserves. Distractedly, I clapped in praise. Fleurie happily pirouetted and bowed on her way back to the kitchen.

Luc was nervous. I was nervous. A crape myrtle leaned in with curiosity over our table, allowing a blue bird the opportunity to fill the uncomfortable silence with a ballad. I was unable to speak, frozen. Thankfully, Fleurie returned with an elegant watercress salad dressed with a necklace of succulent shrimp, buttery gigante beans and a scattering of hazelnuts. Before she took the tray of our empty soup bowls away, she chimed, "Gabrielle, I wish to visit the famous Levain Bakery. Is it true that a line circles the block every day for your *tarte du jour?*"

I blushed at her flattery and quickly complimented her blackberry-lemon clafouti. I knew the recipe well. It had been one of Sister Karis's favorites. All was starting to make scary sense.

Luc reached over with his linen napkin to brush a bit of toasted coconut from my cheek. The hairs on my arms lifted at his light touch. I wished someone could explain the chemical reactions that were set off each time he came near. We stood and bowed our gratitude for Fleurie's special lunch. I would never forget it.

Her eyes twinkled. "Well, you just wait for my dinner this evening. Now, Luc, show Gabrielle *la domaine*. I think she will especially enjoy the gardens. Master Liu has just returned from his pilgrimage east. How about half past seven in the library for a cassis, your favorite?"

Luc smiled and agreed to her schedule. We made a grand tour of the entire house. I especially loved the Rose room. The walls were pink coral, and a large painting of museum proportions covered the entire back wall. It was a garden scene. I was fascinated by the light source. Every blade of grass, dewdrop and blossom pulsated with light. I found myself wanting to take off my shoes and run even for a moment in the serenity of this lush Eden, the place of dreams.

I followed Luc next into the library. The walls were floor-to-ceiling books. A carved mahogany ladder allowed for reaching the treasures on the top shelves. At the back of the room was a lacquered, ebony baby grand piano.

"Do you play the piano, Luc?"

"I used to. My father taught me; it was a shared love between us. We would scribble notes for a new song for my mother. But that was a long time ago. I haven't played since..."

"Will you play something for me now?"

Before he could answer, Fleurie fluttered in, carrying a bucket of freshly cut flowers from the garden.

"Gabrielle, I wondered if you would give me a little lesson in the kitchen this afternoon? I should like to know your recipe for the perfect molten-chocolate cake."

Luc shot Fleurie a look that sent her scurrying from the room, but I called after her, "Of course! I'll meet you, say, around five? Set the milk and eggs out to reach room temperature."

Luc led me next up a medieval, curving stone staircase to the top floor.

"As a child, I loved this secret staircase. I'd dress up as a Knights Templar, wooden sword in hand, and stand guard in this turret room like a real royal guard," he said. I had Fleurie prepare the room for you because it provides the best view here."

The walls were tufted in a lavender toile fabric. The same toile looped and was tied back with velvet cords at the corners of the four-poster canopy bed. An emerald-green moiré chaise lounge beckoned at the window, encouraging a reclining peek at the rose garden below.

Luc opened the pair of French doors, and I followed him out onto the curving balcony.

"You can see the stables, the vineyard, and the fruit and vegetable garden from here. If you look just there to your right, you will also see the roof of the old gate house, now my studio."

His arms surrounded me, kissing me deeply. I went blissfully limp in his embrace, not seeing or caring about the grand view.

Coming up for air, suddenly too warm, I pointed toward the pond. "What is the ivy-covered building there?" And again, Luc's mood shifted.

"That is the chapel. I cannot tell you much about it. It has been quite a long time since I have visited that dank, empty place."

I reached for Luc's hands and looked up into his face. I was surprised that he did not look away. For the first time he did not blink or turn away from me.

"Go ahead. I know your gifts. I no longer wish to hide anything from you."

My breath slowed to allow the visions to take hold of me. First I saw a little boy blowing bubbles and chasing them across the yard before they burst and disappeared. I could hear him calling to a woman whose face was hidden from me.

"Make a wish, *Maman*. A big wish for the whole world."

I wondered who the woman was. Before I could see closer, another vision began. This time it was Luc as a young man, dressed in a white lab coat, a stethoscope around his neck, leaning over the bed of a child. He was laughing with a young girl, whose face was pale and yet her eyes so bright.

I heard him say, "Now, ma petite Alma, tell me again about the chocolate fountain in the window of your chocolate shop. And will you promise to sell triple-chocolate ice cream? It's my favorite, you know."

I did not recognize this Luc. He bubbled over with confidence and hope. He was trusting, still displaying a little boy's surety that dreams did indeed come true. Good would triumph over evil always.

The next vision hit me like an angry storm of locusts. I gasped. The room darkened, except for a single fluorescent light that sprayed a nauseating green glow across the room. Little Alma was on the steel surgical table. Luc's eyes were closed, his hands working furiously with the shiny scalpel. He was urgently but calmly calling for more oxygen, more blood, while at the same time flashing pictures in his mind of a fantasy chocolate shop. Trying his best to salvage Alma's dreams, Luc was desperate to save her.

I heard that same little boy from the first vision pleading, "Holy One, please don't do this. Take me instead. You can save her. She is one of your most precious, filled with so much light."

His intimate conversation was interrupted by the monotone drum of the monitor and the nurse calling the time. Luc beat relentlessly on Alma's chest, trying to revive her little heart.

"I beg you, come back to me! We'll build the chocolate shop!"

I recognized the dark shadow of death descend over the room, followed by the lighted outline of wings. Luc looked up and saw them too. But he closed his eyes. When he opened them next, they were opaque, scary. He leaned over the table and curled his arms around the child, holding her and his faith for the last time. In that moment, Luc denied his gifts as an angel, as a healer, and with a vengeance, he rejected his Creator. Here was a fallen angel now in danger of damnation.

I started to lose the vision through my tears. I couldn't continue. It was just too painful. But then a face I knew appeared. It was Pierre. He was kneeling before Luc.

"Please look at me, son, he said. "I know you are hurting, as you should be. I am hurting with you. But I saw petite Alma home. Please don't do this. Don't abandon the Light. Allow me to carry your faith for you until you are strong again. Please don't leave us."

Luc turned his back on his father and walked straight into the Darkness.

I released my hands and returned to the present. The stranger standing before me was cold, his eyes empty.

"Luc, you are one of us, aren't you? I saw your fingers, the light in them, when you sewed me up. And my ring faintly glowed in your presence. I knew it did. Your gifts—they are exceptional. You can save people. My God, your father is Pierre, the esteemed Guardian? And your mother is dear Lille?"

Instead of answering, he took me in his arms and pressed his lips desperately to mine again. I opened myself to him unconditionally. The desire was rising in both of us. My eyes were closed, but I knew I was glowing with love in the space between us. My spirit expanded, determined to give over to him my Light. I would save him. That was the answer. My faith would be enough for him. It had to be.

At every point that our bodies touched, I sparked with light. But my light could not pierce his armor.

"Gabrielle, it's no use. You are too late. You were destined for that naive young man in a doctor's coat. But he died the moment he realized we were left alone here on earth. I refuse to serve a Creator who allows such misery. Don't you see? The Dark One reigns here on earth. No amount of light can change that. Not my mother's, nor my father's. Not even your extraordinary gifts can change that. Hope disappoints every time."

His words frightened me. I remembered Laila and my own horror. Doubt crept into my heart. Luc was bitter, hurt, disappointed in the One in whom he had trusted to make things right here on earth.

I lowered my head and began whispering prayers.

Feeling the flush of new hope return to my cheeks, I lifted my chin to gaze back into the emerald eyes of my fate.

"But what about love? I love you, Luc. I will give you all of my light. Doesn't that count for something?"

"I will not allow it."

He whirled away from me and was gone. I came down the stairs, my spirit exhausted, and Fleurie pointed off in the distance.

"He's headed to the gatehouse."

I could see Luc striding angrily down a path cut through the trees, the dogs following close behind.

"You mustn't give up on him, Gabrielle."

I nodded, trying to smile, tears on my cheeks and set out after him.

CHAPTER 28

It was approaching dusk. The forest was now mysterious, nearly magical. I followed a meandering path, groomed over time by the hoofs of horses and the delicate feet of deer. I imagined I was processing up the center aisle of a darkened, perfectly still cathedral. The fading light reflected eerily off the shimmering white trunks of the silver birch trees planted in the altar of the earth. They glowed like candles on either side of me. The forest was a natural burial ground for all the fallen trees, the evergreen saints. Now velvet moss and lacy ferns thrived in their brokenness. I caught up with Luc. Again, the invisible veil had fallen between us.

"Gabrielle, trees come down in the forest every day. We hardly stop long enough from our own lives to hear their crash or to pay respects to their roots still twisted deep with others beneath the soil. I am tired of the unpredictability of life here—our lack of control. The forest gives little or no warning before another tree topples. It just quietly folds back into itself. And the forest continues on. Life continues on. I am weary from all the trees falling around me. All the Lailas. My precious petite Alma, whom I couldn't save. My father has it all wrong."

"Luc, I don't know what to say to change your mind. What you lament is true. But I still have hope. I trust in my Beloved. I believe in miracles. I cry like you for all the pain that's here. But Luc, I believe in love. And love never dies. That is the beautiful miracle. Say you believe in love too. Allow my Light to come inside of you. I freely give you my body, my spirit, my light, my all. A life apart from the Light is too scary. I can't bear to lose you to the Darkness. Come back to me, come back to us."

But Luc didn't hear me. He had fled the pain again, gone beyond the forest walls of this green chapel. I was left to find my own way back through the despairing shadows. I turned in a circle and felt the trees pressing in on me. The dark uncertainty of this life weighed heavily. Was Luc right? Was the Holy One apathetic to our plight? Was all for naught? No, no, no. What about the way I loved Luc? I was willing to give up everything for him. Looking heavenward, I called to my father. My mother. The Holy One. Someone to help me hold up the light. Help me to save Luc.

Had the time arrived for me to peer into the face of Darkness? Pierre had said, "Every creature must earn their faith on this side. The hope being that through the darkness they would have the strength to still hold up the Light. To live in hope."

The soft melody of an owl drew me out of myself. I looked up, and there he was, perched on a branch of the birch. His familiar luminous eyes were two white moons surrounded by a ring of soft chocolate. I lost myself in his penetrating, compassionate eyes. The owl turned his head from side to side, engaging me in his own important spiritual discourse. I sensed an urgency in his message. Here in this forest, I felt the mysteries of the universe calling me, like in a dream. All was for good, the Wise One seemed to communicate. Luc called to me from the gatehouse, and I looked that way. When I turned back to my bard-feathered friend, he was gone. Had he been there? But I had my answer, the Creator's answer: All things work for good for those who love and hold fast to hope. It was time to put on my armor, fighting for Luc, for love. I knew the time had come for me to face the Darkness on my own.

I mourned for that young doctor with miracle hands, who once believed all could be made right in the world. Now he suffered from a malaise that plagued most of humanity, an angst and doubt that crippled one's ability to trust in the tremendous imagination and compassion of the Creator. The only way forward was to love with all my heart. This was the message of Gabriel I must proclaim.

The stone gatehouse, a miniature of the château, was covered in vines except for a large steel-arched window. There was a single gas lamp above the door and a large pottery bowl of water for the dogs on the sloping front stoop. I hesitantly stepped inside and shuddered at the heaviness, the

Darkness I faced. On the wall was a collage of black-and-white portraits, carefully pasted together, the glue like streaking tears dried coarsely upon their faces.

"Luc, did you take these? You are very talented. I can actually see through their eyes to their spirits. Who are all of these people?"

He called from the backroom. "They are the fallen trees. Someone in the forest has to remember them. Sophie paints the fantastical world beyond a damn gilt door; I go for the reality of here and now."

I stepped deeper into his studio, touching each picture, as with a priest's blessing. Luc came up behind me.

"That one was taken in Haiti. Her name was Glorianna. I saw her playing in the folds of her grimy tent. Her family lost everything when the earthquake hit, including her papa. Her mother was forced to leave the child alone at the tent in order to make a couple of dollars for fresh water and bread. She only had her body to provide for her family. Glorianna's mom had no idea that her customers would come looking for her and take her daughter instead. Once the animals had their way with this beautiful eight-year-old, they literally kicked the life out of her. She never had a chance."

Luc moved to a large family portrait that covered an expanse of the wall.

"This one here is the Kahil family. They lived in a village in West Africa. Every member of the family died in shame; the specter of *AIDS* spared no one."

I was drawn to another photo, the most beautiful face looked out at me.

"Luc, who is he?"

"His name was Roberto. He was a kind boy, so full of courage. His mother brought him to New York from Santo Domingo. The cancer was like a freak weed that no amount of fire could destroy. I sat with him as the red poison streamed from the translucent bag into his veins. I held his head in my lap, begging for his life. He was much stronger than me. When I saw the flash of wings in the corner of the room, I went after my father with a broom. But Roberto grabbed my hand and said, 'Let me go. Your father has come especially for me.'

"That was the last time I spoke to my father. How could he come for Roberto? The boy deserved a life. All of these people deserved a life. Don't you see? How can you trust in a God who allows this to happen? Who can watch a brave Roberto honor the Holy One even as the cancer takes communion on his flesh and bone? I heard Roberto's prayers. I heard his quiet pleas, teeth gritting, when no one else was listening. He never stopped praying. He even prayed for me, that damn stupid boy. And the Holy One did nothing. He made him suffer to the very last breath."

"But the Creator sent your father to take Roberto to the other side. That is proof we are not left alone. And you were there with Roberto faithfully to the end. That's love, Luc."

"You are naive, Gabrielle. What is the point of being here if we are only to suffer? It's too cruel."

I didn't respond. But I heard my spirit speaking from inside of me: *Because I love you. And you love me. And Roberto's mom loved him. And Pauline loved petite Alma. And their stories continue on. They are okay. Love never fails.*

I spoke aloud. "I wouldn't trade even a painful death if it meant I would never get to feel as I do for you right now. Even my new wings—I'd give them to you. I love you, Luc. I love you from the very place of my soul's light."

But Luc didn't hear me. He was back in the dark room, ranting, "I must fight the Holy One. Fight for every child, mother, father, tree. I take their pictures. I hold them up to the heavens so the Holy One will wake from a careless slumber and take notice. Their eyes—I want the Divine One to see them. I learned that from my father. The eyes tell all."

He was right and yet terribly wrong.

The phone rang in the studio. A reprieve. Luc excused himself and took the call. I was left to touch the eyes of the spirits in the photos. And their eyes indeed told painful stories. Narratives that frightened me. I saw Roberto's fear, the confusion in Glorianna's eyes and the weary sadness in the matching eyes of the Kahil family. None of these brave souls ever had a chance on this side, and yet they were promised it would be different through the Door. No more tears, just the province of joy. I believe; help me in my unbelief.

I wanted to scream at Luc and convince him that love is promised to conquer in the end. I wanted to assure him that he would see petite Alma again one day.

When babies go hungry, or when little girls lose their innocence by the dirty hands of another, or when cancer eats away at the flesh, the spirit prevails. The Divine One does not betray a single one. Anger spurred Luc's courage. He actually ran like a kamikaze toward the pain of life. But his spirit was in suicide mode. He had missed the point of it all.

I ran out of the studio and stumbled through the forest. A swarm of ravens raised up like a dark cape around my shoulders. I forced my feet forward, anything to escape the abominable shrill of their caws. They wanted me to falter, to give in to the darkness like Luc. Be still, I told myself. Open your heart and allow the Light to lead you.

The chapel doors opened ahead. Luc had said that no one had ventured inside in years. It was like a magnet had me in its hold, and I was being drawn toward the stone structure, the steeple nearly hidden beneath curling ribbons of ivy. I stepped inside, and the doors of the tabernacle closed behind me. I was safe. The chapel was dark except for one miraculous candle glowing in the center of the altar table. Though dusty, the air smelled of roses. The benches were empty, and yet I knew I was not alone. I sensed Lille, Pierre, Karis, even my parents, floating on the edge of my reality. I ran my fingers over the ends of the pews as I made my way toward the supernatural Light. I knelt, placed my hands together in prayer next to my heart, and I waited. I had no words. I looked up into the beams of the vaulted ceiling, somehow not surprised to see the owl again staring benevolently down at me.

A calm, otherworldly voice broke the silence.

"Gabrielle, you choose with each breath; hope or despair, light or darkness. The choice is always yours. Roberto, Glorianna, the Kahil family, petite Alma and Laila are with me. Now you must be brave. Shine for Luc before it is too late for his redemption."

The voice was unlike any I had ever heard on this earth—pure, powerful, holy—it brought me back into the Light. I knew right then that I would follow this tender voice wherever it led me. My beginning, my end, my eternity.

I looked around then, but no one was there. I was alone. Only the aroma of roses still floated delicately in the air. I felt at peace as if nestled beneath gossamer wings. I was warm, safe and hopeful again. I wondered if this was how Laila had felt tucked beneath Baabar's wings. A wind blew through the chapel and knocked the candle off the altar. My full span of wings extended, and I levitated, going high above the chapel, the trees. I was beyond the earth now, wrapped in the Holy Light, and the universe made sense.

Slowly I dropped back to my knees at the altar and surrendered to a vision. I saw Luc leaning over a bed. He was crying. I heard Lille's voice: "She called for you." I could make out the faintest outline of wings in the four corners of the room. And then I saw my braid on the pillow. My cheeks were leached of color. Outside the window patiently sat my faithful owl, his wise eyes ever intent on my fragile figure shrouded beneath a sterile white sheet. I also could just hear the faint victory shrill of ravens in the distance. This was a vision of a future I didn't like. I prayed for the light to sustain me for whatever was to come.

The vision released me abruptly. I found myself on the floor of the chapel, wrapped in a blanket of dried leaves. There was no light, no candle. The room smelled of wet earth. I looked up into the small rose window above the doors. Two dark eyes stared back at me. Was it the Owl or the Raven?

I stepped out of the chapel into the fading light of the day. The dogs were playing retrieve by the pond. Fleurie, in her ruffled apron, was waving for me to join her in the kitchen. Yes, I thought, flour, eggs, sugar and a big block of chocolate were just what I needed. I refused to allow the last vision to haunt me. In the kitchen, Fleurie tied me into an apron with bluebirds hand-stitched across the front. Focused on the French classic *un moelleux au chocolat,* I started to concentrate and relax. There is nothing quite like the sensuous moment the teeth break through the chocolate walls, releasing a river of warm chocolate upon an eager tongue.

The kitchen was bustling and warm, clearly Fleurie's home as it was mine. It was a cheery space for cooking boasting a massive fireplace, its mantel hung with all shapes and sizes of hearts. Little paper lanterns with glowing white lights inside were strung from the rafters. I looked up to see a skylight in the beamed ceiling providing a perfect light on the antique wooden baker's table. Yes, I could surely take up residence here.

Fleurie proudly laid out all the ingredients. I was delighted to spot a block of cacao wrapped in the Petite Alma Chocolate Shop's pink and brown striped paper. It was the perfect 61% cacao; anything greater left the cake tasting bitter. Fleurie cooed, "Gabrielle, might we make a few extra of the chocolate cakes in these heart ramekins? I want to barter them with Monsieur Toulouse in exchange for his fresh eggs and churned cream."

I gave Fleurie a mischievous smile. "And may I ask who this monsieur is?"

Just the mention of his name sent her coughing, a bloom of red rose in her cheeks.

"Oh, just a friend. He is often leaving me little gifts on the back steps."

"Well, let's make these extra special then. I have a trick for a mirror glaze on the top that never disappoints. First, you must butter each ramekin, on the bottom first, and then the sides. This ensures the cake will rise to a perfect height. While you do that, I will chop the chocolate and melt it slowly in the *bain-marie*. Next, we'll fold in the eggs and butter, the sugar and cornstarch last."

We worked pleasantly next to each other, as if we had always been friends. While Fleurie put the ramekins on a baking sheet in preparation for the oven, I prepared the *glaçage miroir*: cocoa powder, heavy cream, sugar, gelatin and hot water. We finished the cakes with a coulis of raspberries and sprigs of mint. Fleurie could not stop chirping, *"Magnifique, magnifique, magnifique,"* as she danced a jig around the kitchen. A nice reminder to be grateful for the simple joys.

Perching happily on the counter, I invited Fleurie to join me, the cherry-red mixing bowl between us. We took turns dipping our fingers into the few remaining swirls of chocolate batter. Looking at Fleurie, I got the giggles at her chocolate mustache. But then Fleurie turned serious.

"Luc was such the tender child," she said. "I remember when he brought into the kitchen a wounded butterfly, its beautiful wing nearly torn away. He was determined to find a way to sew a new wing on so the creature could fly again. He just refused to believe that the butterfly's life was over. Gabrielle, he is still trying to sew wings back on. It's killing him."

I passed her a linen napkin to wipe the chocolate and brush away the tears. "He will not allow anyone to get too close. I know it's the fear of not being able to save them. It was so sad the day he put down his scalpel for good. We all knew of his gifts when he was just a boy. But now he is angry at the Holy One. And his anger is eating away at what remains of his Light. He goes from one place to another and—*mon Dieu*—takes those gut-wrenching pictures you saw."

I heard steps in the hallway. Luc entered through the butler's pantry into the kitchen.

"Fleurie, stop! I see Pierre and Lille have bewitched you, too."

"No, my dear boy, I believe they just know the truth. Sit down. Have one of Gabrielle's *très bon* chocolate cakes. I'll fix you a cup of my special tea."

There was tenderness between them. She had been there for Luc through his boyhood to his manhood. The good and the bad.

"Not this time, Fleurie. I have to make plans. I leave for Libya tomorrow. Already seven hundred dead. The dictator is determined to pave his palace with the tombstones of the innocent."

"Dear Luc, let them take care of their own. You can't save everybody. Stay here. Stay with Gabrielle. She needs you too."

"If I don't go, how will the Holy One see the devil's progress? Or the world witness their Creator's gross negligence?"

I looked at Fleurie's stricken face and knew mine held the same expression of dismay.

Rising, Fleurie stammered, "I will start on dinner. Shall I make arrangements to see Gabrielle back into Paris in the morning?"

"No, I owe my mother and father a safe return for her." Nothing escapes their angel eyes."

Fleurie sighed. "As nothing escapes you, my love. You, too, are one of them, whether you like it or not."

With that observation, Luc disappeared up the back steps to his room. Tears streaming, I escaped to the garden. Fleurie called after me, "Make acquaintance with Master Liu, our gardener. He is lilliputian in stature but as wise as that silvery braid is long down his back. He breathes in wisdom. You'll see."

CHAPTER 29

I followed the rocky limestone path, edged in a lace of thyme, and entered a secret garden through a quaint, rickety twig gate entwined in honeysuckle. The air was sweetly perfumed, and a troupe of bees danced in and out of the honeyed blooms. On either side of the gate were beds of blue salvia, lilies, phlox and delphinium. Climbing pink roses stretched their prickly arms over the stone wall. I heard a mockingbird splashing in the birdbath at the garden's center. Two hummingbirds flirted above my head and heralded my arrival. My equilibrium was quickly restored in nature's embrace.

Master Liu was gently tilling the earth with only his fingertips. He waved his hand for me to join him under a weeping willow, and I instantly felt the caress of his light. A sublime peace washed over me.

"Mademoiselle Gabrielle, I see we finally enjoy the same fragrant air. I have heard much about you. Join me here in my meditation garden."

I was surprised by his diminutive physical size. But his seraphic presence was exceedingly grand. Master Liu wore a simple white cotton jacket, trimmed in black silk. His rich blue work pants bore a thick crust of the emerald earth at the pads of his knees. At his temples, the silky hair was pure white. But it was the silver braid, woven down his back and nearly trailing the ground behind him, that mesmerized me.

At that moment, Master Liu looked up at me, and immediately his hypnotic eyes transfixed mine. They were silver, and I could see myself in them. Never had anyone delved so deeply. Without any fear, I became utterly vulnerable to him. He could see me, know me, as no other had before—my fears, fragility, foibles, but also my dreams, all that I had carefully hidden behind the baker's smile. Then I realized he was gently piercing my soul. Light went into light. When he spoke, each angelic word wrapped my spirit in a tender embrace. I felt as if his words were drawing me home.

"The light of my spirit bows to the light of your spirit. Remove your shoes now, for we are standing on holy ground. I am honored to be your teacher this day, angel Gabrielle. I can show you the bridge between creation and the Creator, a transcendent exercise indeed."

I set my shoes on the twig bench and sat down next to Master Liu. His bare feet were tattooed in beautiful designs, colorful inked symbols of earth, wind, fire and water. Without another word, he took me under his invisible veil of tranquility. A diaphanous fabric extended out from his hands to lightly drape my spirit. A supernatural peace fell in beautiful layers all around me.

Master Liu became my sage old grandfather, a twinkle in his eye. He embraced the path behind and the one ahead, the good and the bad, knowing that both were intrinsic to finding one's truth. He communicated to my spirit in the tongue of angels. I don't know how long the meditation lasted, but I awoke from it refreshed, ready for the most important lesson.

He began, "On the pilgrimage of life, we must take seriously the whisperings of the soul. A longing for the sacred becomes the journey. My brother Buddha called this Enlightenment."

Dreamily I watched as Master Liu bent down and brushed his hand across the green moss beneath our feet. The surface flickered with light. He touched, one by one, the roses on the stone wall behind us, and they too sparked with light. Next he reached out to my heart, and shockingly, a glow spread through me. I shuddered in ecstasy.

"Gabrielle, every single cell of creation bears a tiny spark of the Creator's Light. And this light is a gift, a piece of the Divine. When we are separated from it, we suffer on the wheels of life. The Darkness comes. The emptiness comes. It cannot be filled with work, pleasure, earthly power, golden coins or cleverness. Only the Light, the divine sign of love, will work. Our friend Luc runs from this Light, not trusting in the power of love. But we are gifted with glimmers. Just as I awakened these blooms, you may awaken him with your own gift of a glimmer. Show him your soul as you have done for me here today. The Darkness has no power when confronted with the purity of love."

Master Liu took my hands in his and looked into my eyes again, and instantly I felt an electric transmission. It was a supernatural energy that rocked me, then took away the strain of the last few hours, leaving me in a state of perfect peace. My breathing slowed to a near stop. I was transfixed again by his silver eyes. Each aperture became a tunnel of pure white light flowing into me. Without saying a word, Master Liu whispered to my spirit to follow him. He gently took my hands and placed them, palms open, upon my knees. I was breathing in an exact rhythm with him. A slow, measured intake of breath through my nose, held for a trinity of seconds, then released in the same way. My heart was massaged, the mighty muscle rubbed smooth so that it contracted and expanded with a perfect ease. Every muscle in my body took the cue of my heart and softened. My spirit was light within me. I floated free, unencumbered. Nothing—not my past, not my fear for Luc, not my mortal body, not even Time—could weigh me down. I heard Master Liu's voice on the edge of my free-flying consciousness.

"Gabrielle, this is who you are—an instrument of Light. No one and nothing can ever take that away from you. Seek the Source of your power. It will always be available to you. The love and the power of the Holy One are yours."

Master Liu was kneeling before me. His voice brought me back into the space of my body.

"It is a joy to be a gardener, Gabrielle. Clearing away the brambles and debris, I plant seeds and nourish them until they have the courage to open to the world. Remember each seed, each creature, is created with a modicum of light, then released into this world for an allotted time, with a holy purpose. While apart from the Divine Source, there is struggle, but it is momentary. Luc forgets. Remind him."

All I could think about now was Luc. He had let all the suffering of the world cover his light. His garden was wild and overgrown; nothing could grow there. He only saw flesh and bone and its decay, blind to the mysteries of love and forgiveness and redemption. What must I do?

Master Liu whispered, "Love answers every question. It is the salve for every wound. It provides the Master's key into eternity. We live in an imperfect world, and yet inside each one of us is the capacity to love perfectly. We cannot stop the suffering of this world, but we can transcend it with love." Quietly, Master Liu bowed and returned to pruning his roses. Our lesson was finished.

Now it was my turn, my destiny. I looked up into the sky; the eyes of the clouds were heavy and rimmed in kohl. The storms were coming. But the angel Gabriel was ready. It was time that I took my position. Gabrielle, the baker, must become a warrior in the name of Love.

CHAPTER 30

Fleurie had kindly set down lanterns along the path, their candles flickering brightly. There was a large heart, twisted together from the twigs of a cherry tree, and dressed in twinkling lights. It was laid casually against the stone wall of the house, an ebeneezer. I chose to take it as a subtle nudge, painful or not, towards love.

The house was quiet, a whisper here and there. Each room was lit with candles that appeared to whisper to one another from their seats high above in their gilt thrones. I sensed that even the house was holding its breath in anticipation of the night ahead. Then I heard my name in a heated exchange between Fleurie and Luc in the salon. My curiosity edged me forward. I wished it hadn't. The dagger of Luc's words reached me before I could make a grand entrance.

"I will put as much distance as possible between us. Gabrielle is a believer. All of you have tried to protect her since the day she was born. I will not hurt her. If she is destined to become what you prophesy, then I shall not stand in her way. I'll go as far away from her as possible."

"But don't you see, Luc? You are part of her destiny, a big part!" Fleurie cried.

"Fleurie, I am not to be one of you. I have made my choice. Please just let me go."

"I will never do that. You forget, there are prophecies about you, too. It will take both of you to...or—"

"Hush, I don't want to hear that nonsense."

Fleurie stormed from the room and did not see me hiding in the shadows. I followed her back to the kitchen where she sat, defeated, at the farm table, her face buried in her hands. Her tears fell like pearls from a broken strand.

"My fear has always been that something would happen in my life so terrible that I would lose my faith, like Luc. Can you imagine the pain and darkness of living apart from the Holy One? The world can be so cruel. The Dark has him in its clutches. What can we do to save him?" Fleurie shook her shoulders, rose and went to check the roasting lamb, leaving me to face Luc. I returned to the salon. Luc, corkscrew in hand, was about to open a bottle of red wine. I crossed the room and grabbed his arms so he could not look away. I wanted him to see in my eyes what I was willing to give him. Everything. All my love, all my light. Luc would have to see that I was offering him my very soul.

The lights flickered wildly in the chandelier above our heads. We stood before each other, touching yet not touching. I wanted him, all of him. I stood, eyes wide open, in full surrender. The wind swirled, thunder cracked, and the lights went out. The room was eerily dark and Luc suddenly took me in his arms as if he were drowning. Our lips touched. Our hands reached, caressed. Our hearts beat as one. Clothing, inhibition—all fell away. We melded together at last. We were two brilliant lights uniting, perfect together, freed from time, space, even our mortal bodies. I beheld his essence, and nothing was more beautiful than Luc's soul. It was indescribable bliss.

Luc whispered love words. I felt him deep inside me. We were meant to be together like this. But then the thunder boomed, and Luc tore away too soon, the Light show over. I could not hold onto him.

I sank back to the floor. "Luc Bessier, you are a coward!"

He turned back, "I will not watch you suffer, or suffer myself from the losing of you. Love proves tragic, again and again."

I screamed, "Run! Run as far as you can, but you can't escape what you saw in my eyes tonight. Love will endure everything—you'll see."

I did not see him again that night. The storm continued to rage around the old château. I found Fleurie in the comfort of her kitchen, upset about her overcooked, dry lamb with mint sauce. I had lost my appetite, and I thanked Fleurie for her efforts and went upstairs to bed. But sleep betrayed me too.

In the morning, the sun danced through the lace curtains. Fleurie knocked hesitantly on my door and quietly set a tray by my bed. She proudly lifted the silver lid to reveal a plate of egg-washed brioche and warmed cinnamon milk for dipping.

"Sometimes the Holy One chooses to teach us something in the waiting. Be patient," Fleurie said.

I heard Luc's bike revving in the graveled drive below my window. I quickly dressed and made my way downstairs, my mood more than somber.

Fleurie said, "Gabrielle, traveling mercies. I have wrapped a couple of *pain aux raisins* in the napkin, two apricots and a thermos of café au lait. You are always welcome here."

Fleurie and I exchanged a parting kiss on the cheek. She whispered in my ear.

"Until next time, *chérie.*"

And we were off as quickly as we had come, racing through the old gates. I gripped the seat of the bike, refusing to hang on to Luc's waist. In the fury of our departure I barely glimpsed the Raven perched on the stone pillar. Unseen but heard was the owl, hooting from a nearby majestic tree near the main entrance. A desperate duel had begun for a lost soul and an angel of pure Light. Our fate, the winner's prize.

We finally pulled up to the sidewalk in front of the tall doors of 11, rue de Bourbon. I unstrapped my helmet and laid it on the seat.

I turned back to Luc. "You do have a choice. We each do. You can choose the beauty or the ugliness. You can seek the Light or succumb to the Darkness. You can choose love…"

Before I could finish, he was turning the ignition and storming away. I looked up to the gargoyles and whispered a desperate plea that they protect Luc's remaining light. Then I saw the Raven— strutting, cawing, head bobbing.

PART NINE

Carry On

Holy Angels, our advocates, our brothers, our counselors, our defenders, our enlighteners, our friends, our guides, our helpers, our intercessors—pray for us.

— MOTHER THERESA —

CHAPTER 30

Baking was my solace. I stepped right back into the routine of the bakery. Thankfully, Pierre and Lille were away, and I was careful not to allow Baabar into my eyes. I knew he would see my pain and try to take it into himself. Twisting sweet dough into crescents, I reeled off a rapid-fire list of questions for my friend: "Baabar, how is Laila's mother? And Hakiim? May I go and visit them today with you?"

"Gabrielle, I have much to share with you, but first you have Violette waiting in the tea salon. I prepared mint teas."

I took off my apron and joined Violette at the small round marble café table by the window. I was suddenly taken aback by my friend's beauty. The flush of her cheeks had finally returned. Violette's long hair, the color of wheat, was divided into two golden braids. Her face was freckled by the sun, her aquamarine eyes bright once again. One could not miss the new lines, tiny wrinkles that branched out like tributaries from her eyes. But they had served her well over these last months to carry the grief away. There was a new peace in her face—more like gratitude for making it to the other side of grief. Today she was bursting with excitement.

"Gaby, *ciao, mon amie.* Did Baabar tell you?"

"Violette, I have missed you. And yes, Baabar told me you are starting the Friday meals again. I am thrilled. I have missed the bonhomie of the flower market. I have missed you, especially. May I help you do something for the celebration tomorrow?"

"The party is really to be a surprise 'welcome home' for Leif! Madame Goriot received the postcard yesterday. I want everything to be perfect for him. I want him to see that we need him here…that I need him here."

Her voice quavered, and I recognized the same hope in my voice when I had offered my past, present and future to Luc, only to be denied. I hoped she would have better luck.

"Violette, this is just what the flower market needs! Hope for a new day. I am envisioning pistachio meringues, raspberry tuiles and savarins! Let's start with Gaston. He still cycles on the weekends, right?"

She nodded excitedly.

"I will create a grand *Paris-Brest* in his honor. Imagine a round pastry bicycle wheel filled with dark chocolate crème. And for Madame Rousillion, I will make her strawberry heart cookies, a spoonful of chocolate in each center. For Madame Lucier, a proper lemon tart with a gingerbread-almond crust. The La Chapelle twins are easy: I will prepare a tray of éclairs, chocolate and caramel. Something special for everyone."

Making copious notes in my catering journal, writing each person's name under his or her sweet gift briefly took my mind off Luc. Others were happy and I would be content with that.

Violette's smile was contagious. She purred with a new twinkle in her eye. "Have you forgotten Leif?"

"Oh, no, chocolate mousse, of course, his favorite—with florets of white chocolate that will look like the orchids he adores. And for you, my dear Violette, it will be my pièce de résistance!"

Anticipation flashing in her bright-blue eyes, she asked timidly, "Do you think it's possible to miss your destiny when it has been standing right in front of you all the time?"

I sighed. "I fear my destiny is made with flour, sugar and cacao beans. But you, my friend, will surely find your happiness. You have the courage to open your heart again. Now I must get busy in the kitchen."

Violette clapped her hands and merrily set a saucer of sweet milk in the windowsill for Bijoux. He happily purred words of gratitude. Back in the kitchen, I found a note Baabar had left under my rolling pin: "Will be back. Naima needs me. Trouble in the Maghreb."

Now alone, I was left to replay Luc's cruel refusal of me. Thankfully, the bakery was my sanctuary, and now I had Violette's party to focus on. Quickly I set about preparing sweet dough, stretching my arms across the table and rolling the pin back and forth. I scooped my hand into the tin and brought out one scoop, then another, of flour to dust each layer of the pastry dough. I was happy for Violette and offered up a quick prayer for her growing courage.

The sisters would be proud to witness my sincere attempts at heavenward supplications. They had known I found prayer to be a suspicious enterprise, too nebulous for my comfort. The intimate exchanges at the prie-dieu between Sister Karis and an invisible Presence had seemed ridiculous to me. She would light a votive candle, unfold a woven tapis and kneel upon it for hours in conversation. I thought we could have been baking more bread. So detailed in her conversation, she even prayed for my silly finger, burned by hot caramel on the stovetop. Nothing escaped her litany of the day. I see now that Sister Karis's life was one long beautiful prayer.

It struck me that now I too had my own daily litany. Words bubbled up and spilled out over the edges of my spirit. I was desperate to pull at the invisible thread that connected me to the Divine. I could no longer traverse the pilgrimage of life here alone.

With six trays of pastries in the ovens, I untied my floured apron and tucked it under my knees, then placed my hands together and slowly lowered my forehead to the bakery floor, just as I had watched Baabar faithfully do every single day.

"Holy One, I come to you now, your angel of Gabriel. Please help Baabar save his people. I fear what is ahead. I'm frightened by Hakiim's eyes. They are full of hatred. I pray you will turn him back to the Light. Guide Violette, who has already lost so much. Help Leif be worthy to receive the gift of her heart. Luc—what can I say? I fear I can't save him. I ask for your mercy now."

The endless tears were dampening my apron. I could see all the faces I loved before me: Serene, who no longer recognized her husband and children; Madame Charpentier, who still, after fifteen years, curled up in a ball many nights, violently slapping her legs in penance for the child lost; Leif, on the plane, full of fear for the next step; my Luc, perilously close to edge of the Deep. Helplessness so close to hopelessness.

Suddenly, a presence surrounded me. I stayed very still, nose to the mat. One hand, then another, and another, and another touched me until my back was covered. They were warm, comforting, pressing straight through to my very soul. I knew the language they were whispering, the tongue of angels, blessing me, ordaining me for what was ahead. I sighed in relief, knowing that whatever was to come, I would be okay. No wonder Sister Karis had kneeled in prayer every day.

A tap on my shoulder caused me to rocket up in surprise.

"Gabrielle, are you asleep, child? Are you all right?"

It was Pierre kneeling beside me with one of the linen kitchen rags. He was trying to wipe away the flour that must have toppled over on top of me from the table above. I was covered head to toe in white dust. I quickly looked around to see if there were footprints behind me to prove that I had indeed been visited, touched. But I saw nothing, only the cracked-tile bakery floor.

"Pierre, something just happened to me. I felt hands or wings holding me like a newborn baby. They whispered in the language of the *Angel Holy Book* in the library."

Pierre smiled. "There is a balm in Gilead! Great, isn't it? You are never alone. Now, you better get busy. The fête at the flower market is just two hours away."

As he turned to leave, he put his hand on my shoulder. I instantly recognized the imprint. My eyes met his, and my spirit bowed in gratitude.

It took two of our brass chariots to transport all of the desserts to the flower market. I heard the music as soon as I crossed the bridge, pushing the heavily laden carts by Notre Dame. Bernard, the street performer, clicked his heels, cocked his head and grinned. The old monk sweeping the chapel steps stopped and nodded his bald head. Oh, the sweet secret that angels lived all around us.

I stopped to carefully lift the cart up onto the sidewalk and someone tapped me on the shoulder. A beautiful Japanese family stood in front of the cathedral and motioned to ask that I take their photo. When I looked through the lens, I saw not the smiling family but instead the gargoyles suddenly distorted into the shapes of ravens lurching out at me. I shook my head, blinked, and the laughing family returned. I quickly captured the moment and returned the camera. Looking up, I was grateful to find a bright-blue sky. The familiar outline of Notre Dame's gargoyles blended harmlessly again into the stone facade of the building. But in my heart, I knew the Darkness was mounting an offensive. I whispered prayers the rest of the way to the market.

Each stall in the flower market was strung with twinkling lights. It was a true gypsy celebration. Tables were lined up the center of the arcade, covered with red-checked tablecloths. An assortment of crooked, dented, tarnished but beautiful candelabras sporting pink, orange, red and purple candles added a romantic, soft glow. This was a flower market, so each merchant made a special contribution. There were fuchsia peonies, a cactus plant with a spiked crimson bloom, elegant white roses in different sizes of crystal vases, a large tin bucket of sunflowers and a pair of lemon trees to perfume the air. Sitting prominently in the center of the main table was the Rothschild's Slipper orchid—Leif was back.

A smorgasbord of food fit for any gourmand magically began to appear. Madame Lorient had spent the day perfecting her family recipe of duck cassoulet. Claude brought a spit-roasted pig from his farm outside the city, mounted on a metal board secured to the bed of his delivery truck. Violette prepared a dozen ratatouilles from her grandmother's Provençal recipe. *La Poissonnier,* run by Monsiuer Gateau's brother, Lyon, contributed five platters overflowing with raw oysters, littleneck clams, grilled lobsters, *crevettes* and crabs. The twins proudly carried in two of their mother's famous potatoes gratin, each with six layers of Gruyère cheese. Mademoiselle Elizabette arrived late, bearing a colorful canapé tray of roasted eggplant, cherry tomatoes, zucchini and chanterelle mushrooms, all bathed in a citrus-thyme vinaigrette. The Levain Bakery sent *boules* of rosemary-olive bread, along with my dessert bounty. Altogether, it was a potluck communion table, the breaking of bread and sharing of wine nourishing far more than the stomach this night. Even without the flowers, romantic lights and beautiful food, I knew these people would see one another through whatever life brought them, both the joys and the sorrows. This was family incarnate.

Louis, who had sold me my beloved bird, Sucre, played his violin, and the children danced around a circus of barking dogs and squawking pigeons. I looked over the happy crowd and gave thanks. As in a fairy tale, Violette made her entrance. Leif saw her first. At that exact moment, Louis changed up into a beautiful sonata as our market princess made her way through the crowd. Everyone stopped what they were doing and watched as Violette walked straight toward her destiny. I saw her moment of hesitation and then her determined smile. It took courage to love again.

Leif set down the wooden crate of bottles of rosé wine. Their eyes met, and I could feel his worthy heart beating for her. Leif was stronger than his brother had been in every way. He knew his future stood before him now, and he would not miss his chance at happiness. He would tell Violette that he had loved her from the very first time he had seen her pedaling that rusty red bike through the market, blond hair flying behind her.

I thought to myself, *You may lose what you believed was your everything, but that doesn't mean the story is over. The opportunity to give and receive love is never over. Who else needed to hear this? Oh, Luc, where are you now?*

With everyone in the market family gathered, Louis stepped off his crate and invited the children to follow behind him as he danced and serenaded the crowd in and out of the tables. The adults then joined in, and before I knew it, I too was drawn into the curling ribbon of smiles, clapping hands and tapping feet.

Little Jacques was pulling at my pants leg, and suddenly the air changed. Something was dreadfully wrong. Spinning around to face the rear of the market, I saw a grim Pierre standing on the edge of the celebration. There were dark shadows where light had just been before. He motioned for me to come. I felt the Darkness pressing in.

"Gabrielle, something is happening in the eighteenth arrondissement. You must go immediately. Find Baabar. Take this scarf to cover your head."

I turned back to the dancing party and waved to Leif and Violette, whose hands were intertwined. They were leading the parade now in a joyous serpentine around the perimeter. Hope has this mysterious way of taking the spirit by the hand and leading it out of the Darkness and back into the Light. That was my wish for Leif and Violette tonight. My eyes teared up, and I said a quick prayer of thanksgiving. Sadly, joy and sorrow live side by side. I turned away to face my fate. The battle had begun.

PART TEN

In the Clutches of the Raven

Into this silent night
As we make our weary way
we know not where,
Just when the night becomes the darkest
And we cannot see our path,
Just then,
Is when the angels rush in,
their hands full of stars.

— ANN WEEMS —

CHAPTER 32

The joy of the flower market followed me all the way into the metro but refused to join me on the train. Inside the car, the air became thick with dread. The fluorescent lights flickered on and off with every jolt of the train on the rails. The oncoming darkness increased my apprehension. I could smell the fear, subtle at first, but increasing with each stop, as the train moved closer to the Clichy-sous-Bois station. I closed my eyes, breathing rhythmically, traveling inside myself, just as Master Liu had instructed me. The Light grew stronger within me. I was ready now.

Baabar had warned us about the mounting bitterness of the young Franco-Maghrebs. They would fight for their dignity, sadly excited by the thrill of martyrdom. The French police did not distinguish them as Algerians, Tunisians, Moroccans or Berbers. They were just the *banlieuesards*, the villains of the Muslim ghetto. It had started off as another peaceful demonstration. Baabar had helped them organize a silent parade in the Clichy-sous-Bois square to bring attention to the plight of the immigrants who were barely surviving. He had wanted to expose the poverty of children living in squalor, right under the belly of the most beautiful city in the world. Hungry youth had resorted to setting traps to capture the edible rats living in their apartments. Today the rodents were hung on sticks to brandish in the parade.

No one could have predicted the bubbling rage would spill over into such wretched violence. The peaceful demonstrations had quickly transformed into a ghetto war. The protesters had turned bestial, thirsty for blood, reckless, eager for destruction. The hot "young bulls" were determined to gore the establishment which had continued to bait them with empty promises. They stole cars, then set them ablaze with homespun Molotov cocktails.

In the morning, there would be a makeshift banner waving from a window with the tally of cars set on fire the evening before. The Maghreb misery was now a growing flame. It would quickly spread, making its way up the hierarchy until the powder keg of rebellion exploded.

The French president authorized the police to put down the riots using any measure necessary. Every man in uniform reported for duty in the streets of the French Maghreb. A mandatory curfew was issued for the surrounding *banlieues* with a strict order that any infraction would result in arrest. Word spread, and like a domino, the riots stretched outside of Paris to the Maghrebs of Lyon, Toulouse and Arles. Reporters flocked to the wretched scene for a choice picture of the cemetery of burned cars, looted shops and nameless dead bodies. The police detained several hundred Muslim youth. And yet every night the sky was ablaze, smoke plumes twirling in the dark night, encouraging the reckless brothers to more violence. There would be no retreat this time. The Darkness had mount an offensive; the battleground was swarming with ravens. Where was the Light?

Hakiim went missing and Baabar feared for his young life. Quietly, word spread, one veil to another, for all women and children to remain inside. Shops closed and streets were barricaded. The officers joked with Mahoumed at the corner *tabac* that the young boys had finally grown tired of the game and had run to hide in the folds of their *mamans'* abayas. If only that had been true.

The police were loitering outside the cafés, rolling their cigarettes for the evening ahead, taking one last shot of espresso, when the first bus exploded. Nightmarish shrieks pierced the air from the human candles trapped inside the burning steel vehicle. The policemen froze, unprepared for this latest unleashed fury. The hours ahead would prove devastating. The smell of charred flesh was effective at suffocating the spirit of all those terrified on the sidelines. The scene of destruction was sickening. Led by Hakiim, the *banlieusards* were cleverly hidden behind the flowing veils of their mothers', sisters' and wives' burkas so that they could move undetected across the city, explosives wrapped around their bellies and Molotov cocktails concealed deep in their pockets.

I could barely squeeze through the panicked mob of women and children who struggled to escape the inferno, seeking refuge on the train. I fought my way against the crowd up the stairs, covering my face with my scarf to shield it from the choking smoke and grisly smells. One never grows accustomed to the scent of burning muscle. When the iron-rich human blood reaches boiling point, it releases an acrid metallic perfume that clings to the hairs of the nostrils for days, and to the spirit forever. The crisp remnants of hair burned up to the edges of innocent scalps would leave a permanent sulfurous residue upon the bus's leather seats. An unforgettable tattoo of death.

At the top of the stairs, I first saw the firefighters spraying a flaming bus with an inadequate amount of water, their hoses clearly no match for the combusting gas fires that had already silenced the passengers inside. I crossed the street and made my way to the building where I had last seen Naima and Hakiim. Crying and gasping from the tear gas, I opened the apartment building door to find no one. I quickly grabbed a blanket off a cot on the floor and wrapped it around my head. As I turned to leave, I heard a whimper from the apartment across the hall. Opening the door, I found Naima leaning on her cane and looking out the window at the terror on the street. She was chanting an ancient song of lamentation.

Looking through me with dead eyes, she said softly, "They drove him to such evil. Hakiim—he was always the sweet boy, breaking his heart for all the world. Now look at him. If you are looking for Baabar, you'll find him at Mamouna's tea shop. He promised he would bring Hakiim back to us. But I fear even he cannot save Hakiim now. We are standing at the gates of Jahannam this night."

She turned back to the window, engulfed in silent agony now.

I made my way to Mamouna's tea shop two blocks over. A policeman broke free from his barricade behind Amir's storefront. Yelling in rapid-fire French, he chased me down the street. I did not see the bus careening around the turn, its windshield wipers crisscrossing the spewing flames across the glass. Baabar, my glorious warrior, suddenly appeared from nowhere. He had seen me first and was running for the bus. A second explosion tossed us both to the ground. Pain ricocheted through a burst eardrum, but I was determined to reach Baabar.

Youth with torches and torn red-cloth flags danced manically around the burning bus, screaming like a pack of coyotes, dark heads thrown back in violent joy. All I could see through the smoke-belching windows was an elderly woman, flames licking her long, bony fingers as they fought to remove the hat burning atop her silver-haired head. A little boy was being shoved through an impossibly narrow opening at the driver's window, his mother frantic to push him to safety as her dress caught flame.

I didn't think. I just ran to the door of the bus. The hot metal singed my fingers, but I did not feel it, a strange blessing. I dug into the rubber center crease and flung open the door. Once inside, flailing arms were reaching for me, pulling me in deeper so that they could push themselves out. I found the silver-haired lady first, her charred face nearly unrecognizable, her dark eyes now peaceful. I shoved her down the exit steps anyway and turned back to help the unconscious mother of the freed child who was awkwardly slumped over the steering wheel. I pulled her into me and could feel the flames leap for new flesh. Dizzy and disoriented, I somehow got her into the arms of the fireman who had bravely crawled in after me.

I heard him from far away, screaming through his oxygen mask to get off the bus, but I saw more people to save. Somehow I reached the back of the death bus, climbing over the bodies already sacrificed down the center aisle. It was cemetery quiet. Suddenly, I heard Master Liu's voice speaking softly to my soul. I bowed my head in thanks for his gift of peace. I no longer felt the burning. I left my painful body behind. Only my spirit could help me now.

Then I heard Baabar's magnificent deep voice, "Gabrielle, the bus is going to explode! Get down!" One second. That's all it took. One life exchanged for another. I felt his body fall hard on top of mine. Our faces were so close that I could not distinguish who was breathing. There was not enough air for both of us. My lungs panicked for a breath. And Baabar, my savior, breathed into me, for me.

I remembered the time when I was eight and burned the tender inside of my right arm. I had carelessly reached into the oven to grab a tray of *palmiers* and ended up with a second-degree burn. I was left with only a small scar, but the smell of my own burned flesh still haunted me. Now the flames engulfed my whole body. I watched as in a dream, as fire lunged at every part of me, the dark enemy greedy to ravish my angel flesh. How long would this take? I wondered. I moved in and out of consciousness. An indescribable pain near my left breast jolted me briefly awake. But the smoke engulfed me, and all I heard were the ravens screeching in triumph. They had finally come for me.

Baabar would not go down without a fight. His giant body provided a protective tarp from the flames and deadly smoke. He laid his lips gently upon my open mouth. I could just taste the mint from his morning's tea. His last breath was so strong, like a blessed wind as it entered my body.

Baabar lifted slightly so our eyes could meet. "Gabrielle, I am your Protector, always." He smiled, and then he was gone.

A white light unlike the angry flames encircled us. The next thing I remembered was the blackened face of Hakiim over me. I struggled against him, to go to Baabar. "No, no. Save him, not me," I cried. Hakiim refused.

"Gabrielle, Baabar is gone. Don't fight me. Allow me to save you. Turn your head. I beg you, let me do this for my brother."

I quit struggling then and rested in Hakiim's arms as he carried me off the bus to the medics. He turned to go back for another victim. Then I heard the shot. And Hakiim's body, his strong young self, full of promise, fell to the pavement. I screamed and begged the fireman to go to him. But it was over. No one cared about one rebellious Muslim youth dressed in his mother's burka.

Nearly unconscious, I whispered, "Luc, we are in the forest, and a tree, a beautiful tree, has fallen."

The Darkness took me.

PART ELEVEN

Light Dreams

O Lord, you have searched me and known me. ... You hem me in, behind and before, and lay your hand upon me. ... Where can I go from your spirit? Or where can I flee from your presence? If I ascend to heaven, you are there; if I make my bed in Sheol, you are there. If I take the wings of the morning and settle at the farthest limits of the sea, even there your hand shall lead me, and your right hand shall hold me fast. If I say, "Surely the darkness shall cover me, and the light around me become night," even the darkness is not dark to you; the night is as bright as the day, for darkness is light to you. I come to the end—I am still with you.

— PSALM 139 —

CHAPTER 33

Lille, Sophie and Pierre rescued me to a safe haven on a hilltop overlooking the sea. The medical world had done all it could, and now the angels sought alternative healing from one of their very own. The illustrious angel Odette, from the line of Raphael, was my last hope. I was so very weak in body and spirit. They were fearful that the Dark One would find me and finish the job. Desperately, they tried to secure a little more time on this side for their young light-bearer.

Odette's stone cottage was perched on the side of a cliff in a grove of sturdy olive trees; it enjoyed a seagull's view of the sea. Odette had known my mother long before I was born. She too was a well-known healer and now my last chance. Like my mother, Odette could be tender but also fearless. Her hair was the color of shimmering raindrops in the sun, silvery and soft, flowing down her broad back. Odette was large, her features blunt; she was strong as an ox and always ruddy cheeked as if just returning from a brisk walk through the olive grove. She wore a turquoise-beaded necklace with a healing-stone pendant around her neck; she would often rub the smooth amber between her thumb and forefinger when solving a problem. And you always knew of her presence in the room by her clean scent of verbena and eucalyptus. Like Lille, Odette could make things seem possible when all vowed them impossible, and I needed that now.

She and my mother had met for the first time at the healing springs in Hungary. Both had come with sacks of empty bottles to fill with the miraculous mineral waters. They became fast friends. Odette knew first that Valentina was with child. And Valentina prophesied that Odette would one day save that child. Odette had prepared the rose oil for my mother, despite the fact that they both knew I would not turn in the womb. And Valentina made a last stop at Odette's house on the way to Santiago de Compostela. Neither my papa nor Odette knew then that a little bundle of recipes for ointments, salves and medicines, left by my mother in a tin, would be used thirty years later to try and save me.

The medics in Paris, who specialized in burn victims, had spent nearly sixteen hours trying to remove the woolen blanket I had carelessly wrapped around my face as a shield from the fire. The art was in the detachment of the blanket without taking the flesh with it. I lost all my eyelashes and eyebrows. I would forever bear a constellation of white scars like tiny tears, down my left cheek. As luck would have it, the greater portion of my hair was saved only because, by nervous habit, I had tied it up in a bun on the train.

Several of the medics suffered second-degree burns on their fingers just from handling my body. They had fastened my body to an aluminum pallet and repeatedly immersed it in a bath of ice water. Never had they seen a body smoke like mine did. The water sent up clouds of steam with each immersion. Everyone, even the circling angels thought I was gone several times. But somehow I survived. I would never look the same. My youth and innocence lit up the sky that night, only to fall to the ground in a pile of ash.

For a long time I had no concept of where I was, nor did I feel connected to my body. I would learn later that I moved in and out of consciousness for nearly a week. Six weeks later, my doctors in Paris had achieved all that was possible, and I was carefully moved to the south and given over to Odette's care. She created a rigorous regimen of linen compresses of witch hazel with hyssop and lavender oil in the morning, followed by a special recipe of aloe and chamomile in the evening. In the first weeks, Odette applied freshly mashed and moistened chickweed leaves to my hands and chest. She bathed my lips and face with plantain juice for its antibacterial properties and to encourage growth of new skin cells.

Lille said many days she would lean close to my face and touch her nose to mine to make sure I was still breathing. My arms and legs were tied down to the bed for my own protection. As the weeks went by, the nerve endings began to heal, which caused excruciating pain. I became like an animal, caught in the trap of my own skin. Imprisoned in the bed, I screamed for it to end. Lille worried her tears would contaminate the linen bandages. What no one knew was that my skin was not the direst problem. There was a grave internal wound that went unnoticed—my heart. It had mysteriously received the greatest trauma. It would take more than the sea air and a cornucopia of herbs and salves to heal it.

Odette and Lille were very careful to keep my presence a secret out of fear that the Darkness would come for what was left of me. My angel spirit remained in danger; evil feeds on weakness. And it was my spirit, my Light, that Odette and Lille were fiercely determined to guard.

That is what happens on this side of the mysterious boundary of life. We suffer a blow to our humanity with the power of a cannonball that tunnels a hole straight through our core, exposing the soul to the darker elements of living. Whether it's from a broken heart, a tragic diagnosis, a grave loss or the oppressive presence of evil pressing in on all that we know to be true and good in the world, regardless, each has the power to crush the spirit. An opening, imperceptible at first, lets the Darkness worm itself inside. First there is anger; then it morphs into doubt and finally despair. Luc went through this. Now it was my turn. The reign of Darkness is well versed in its ability to seduce the spirit when adversity overwhelms it. The spirit loses its resilience. Melancholia draws a curtain across the whole story. The eyes, the windows of the soul, are blinded. And soon all efforts to seek the Light are abandoned.

Lille begged me to focus on my inner Light, but giving in to the Darkness was easier. Self-pity makes the devil grin. Also, my guilt proved razor-sharp. I was the reason Baabar would never be the savior for his people of the Maghreb. I missed him so much and blamed myself for what had happened. When I closed my eyes, I relived that night over and over again. Where were my wings then? Now? Lille kept telling me to wait, to heal, to look deep inside. All I saw was tar—sticky, smothering tar. The whole angel community rallied around me, doing their best to guide me back into the light again, but secretly feared I was already in the Raven's clutches.

CHAPTER 34

When Odette purchased the hilltop *bastide* overlooking the sea, many in the village whispered that a witch had come. It was only when she healed the mayor's wife of psoriasis, so debilitating that she could not leave her house, that Odette became not only a part of the community but one of its most cherished citizens. The villagers clamored for her herbal teas, ointments, poultices and oils. On a shelf above the kitchen window, with the best view to the sea, were dozens of glass jars with blue-enamel tops, labeled in Odette's hand: chamomile, eucalyptus, geranium, garlic, and lavender. An antique armoire, formerly the resting place for dowry quilts, linens and tablecloths, was now Odette's magnificent medicine cabinet. Discarded wine crates were filled with beakers labeled and ordered so that she could grab the aloe vera, balm of Gilead, kukui nut oil, hyssop, tea tree oil and witch hazel with ease.

The lines stretched around Odette's house every Saturday, all with hopes of a cure for whatever in life ailed them. There were the regulars, like ten-year-old Jean, who came with his mother each week despite his loathing of Odette's onion juice and baked garlic, proven cures for his epilepsy. A trio of menopausal women, tired of feeling like angry, shriveled prunes, climbed the hill for Odette's miraculous powders made from the dried skins of pomegranates. When mixed with water from her natural spring, they created a natural balance in their hormones. Many an aging gentleman feigned an illness to get her secret pouch of pistachio nuts and pomegranate seeds for increased sexual vigor. New mothers arrived frazzled and desperate for Odette's chamomile tonics for newborn colic, as well as her special jar of rose-lavender honey to calm their own fragile nerves. Odette listened to each and every plight. Compassion proved to be her greatest cure. She knew all too well that every ailment that presented on the outside usually pointed to a greater need on the inside. And I was no exception.

Odette had created a little Eden on this seaside hilltop. Her garden flourished with medicinal plants and flowers, vegetables, fruit and olive trees, and even a couple rows of grapevines. Her home was a potpourri of fragrances, and the kitchen farm table was frequently covered with wicker baskets of peppers, zucchini, potatoes, wild onions and arugula. The open fire pit was ready with fresh kindling to light beneath a heavy cast-iron pot for her healing soups and miraculous healing potions.

Down the road, Odette was the chef at *L'École des Filles*. In a twist of fate, Odette purchased the old girls' school the night before it was to be torn down for a petrol station. She could not bear to see the enormous, spreading Tilleul tree in the center of the schoolyard cut down. The villagers laughed: "That crazy Odette started a restaurant to save a tree." But they all became believers when they tasted earth's bounty in her quaint, healing bistro. The cobblestone terrace provided seating for only twenty-four for lunch or dinner. And she was always packed. The whole month of August was a sabbatical, and a wooden sign on the gate read, *"l'école fermée,"* to let people know it was a time of rest.

There was a set menu each day, inscribed in chalk on a large blackboard propped against the Tilleul tree. It was inspired by whatever spoke to Odette on her morning promenade through the garden. She also counted on Antoine's nets, still slick from the saltwater of the sea, for fish on Tuesdays; and on Gerard, the butcher, for his best cuts of beef and lamb on Wednesdays. Odette kept her own prize chickens in a coop behind the old schoolyard for Thursdays. Fridays were *un grande surprise!*

Odette paid tribute to the history of *L'École des Filles,* once filled with happy schoolgirl chatter, by keeping many of the old wooden two-seater desks, which were now home to water pitchers, trays of butter and woven baskets of silver cutlery. Scattered about were wooden pencil boxes, abacus sets and globes filled with flowers. The old assembly room for the girls was now a culinary kingdom, the kitchen. Three wooden professors' desks were now prep tables, and the chalkboard on the far wall had the day's recipes scrawled across it.

When the first course was ready, Odette would ring the old school bell, and each patron would file into the kitchen like eager pupils and take a plate. As all were eating, Odette would prepare the next course. On the second ringing of the bell, everyone would return with plates licked clean, in great anticipation of selecting a main-course platter.

Old and new photos in mismatched frames lined the walls of the old school library. Happy prints of Odette's garden, her olive trees and beehives, many of her jolly patrons and, of course, the blue ribbon award for her winning recipe of *Fleurs de Courgettes*. Imagine lemony flowers from the schoolyard garden stuffed with red peppers, squash, onions, black olives, tomatoes, garlic and basil, and topped with a dollop of Odette's own goat cheese. This dish won over the curly-mustached food critics and earned *L'École des Filles* the coveted gustatory star.

Odette was a gifted teacher, too. Her fortunate pupils sat in complete awe of her every culinary discourse. Odette called it her "kitchen arithmetic." You take a humble vegetable, add a splash of fragrant olive oil, include a trio of fresh herbs, and—voilà—you have your greatest sum. Dessert provided another lesson opportunity. A simple clafouti, chocolate mousse or tarte tatin, and you could count on the "Eurekas" all around.

But Odette was first and foremost an angel healer. One of her regular lunch patrons was a statistician who claimed he could prove that anyone who found himself in Odette's care could be guaranteed a significant percentage increase in his or her life span, or at least a spike in the joy quotient.

My coming to the *bastide* would prove Odette's greatest challenge. She tended to me in the morning, left to prepare lunch at *L'École des Filles*, returned in the afternoon with cool compresses of St. John's wort oil and tamanu oil, and then hurried back to the schoolhouse for the dinner seating. Lille never left my side. While Odette wrapped me in gauze and honey, Lille nursed me with her constant prayers.

Weeks passed in the exposed beamed room of the stone cottage attic. I had the best view of the sparkling sea. Odette's abode reminded me of an artist's studio. Each room was unique and painted in color washes of lavender, eucalyptus and burnt sienna. They magically changed hues like a chameleon depending on the posture of the sun. The floor was tiled in celadon and was cool to the bare feet. Every window remained open day and night so the sea air could work its magic. For centuries people had made pilgrimages to the south. Maybe it was for the quality of light, the promise of warmth or just to enjoy the beauty. Regardless, all journeyed here for healing of some sort. And Mother Nature willingly opened her arms, mysteriously knowing exactly what each spirit needed.

My body was charred on the outside, my organs nearly suffocated by the inhaled poisonous smoke from the explosion on the inside. My heart was a ticking time bomb. But even more damage had been done to my spirit. I heard Lille telling Odette, "We must reanimate her soul if she is ever to deliver the Message again." I was ravaged, and yet I still retained the Light, she believed. Odette and Lille were determined to heal me. And so the daily ritual continued, the tending to my body and soul by two special angels who believed I still had much left to do on this earth.

In the beginning I was a pliant, docile patient. This was a blessing because it allowed Lille and Odette to nurse me like an infant. All those fruits and vegetables, oils and ointments, began to work. They were able to decrease inflammation in my body, boost my immune system and provide antibacterial properties to ward off infection. Odette cleared a new area in her garden and solely dedicated it to fruits, vegetables and herbs for me. She planted asparagus, brussels sprouts, two new blueberry bushes, broccoli, onions, potatoes and basil, just to start. Odette prepared purees blended with spices like turmeric, cinnamon and ginger which had for centuries proven their valuable healing properties.

Lille spoon-fed me, forcing open my blistered lips. There were many scary moments when I would stubbornly refuse to swallow because of the pain. She had to drop her kindly demeanor and become a tough sergeant, not afraid to pinch my cheeks or spend hours coaxing me for the reward of three spoonful's of soup. Then I became an incorrigible patient when I regained full consciousness and saw in the mirror the ugly beast staring back at me. My pride and the inescapable presence of darkness chipped away at my will. I was sure that the only reason I was still breathing was for the penance owed for the lives of Baabar and Hakiim. Oh, the Raven was happy.

Lille and Odette, however, would not be deterred. Honey became a secret weapon. They not only wrapped my body every evening in a thin glaze of either a rosemary or eucalyptus honey dressing, but they also included honey in every recipe. Raw honey proved unrivaled in its ability to protect and heal my body. I owed the schoolyard bees much for their tenacity in the hive. It was their honey that miraculously allowed my skin to soften instead of harden in scars.

My body proved malleable, even thankful for the daily massages and therapy. I was able to move my arms and legs again. I knew I was beginning to heal when the neurons of my olfactory senses awakened one morning to the scents of lavender, mint and camellias in a vase beside my bed. I next regained my voice. My first words since the accident were more like blood-curdling screams.

Thus commenced the nightmares. I saw them as fitting punishment. They were always the same. I was trapped beneath Baabar's body, screaming for him to stop breathing for me. Some nights I would see a dark specter choking Baabar as he struggled to give me his last breath. I lunged for it, only to wake with Lille forcing me back into bed.

But the worst of the nightmares were about Luc. I could hear his motorcycle. I would joyfully call out, "I knew you would come! I've been waiting for you, Luc!" Next I would be running through a labyrinth, the same as my dreams before, except now the walls were not fragrant green and soft to the touch; they were black and smoking.

I had seen it happen before in my visions for others—the loss of a job, a marriage, a child, a dream. That was all it took for the insidious Darkness to come calling. How easy it was to turn away from the Light. The Darkness overwhelmed. I had no energy, no radiance. And my heart muscle was secretly growing weaker by the day. I was afraid. I no longer had the energy or will to project the Light, stretch my wings, or deliver the message of Gabriel. I had allowed life to defeat me. I feared the Raven had finally won.

CHAPTER 35

I wanted to feel my skin peel away, strip by strip, the flames searing the flesh until there was nothing left—my debt paid by my life. But I was one of the Chosen, not to be lost to the Darkness without a fight. And so came the "light dreams." At first they were just flashes, like little fireflies lighting up the darkness in my soul. Then I had longer dreams, where my spirit was led through a tunnel of technicolor. I fought the dreams as long as I could, afraid of where they were leading me. But I was no match for the Divine.

Jobe, the gatekeeper, was sent on my behalf. He mysteriously stepped into my dreams one night. I knew it was him by the sound of his keys jangling. His form was traced in brilliantine light. Glowing before me, he reached for my hand. This went on for several dreams until one night, speaking in the angelic language, he ordered, "Take my hand. Walk into the light, Gabrielle." But I was too scared, too ashamed. Finally, he pulled me close, and I felt his light enter me. By giving me some of his precious light, I was made stronger. I took his hand. "I was sent as your guide, Gabrielle. You are safe with me. Step through the Door."

This was no ordinary door. It reached higher than my eyes could see, shimmering, trimmed in gold and precious stones, whose patterns changed every time I blinked. The Door opened immediately, and an arrow of light pierced through my being, expanding and healing as it went. I became one with it. I could hear voices whispering all around me, but I could not see who or from where they were coming. I began to wonder if I had died. Maybe my heart had finally stopped. But then a woman's voice rang out.

"Gabrielle, we are all here with you."

"Who are you?" I said. "Where are you? Come out so I can see you."

"First you must step through the Door. You are still standing at the threshold. We will remain invisible to your human eyes until you step through the Door. Courage, dear little one."

I stepped hesitantly forward into the warm, caressing air. I could not take enough of it into my lungs. With each breath, I felt stronger. Loss, disappointment and hurt were shorn; it was as if all the bad had never happened. I was new again. I was healthy, beautifully lighted on the outside, but especially from within. My pride and fear were refined away by the light. I was reborn.

Walking now through a sheer, billowing curtain trimmed in gold, I came to a bench carved from acacia wood and overlaid in gold. Beside the seat was a bronze basin filled with a sweet-smelling oil. Then I heard the familiar voice once again.

"Gabrielle, this is the Mercy Seat. Sit here, dip your finger into the oil, touch your forehead and allow the oil to drip down into your spirit. It will remind you again who you are, one of the Chosen, beautiful and wonderfully made. There was a silence and then I heard the words I had so longed to hear.

"And you are my daughter. I am Valentina—your mother."

The tears were instantaneous. I recognized her voice; the same one that had whispered my name the day I took my first mortal breath. I now remembered her first words to me: *"You will be called Gabrielle. And all will remember you on earth for your light and your love. You carry the soul of God within you, a living message of hope for the world."*

I even remembered the sweet sensation of her kiss on my forehead. And then she was gone. But here she was before me now, a vision of light. Valentina was flesh but not flesh, nearly transparent, an indescribable radiance. Then I looked into her loving eyes. An angel's eyes, indeed. I saw myself in them.

We crossed the holy threshold together. I reached up with my other hand to run my fingers across the bejeweled door, and the gems spilled like rain across my path. I heard my mother's tinkling laughter.

"Gabrielle, welcome to joy."

Then we were in a garden, clover tickling my bare toes and the morning dew cleansing my feet before we headed down a golden moss path laced with sweet-smelling herbs. I was elated to hear the familiar sound of birds singing high in a eucalyptus tree. All that was good in the world was here, except now perfect in every way. I was so relieved to be out of the Darkness. I knew I would find no death, ravens, dark shadows or hurt here.

We continued over a bridge of silvery bamboo, the brook beneath in happy conversation with the warm wind. I thought of Master Liu and stopped to admire the graceful arms of a blue-green weeping willow dipping its fingers into the clear spring. I closed my eyes and sighed in relief, for I was Home.

"We have all been waiting for you."

Valentina pointed with her lighted hand to a group of Angels gathered on a knoll near the perfect brook. Each was luminous, haloed and broadly winged. One laugh was unmistakable. Sister Karis was more beautiful than I ever remembered. She was speaking to a man, who turned in a starburst of light toward me.

And there he was—my papa. The same eyes of the wise owl who had watched over me all this time. Smiling, my father came to greet me. When his radiant spirit leaned in for an embrace, I felt a jolt of raw energy. It pulsed through my entire body, and my knees gave way.

"I am sorry, Gabrielle. You are still clad in your human body. It has never experienced the potency of love on this side of the Door. Love at its purest is quite powerful."

My whole body tingled. Light was filling every cell from his one touch. I did not know how to respond to this kind of joy. I wanted to open my chest wider to take in more and more of the white light streaming from Sister Karis, Valentina and Papa.

Sister Karis turned to Papa and spoke in the angelical language. "You must tell her now. She is still living on earthly time."

Her words were luxuriant to my ears. I sat down on the lush moss blanket, and it was as if I had always been here with them. Time had no meaning. Everything was simultaneous here. With each breath of celestial air, my body became lighter. They saw me as the Creator must, no longer caught in the web of time nor burdened by a perishable body. I was pure angel, and my soul was perfect energy now.

Papa spoke. "Gabrielle, you have not completed your task on earth. You must return. I warn you that your human heart is in danger. And only the fallen one has the lighted hands to repair it on earth."

I was not listening. I looked around, hoping to see Laila, Papa Joe and Baabar, even Hakiim. I had no desire to go back. Why should I ever put myself through the hardship of living on earth when I could be here? No wonder no one returns. Papa pulled me into his chest of light. I closed my eyes, so grateful to be Home.

"My daughter, there will be endless lifetimes for reunions. It was such a happy celebration the day Baabar and Hakiim arrived together. Every day is a homecoming with those you love here. But don't you see? There are people on earth who still need your love and light. We are depending on you to bring the Message of Gabriel to a world so in need of hope. Luc needs you, my love. He is an important part of the message of redemption. The road ahead will not be easy. Do not be afraid. Fill your heart with hope so that when he comes for you, you will have the faith to entrust your life into his hands. In this act of courage, you may save him and deliver the Message of Gabriel to the world. Traveling mercies, my daughter."

PART TWELVE
Love is the Answer

At the center of our being is a point of nothingness which is untouched by sin and by illusion, a point of pure truth, a point or spark which belongs entirely to God. ... It is the pure glory of God in us. ... It is like a pure diamond, blazing with the invisible light of heaven. It is in everybody, and if we could see it, we would see these billions of points of light coming together in the face and blaze of a sun that would make all the darkness and cruelty of life vanish completely.

—THOMAS MERTON

CHAPTER 36

The familiar hooting of the owl, faithfully perched outside the window of my balcony, woke me. I lurched up from the bed and looked around for Karis, Papa and my mother. But all I found was Lille and Odette whispering in the corner. Lille had been crying.

Odette consoled her. "Lille, no one realized that she suffered a mortal injury to her heart. They thought it was only a flesh wound. The skin healed so beautifully; there is barely even a scar. I thought I was only to heal the burns across her body. If I had only looked deeper, seen how damaged her heart truly was. I am surprised she has held on this long."

Odette and Lille had immediately called in reinforcements when I took a surprising turn for the worse. The doctors who reexamined me spoke medical jargon to explain my dying heart. But I knew what was wrong. The Raven was devious and had cleverly gone after my heart, the source of my Light. It was barely a flicker now. My time here was nearly up.

Odette rattled on. "It's Docteur Blanche's opinion that a tiny piece of shrapnel from the explosion penetrated her chest wall. He said there were documented cases of soldiers from the Afghan war, who, like Gabrielle, sustained injury from a foreign object piercing the pericardium, the sac that protects the heart. It then dangerously lodges in the flesh of the heart muscle. The fragment could remain stable for days, months, or even years. Or it could move even a millimeter and be fatal. The only way to ensure survival is to remove the object and repair the heart. Docteur Blanche said, 'Her only chance is a delicate surgery by a pair of miracle hands and a fearless heart.'"

Lille bowed her head on Odette's shoulder. "Cunning of the Dark Deep—a breach to the heart. The Darkness never ceases looking for a way in. Anything to extinguish a true light and stop our mission to bring hope to the world."

Odette buried her head in her hands. "My powers have proven no match for the evil of this world."

Then they heard me.

I whispered, "Luc."

Lille and Odette rushed to my bedside. I saw the look in Lille's eyes at the mention of her son's name. But we both knew that Luc was my only chance.

A beautiful peace descended upon me. It was settled. Jobe mysteriously arrived on cue. They would find Luc for me. In the meantime, Odette closed *L'École des Filles* indefinitely and focused her full attention on preparing my body and spirit for the surgery. Word spread in the village that one of Odette's very own was sick, and the villagers flocked to her aid. Odette pushed my bed close to the window so I could see the evening candle vigil. A luminous ribbon of flickering candlelight twisted up the hill and through the olive grove. They had come for me but also for Odette, in gratitude for all her years of kindness and healing. I smiled; one can never underestimate the power of a multitude's prayers.

Docteur Blanche sent by urgent mail a medical file with details of the surgery protocol. It was a procedure not for the faint of heart, and unfortunately, my earthly heart was plenty faint. A highly gifted surgeon must penetrate the breastplate with a saw. Once the chest was cracked open, the heart would be stopped and life temporarily supported by a mechanical device, pumping the circulating blood. My wounded organ would then be left unprotected, vulnerable to the world. With critical timing perched heavy on his shoulders, the brave doctor would have only three minutes to stop the heart, remove the foreign object, knit the muscle back together, repair the surrounding protective sac and shock the heart back to life with an electrical current. Then all must wait—wait to see if the fragile heart would have the courage to start again. Even the slightest misstep could result in cardiac arrest. The angels would come for me in love, but my Message would be lost. Luc would be lost.

Sophie and Jobe visited all of Luc's old haunts and watering holes. It was Sophie who eventually found him. The moment she heard the news of my heart, she ran to Petite Alma's Chocolate Shop. At first, Pauline furtively claimed ignorance of Luc's whereabouts. He had made Pauline promise on Alma's memory that she would keep his secret. He was ill and growing worse each day. With all of his medical expertise, he could not diagnose his own ailment. He, too, was suffering from a wound to the heart. Pauline, thankfully, told Sophie where he was.

On the night of the Maghreb riots, Luc had been helping refugees flee the Libyan city of Sirte. Suddenly, he experienced a terrible pain in his chest; it brought him to his knees. He tried to ignore it, but the pain was unlike anything he had ever encountered. It made him weep like a child.

When Sophie stormed the storage room of the chocolate shop and found Luc, he was not surprised. He just nodded his head at Sophie's news. He should have known his diagnosis could not be found in the medical books. He had been hurting for me. The Dark One was betting on two for the price of one.

To love another so profoundly, you become mystically one and vulnerable to whatever pain and suffering the other endures. Luc knew that he had to come for me, to save us both.

The risks were now too great to move me. It was too late, they all secretly feared. Hands in the air, Odette brashly announced, "If they can do it in the caves of Afghanistan, we can make miracles happen in this sacred olive grove." With the help of Docteur Blanche's team, a sterile environment for the surgery was achieved. Sophie intentionally did not tell Luc what was ahead. She would leave that to his mother, waiting at the top of the hill. When he arrived, Lille did not have to say a word. It was all there in her eyes. He was my only hope. Everything had led up to this moment. He would have to use his divine gifts, those miracle hands, or lose all that mattered to him in the world.

Lille held him in her arms, as she had when he was seven years old. "Luc, my son, if I could bear this for you, I would. But I believe in you. Be the child who mended a butterfly's wing. You always had the gift. Yours are the hands of the Light. But remember, in the end all Gabrielle needs, like all of creation, is to know that she is loved. Have the courage to give her at least that final gift, Luc."

The room was cool, lit by the one candle in the window. The house was quiet. I could hear my every labored breath. Luc came, and I felt his presence immediately. My hands were tied down to the bed, and I fought to loosen them, desperate to cover my face. I didn't want him to see me so ugly. But Luc touched my face and nothing else mattered.

"We are all gargoyles on this side of paradise, Gaby." He touched his lips to mine. "Remember a gargoyle protects that which is sacred and most beautiful within. You are even more beautiful now. I love you with all of my heart."

Luc unbound my hands and placed them on his heart.

"Gabrielle, forgive me. I am a fallen man. A fallen angel. But my heart has always belonged to you."

He didn't say another word. He leaned down and laid delicate kisses, first on my forehead, then one at each temple. He was marking me with his love. Leaning close, I could feel his breath and then his soft lips. So sweet. He lifted me up, careful not to hurt me. What relief to find my other half again, if only for a moment. Our souls once again united. But we both knew that our bodies were still on this side of heaven. We must play within the rules. Death was very real and close indeed. But that didn't stop Luc from wrestling with Time, pleading on my behalf for mercy. For that, Luc must make peace with another, the Source of our Light.

The surgery no longer frightened me, because now I knew his heart belonged to me forever. I saw the love in his eyes. We were destined from the beginning. I was not sure how my story would finish. But I trusted in the One who had created Luc for me. All would be as it should be. For good, always for good.

Somehow Docteur Blanche had secured all the sophisticated instruments, the monitors and even a metal pallet used in emergency surgery on the battlefield. Angels can be resourceful. It was time to begin.

The anesthesia drip started.

"Luc, please don't be hard on yourself. Loved by you, that is enough for me." Sleepily, I whispered, "There is a place. You won't believe it. I will wait for you at the Door. It is beautiful there."

"Gabrielle, my love, I'll find you."

CHAPTER 37

The only people Luc allowed in the operating room were Docteur Blanche, Jobe and Odette. The doctor and Odette would assist him in the surgery. He required of Jobe to protect the room from the Darkness and to bar the death angels from descending too soon. He needed the chance to attempt a miracle.

He kissed me one last time before I was completely under. I smiled at the owl in the window and then closed my eyes in total peace.

There was one final thing to do before the surgery commenced. He sent the others away. With his hands lifted to the heavens, he asked to return. Return to God. He knew he couldn't do this on his own.

"Holy One, I understand little here. I have strayed. But her love has led me back to you. I love Gabrielle with every fiber of my being. And for that, I offer you myself. Take me, use me, I am willing. I know I have mocked everything that is sacred. You win. Even with the worst the world can do, you redeem it with love—her love. Please save her. Bless my hands this day. Allow me to be your faithful servant again. I am a foolish, stubborn angel. It was always right in front of me. Love. Love is all and enough, always."

Luc called Odette and Jobe back into the room. He walked through every step of the surgery to calm his nerves. And then he gave the nod that it was time. Odette waved from the window to signal to Lille and all the light-bearers to begin their litany of prayers.

Luc did not flinch as he cut through the sternum of my chest. He carefully inserted his hands into the cavity and pinned the edges of flesh over to each side to gain full access to my fragile heart. He nodded to

Odette behind a surgical mask to infuse the medication through the line to stop my heart. She signaled that he had three minutes to work. Luc drew in a breath, my limp heart muscle in his hand. Jobe touched him with his light on the right shoulder, and that was all he needed. Courage. First he removed the fragment, a piece of jagged metal the size of a child's thimble, from the muscle. He quickly knitted up the wound and moved to the pericardium. He was suturing the pericardial layer when something went wrong. Bright red fluid rushed into the pericardial cavity, compressing the heart.

Docteur Blanche was calm in his delivery, as a minute and a half remained on the clock. "Luc, this happened in the medical brief I studied. Identify the source of the bleeding. If you don't, the pressure around the heart will build to dangerous levels. You must quickly unzip the fresh repair of the pericardium, identify the offending vessel and tie it off. And then continue."

Jobe was first to spot the wings that appeared in the four corners of the room. He looked up and said, "Give him time." Brilliant light was everywhere.

Luc closed his eyes, took a deep breath. His fingers lit up inside of me. He began, like he had always done before in surgery, talking about his patient's dreams. It was the only way. Except this time his patient's dreams were also his own.

He spoke as he worked. "There will be a wedding. An exchange of more than rings. Pierre will write a song. Odette will hang colored lanterns from the Tilleul tree and prepare an amazing wedding feast. Jobe will ask if he can change the water into merlot. Pauline will design a chocolate cake, and Alma will bless with a smile from Above. Violette will make a crown of rosebuds for her hair. Fleurie and my mother will create a beautiful dress of cream silk layers with a pink sash. Of course, none other than Sophie will be her maid of honor. And lastly, but most importantly, Master Liu will ordain the union with the Light."

Oh, what could be. If only for another breath and the sound of a strong heartbeat. More precious time. Always, we want more time. Luc remained calm and precise. He looped the final stitch on the sac and motioned for the medication drip to restart my heart. He inserted the slender metal prongs around the heart and jolted it with an electric current. Everyone in the room, including the winged, held his and her breath. The heart lay still. The monitor showed only static. Luc gave it another shock. Nothing. Static again that sounded like a raven's shrill. Chills raced down Luc's spine. This couldn't be.

He whispered, "Take me. The world needs her light more. There is so much darkness. Save me by saving her."

The wings left the corners of the room and glided in around the table. The tears spilled from Odette's eyes. Jobe stomped his foot and lifted his arms to scatter the hovering wings. He calmly ordered Luc to try one last time.

It was the owl who signaled my return. With those wise eyes, Papa was the first to see the flicker of light. The heart muscle then fluttered. Luc gave it another jolt, and life sprang again from my breast. The dark raven took to the night. The death angels returned across the boundary. For the story here was not over—far from over. Let the love story begin.

Farrell Mason lives in Nashville, Tennessee, with her husband and five children. She has a Master of Art Business degree from the University of Manchester, in England, and Sotheby's, in London, and is currently completing her Master of Divinity degree at Vanderbilt University. Her first novel, Alma Gloria and the Olive Tree, is the story of a magical cooking school set on a hilltop in Provence where the guests learn much more than how to make the perfect cherry chocolate soufflé. Lives are changed, bread is broken and shared, and love abounds!

Farrell is passionate about raising funds, awareness and especially hope for kids with cancer. Proceeds from all of her writing go to Memorial Sloan-Kettering Cancer Center in New York City in honor of her son.

YOU CAN FOLLOW FARRELL'S WEEKLY BLOG POSTS
at WWW.BREADANDHONEYBLOG.NET

Made in the USA
San Bernardino, CA
25 June 2014